Half Past Evil

A Novel

Daryl Duwe

Published in the United States of America By Callaway Holdings, LLC.

This is a work of fiction. All characters, situations, and incidents are the product of the author's imagination. Any resemblance to actual people, living or dead, is coincidental and unintentional. Even when actual locations are used to provide context, such locations are used fictitiously.

ISBN-13: 978-0692207895

ISBN-10: 0692207899

Also by Daryl Duwe:

Borrowed Time

ISBN 978-1-4116-5475-4

This book is dedicated to two people.

Dale, my brother, who kicked me in the butt

exactly when I needed it most. I love him

for that, and I'm still waiting to return the favor.

Yolanda, my wife.

She's not only the wind beneath my wings.

She's the wings.

Prologue

Jefferson City, MO

Rafi was getting used to the routine, even liking it, especially on such a wonderful day. It was late August, usually a muggy time in the heartland of America. But a front had swept through overnight, taking the humidity with it. The sky was a deepening blue as Rafi walked his dog, Angel, around the Capitol building and up to his favorite coffee shop on High Street.

The strong, bitter brew reminded him of his homeland. He ordered a large to go and set himself up at one of the small tables on the sidewalk. Rafi sipped and watched as the capital city percolated to life. People came and went, some of them carrying bags of sweets to get the day jumpstarted. Almost all were friendly to a fault, nodding and greeting him and his tail-wagging chocolate lab.

Jefferson City was like that, he had discovered. It was obvious to everyone that Rafi was of some type of Arab descent, but he was widely accepted in a town that is overwhelmingly white and primarily Catholic. "It's an easy place to live," people would tell him. "There's very little traffic, the cost of living is pretty cheap, and it's so safe."

Well, Rafi thought, we'll see about that safe part.

After a while, when no one was near him, Rafi lifted a disposable cell phone from his pocket and dialed a number from memory. It was immediately answered by an automatic public address system in the elevator of a state government office building a block away known as the GOB.

Back in the day, the GOB was the Governor Hotel, where legislators and lobbyists stayed during the legislative sessions. To this day, the stories of what went on in the hotel rooms and a rowdy basement bar are epic. Today, though, it calmly housed a few state government agencies.

A heavyset woman who was alone in the ascending elevator, on her way to work, heard a click over the speaker and what sounded like noises coming from the street. Confused, in an unsure and hesitating voice, she said, "Uh, hello? Is someone there?"

"Shut up," Rafi said sharply, deliberately using a heavy accent. "Listen to me. I have a hostage on the fifth floor. Do as I say or people will die." With that, Rafi disconnected the call, turned off the phone and threw it in a nearby trash can with his empty coffee cup. Then he walked Angel around the corner and across the street to get a better view of the proceedings.

Inside, away from Rafi's view, the woman almost dropped the Tupperware container of brownies she had made that morning for the staff.

"Hello? Hello? Are you still there? Hello?"

Finally, as the elevator arrived at her floor, she scurried her way to the boss's office.

"Jim, you're not gonna believe this."

Jim, his suit jacket already hanging on a hook and his sleeves rolled up, looked at her and said," Not believe what? That you brought brownies again? Why wouldn't I believe that?"

"No! I was just talking on the elevator phone and somebody said they have a hostage and people are gonna die!"

"Who the hell talks on the elevator phone? I didn't know there was an elevator phone."

"Well, it was making noise and it sounded like somebody was on the other end. So I said hello. Anyway, the guy hung up after he said people were gonna die!"

Jim got up from his desk and started pacing. "He hung up? He said people are gonna die? What the hell are we supposed to do?"

"I don't know."

Jim was still pacing. "Shit. I'd better call security and tell them. It's probably a prank. I mean, why call and threaten the elevator?"

Jim stopped pacing and picked up the phone. "I'll take care of it, Marge."

As Marge was leaving his office, Jim called after her. "Hey, did you put some black walnuts in the brownies this time?"

"Sure did."

Jim grinned. "You're the best."

Outside, Rafi had positioned himself at one of the empty tables in front of a local bar with a good view of the GOB. People were still streaming into the building. It was time to kick things up a notch.

He pulled out his smart phone and accessed one of his Twitter accounts, the one that described him as a flirtatious young woman. He tweeted: "911! Somebody has a hostage in the GOB! For real!"

It took about thirty seconds for the re-tweets to start showing up. Pretty soon after that, some of the media tweeters got into the act. Before long, the event had a hash tag: #JCMOhostage.

Rafi tweeted again: "Shots fired! Shots fired in the GOB! I heard them!"

Inside, security was locking down the building. An announcement over the building-wide intercom instructed all personnel to stay in their offices behind closed doors - locked, if possible - until given further instructions.

Security also notified the local police. The local police notified the state highway patrol. Along the way, the report of shots being fired got picked up by somebody official and repeated as a precaution.

Rafi smiled as he saw the tweet from someone he didn't know: "Trooper confirms shots fired on the 5th floor GOB! Time to pray."

The local police cars started showing up next. An officer sporting a bulletproof vest started clearing people off the street. The area immediately in front of the GOB was cordoned off.

Next came the state troopers, and they meant serious business. Some arrived in an armored vehicle and disembarked with assault rifles.

Rafi was impressed with the scale and speed of the response. He watched every move with keen interest. Then he heard the helicopter as it hovered overhead. He didn't know what the helicopter was for in this instance, with a report of a hostage inside the building, but Rafi took careful notice of it and filed the information away.

By now, even some of the politicians in the nearby Capitol building were gawking out their windows and tweeting furiously. "Sharpshooters deployed on the roof of the Jefferson Building!" "There's a helicopter overhead! With a sharpshooter in it!"

The media started showing up next and started posting pictures of each other staring at the gathering rubberneckers.

Then this tweet: "Governor McHenry will be flying home early from a campaign event in Texas to monitor the hostage situation at the GOB."

Interesting, Rafi thought. What was the governor planning to do? He made another mental note.

Finally, somebody in the media called a friend inside the building. Nothing was happening, nobody heard any shots, and nobody knew anything about a hostage. It was probably a hoax or a false alarm.

Immediately, Twitter turned on a dime. The tweets started poking fun at the people who had tweeted all that gloom and doom. The police held a quick news conference out in the street condemning all the unfounded rumors.

The troopers carefully cleared every floor of the GOB and downtown returned to normal in time for lunch. Rafi had learned a great deal that would come in handy later.

Rafi and Angel took another pleasant walk around the Capitol. They paused on the river side and looked up at the governor's office. He wondered: was Governor

McHenry relieved that nothing had happened, or disappointed? The man was less than a week away from accepting his party's nomination to the office of president. This could have been a huge event for him. Instead, it turned out to be a flop.

Rafi was leaning in the direction of disappointment. After all, McHenry was running on a platform of returning to the old days of the Bush Doctrine and the War on Terror. Other presidents, the incumbent included, were treating terrorists like common criminals. Nothing was done until an act occurred, and then the perpetrators (if they ever got caught) were put on trial like common thieves.

Today could have been a good backdrop for that message. But, alas, it was not to be.

"Don't worry, McHenry," Rafi whispered. "You'll get your backdrop. And soon."

Three Years Earlier

He was a meticulous dresser; always had been. So, even though it was a weekend, he put the finishing touches on his red and gray silk tie and examined his image in the mirror. Ship shape. Not bad for a man of 82.

Then he added the day's most important adornment: a lapel pin featuring a bright red Azalea blossom. He had been wearing it for 60 years. Not every day, of course. It was to be worn only when the Azalea Team was assembling at the innocuous-sounding Westchester Garden Club. "Wearing the blossom," as the employees of Westchester knew, signaled to them that the members of the Azalea Team were to be escorted immediately to the private library on the top floor and not to be disturbed for any reason. Only code names were to be used when the blossom was on display, and nobody without the proper lapel pin would be admitted.

That was easy. There were only four lapel pins in existence in the world. It was, the old man knew, the most exclusive club on earth.

Code-named Alpha, the old man had been the leader of the Azalea Team for more than 50 years. He alone decided when the team needed to meet, the last time being some two years ago. It was time to evaluate the decision made at that last meeting and decide if a mistake had been made. If they *had* made a mistake - and it had happened before - they would need to get moving on a course of correction.

After all, the fate of America might very well hang in the balance. Alpha sighed as he thought about it. So much weight on the shoulders of so few.

One last look in the mirror. Stand tall, he reminded himself. Satisfied, Alpha left his suite overlooking Central Park and rode the elevator to the spacious lobby. The doorman saw the Azalea pin and nodded in the direction of a waiting limousine. Alpha nodded his approval.

No words were exchanged; none were needed. Inside the limousine, Alpha reached over and poured himself a short hit of Woodford Reserve.

The entrance to the Westchester Garden Club was completely unremarkable. The address was on the door; that was it. Alpha entered and was immediately greeted by a distinguished black gentleman in a light gray suit.

"Beta is already here," the man said. "Almost an hour."

Alpha was surprised. He was almost thirty minutes early himself. This was not a good sign. Beta, alone in the private library, with nothing but his thoughts and a bottle of Knob Creek.

"And Omega?" Alpha inquired, his eyebrows arched.

"Not yet."

Good. The only thing that worried Alpha more than Beta drinking alone was Beta and Omega conjuring up conspiracy theories among themselves.

Another gentleman appeared and ushered Alpha up two flights of heavily carpeted stairs. The walls were covered in thick cherry panels and expensive artwork. By the end of the second flight Alpha's knees were starting to bark at him, but not too bad.

The third floor of the building was a rotunda with a view back down to the first floor entryway. From here, Alpha could have watched for Omega to arrive, but what would be the point? Elsewhere in the building, other private meetings were taking place. Conversations were under way, some in hushed tones. Expensive liquor and cigars were being consumed. But nothing came close to the gravity of what took place on this floor. The usher unlocked the private library door and Alpha entered. He heard the heavy door lock behind him.

There was Beta. He did not look well. Barely 60 years old and overweight, he looked on the verge of a stroke. His rounded face was aflame with red, his tie undone.

"Good evening, Beta," Alpha said casually. "You're early."

"I couldn't wait," Beta replied, trying to rise from his leather wingback chair and struggling mightily to do so without setting his drink on a side table. "This whole thing is going into the shitter. And the more I think about it, the worse it seems. My God, Alpha, what the hell have we done?"

Alpha walked over to a makeshift bar and poured himself a healthy dose of Woodford Reserve. "Now, now, Beta. Let's not get ahead of ourselves. Let's examine the research and see where it takes us. It might not be that bad. Hell, it might be good."

Beta was about to protest when they heard the key in the lock. It was Omega.

Alpha looked at Omega with a frown of disapproval. The man, barely 35 years old and fit as a marathon runner, was wearing blue jeans and a white dress shirt, untucked, and boat shoes without socks. His lapel pin was clipped to his open collar.

"Do you even own a suit, Omega?"

"Actually, Alpha, I own two. One for when people get married, and a black one for when they get buried. And we're not doing either of those things here, are we?"

Alpha grumbled about decisions affecting the country being done by people in proper attire and watched as Omega found himself a beer, plopped himself in a chair, and slipped his smartphone out of his shirt pocket. Omega was a smartass, but he was a genius when it came to social media and the way the younger generations communicated. His skills were valuable, even if he did offend Alpha's sense of common decency.

The three made small talk about the stock market and the Yankees until they heard the key in the door for the final time tonight.

That would be Zulu. Three heads turned as one as Zulu entered as she always did, with her long and impossibly toned legs striding confidently atop her stiletto heels. Her black dress was simple and short, and the curves her body added to it made it deliciously complex for the simple male mind.

"Hey, Zu!" Omega said as he met her with a hug. "You're gorgeous as always."

"Thanks, Omega." She set her briefcase on the floor and found her bottle of Chardonnay.

Alpha envied them their youth and good looks. Zulu was only in her twenties and one of the brightest political minds in the world. But, he reminded himself, it was her research that convinced them to make the decision they made in this very room two years ago. And tonight they were here to question that decision.

They freshened their drinks and settled themselves into their chairs. Alpha looked at each of them. Then he returned his gaze to Zulu. He was struck by her beauty; he always was a sucker for raven hair.

"Two years ago, based on your research," he said as he nodded in her direction," we made a decision and our efforts were successful, as usual. Given all that has happened in the last year or so - riots in the Middle East, the world economy sliding away, and so on - did we make the right decision? Did we - the Azalea Team - pick the right man to be President of the United States?"

Alpha, Beta, and Omega all looked expectantly at Zulu. She took a sip of her wine, leaned back in her chair and very slowly crossed her impossible legs. "Hell, yes, boys. And here's why."

For the next thirty minutes she took them through it: the bad stuff wasn't the fault of the current president. His heart was still in the right place, and their agenda was his agenda. She told them what they wanted to hear, even if she didn't believe a word of it.

"And besides," Zulu added, "the other guy was far too conservative for us. He was a knuckle-dragging misogynist, for God's sake. What choice did we have?"

15

"Very well," Alpha said. "Suppose we decide POTUS gets a second term. How do we make that happen in the current environment?"

Zulu had come prepared. She laid out a plan that had all three men grabbing for more liquor.

"Surely there's another way," Beta interjected. "You're talking about bloodshed, for God's sake!"

Zulu looked at Alpha to take the lead. He cleared his throat. "Beta, need I remind you that the color of the Azalea bloom on our lapel pins is blood red for a reason. This organization was started by people looking to correct a terrible mistake by the name of Kennedy. That, too, required bloodshed. I don't take this lightly, but we have to stay focused on our agenda."

Beta looked defeated. Alpha called for a vote; only Beta dissented, and it was barely audible.

"Very well, then. We execute the plan, POTUS gets a second term, and this meeting never happened."

1

Three Years Later

August 31

Only a handful of people knew it ahead of time, but today was going to be one of the days that America would never forget.

In St. Louis, excited political insiders were preparing to nominate Missouri Governor James McHenry to be (they hoped) the next President of the United States. The popular governor had been planning this moment for years, which is why he had successfully steered the convention to his hometown.

McHenry was holed up in the Presidential Suite of a downtown hotel, going over every nuance of his acceptance speech to be delivered the following night. Tonight, his running mate, a retired Marine with a distinguished record of heroism that had been documented in a blockbuster movie, would dish up a big pile of pro-American, patriotic red meat that would have the party faithful in a wild frenzy.

The campaign was going quite well, although it was still an uphill battle to defeat an incumbent president with a lot of personal appeal and who was a gifted orator. Still, McHenry carried with him a solid base of support from the middle of the country, and his choice of Sergeant Major Richard Gunderson as his running mate was hailed as a stroke of genius by the pundits.

"Gun," as he was known, had never held political office but was one of America's most well-known heroes. He had single-handedly defeated a wave of heavily-armed Taliban forces in Afghanistan and freed six American hostages while taking two bullets in his right shoulder, shrapnel in his left hip, and two stab wounds suffered in hand-to-hand combat with the last Taliban standing.

The best part was the video clip of President Darling giving Gun the Medal of Valor in a White House ceremony and calling him "one of the most courageous Americans who ever lived." Of course, that was before McHenry put him on the ticket. Now, the video clip had gone viral on the Internet. Gun was golden.

McHenry got up from his chair to pour himself some coffee. He stretched his back and looked at the sun shining through the Gateway Arch. His reddish hair and Irish good looks were slowly giving way to thinner, grayer hair, but he was still remarkably fit for a man in his fifties with his history of drinking and carousing.

He allowed his mind to drift back to a decade ago, when he was serving in the Missouri Senate and still tinkering with the idea of running for governor. Those had been heady days. He was chairman of the powerful Senate Appropriations Committee, moving billions of dollars around on a handshake. His office was a favorite hangout for his chosen covey of lobbyists. The poker nights were legendary. One day, a lobbyist brought in a digital blood pressure machine and the gang started placing bets on who had the highest reading. Bobby "The Belly" Randolph won, of course. At 300 pounds, with a glass of scotch in one hand and a Cuban cigar in the other, nobody else had a chance. And here's the kicker: he lobbied for the health care industry.

Yes, those were good days. He'd had fun in the governor's office, too, but his staff was always warning him to tone it down. At the beginning, McHenry enjoyed going straight from the capitol to his favorite bar - The Rocks - for a couple of pints of Sam Adams for happy hour. He held court, like politicians used to do in the old days, before political consultants and the invention of YouTube. Now that he was running for President, well, he was practically on house arrest. McHenry vowed to bust loose a little bit if he won the election - maybe fly the old gang in for some poker in the Oval Office.

McHenry grinned at the thought, took one last look at the Arch, and got back to work.

At about nine o'clock that morning, with the precision of a fine, hand-crafted clock, eight Soldiers of Allah moved into position at various locations across the country.

In Waverly, Iowa, a pristine town known primarily for a prestigious private college, a man code-named Allam showed up at a day care center in a full clown costume and started handing out colorful balloons.

Outside of Ft. Polk, Louisiana, Askari walked into a Burger King, ordered a hot cup of coffee and positioned himself near the front door.

In Prairie du Chien, Wisconsin, Basil entered a Walgreens and started looking through the antacids.

Hariz strolled into a pancake house at The Legends shopping center in Kansas City, Kansas. He stood by the door, explaining he was waiting for a friend.

Hasan was in Tunica, Mississippi, playing the nickel slots at a casino that was way too noisy for so early in the morning.

In Metropolis, Illinois, the Hometown of Superman, Jasim went to the public library and started reading a copy of Sports Illustrated.

In Gulf Breeze, Florida, Sayid walked into a beauty salon and inquired about getting a haircut without an appointment. When told he would have to wait a few minutes for Gladys to finish up with her blue rinse, Sayid said he didn't mind.

And in Jefferson City, Missouri, Rafi walked into his living room with a cup of hot coffee and turned on CNN.

At precisely 9:11, all of them shouted "Allahu Akbar!" All except Rafi pulled out their folding machine guns and started shooting.

2

The machine guns held 31 rounds in the clip. Allam made easy work of things at the day care center, hitting 18 children and two college kids who had been entrusted with their care. When the clip ran out, there was no one outside the day care center left standing except Allam. He had seen a frightened worker inside the center peek through a curtain, but he didn't care. He assumed she was calling 9-1-1 by now, but what difference did it make?

As the echo of the shots faded away, Allam could hear the groans and cries of those who were hit but not dead. Above him, balloons of many colors floated away in the sky. Allam wadded up a piece of paper and tossed it onto the playground. He calmly folded up his gun, got into his car, and drove quietly away. It was 9:13.

About a thousand miles south of Waverly, Askari was taking his time inside the Burger King. The ten people who looked like soldiers were the ones he went for first, followed by the children and their parents. He sprayed the last six bullets of his clip into the base of the counter where the brave employees had gone to hide. Askari didn't know if he killed them, but he didn't really care. It was 9:16.

There weren't very many people inside the Walgreen's at Prairie du Chien, so Basil had his gun set to fire single shots. He put a bullet straight into the forehead of the check-out girl, pumped two more into a pimply-faced guy who was stacking Charmin in aisle four, quickly gunned down two elderly ladies and one old guy in a walker with tennis balls on the front legs at the prescription counter. Then he switched to automatic and shot the place all to hell, including the pharmacist on duty. It was still only 9:16.

Hariz managed to empty his clip in less than a minute at the pancake house, hitting 17 people. Within three minutes, there were more than a dozen frantic calls to 9-1-1 about some crazy bastard shooting up The Legends. By 9:16, Hariz was merging onto I-435, his machine gun still hot to the touch.

Sixteen people were dead or dying at the casino in Tunica. In the far corner of the casino, several players were unaware anything had happened and were busily gambling away their grocery money. Oh, sure, there might have been some commotion up front, but why give up a prime slot machine that was due to pay off big any minute now? Hasan drove off in the direction of The Hollywood, where he planned to switch cars and head north. It was 9:20.

Jasim headed north out of Metropolis, Illinois, with nearly a full clip. The public library had been almost deserted, which was a huge disappointment. Don't Americans read anymore, he wondered? Where the hell was everybody? He shot the old lady at the reference desk and some fat guy who was online reading the Drudge Report and left in a huff. Jasim was tempted to shoot some people driving in the opposite direction just for kicks, but such a thing was not part of the plan and therefore strictly forbidden. It was 9:22.

Sayid managed to kill everybody inside the beauty salon, including Gladys with her shiny blue hair. With the odor of spent gunpowder still in his nostrils, it occurred to him that there was no one alive to report what happened, so he picked up the phone and called 9-1-1.

"There has been a shooting at the Clip and Curl," he said. "We're all dead." Then he hung up the phone and laughed all the way to his car. It was 9:24.

At 9:25, Rafi logged onto another one of his Twitter accounts. He sent a direct message to CNN: "Call Waverly, IA PD. Children are dead. Lots of them. Many more will die at the hands of Soldiers of Allah. #AllahuAkbar."

Rafi wondered how long it would take for the hash tag to catch on. He smiled broadly at the thought of Americans adding "Allahu Akbar" to their tweets and typing it into search boxes. He walked to the kitchen for a coffee refill and waited for CNN to break in with a bulletin. He figured it wouldn't take long.

3

CNN did indeed call the Waverly cops, after a heated debate within the newsroom about wasting time and effort on "a stupid hoax." They assigned Ricky Smith to the job, an intern on his last day from Georgia Tech. After a summer of fetching coffee and hauling equipment around, Ricky finally snagged a memorable day when he inquired about a report of dead kids in Waverly.

"How the hell does CNN know about this already?" inquired the officer who answered the phone. "We just got the 9-1-1 call a few minutes ago!"

"So it's true? Kids are dead?" Ricky was frantically waiving at the assignment editor.

"Yes, apparently so, but we don't know a helluva lot. Our officers just got there. How did you guys hear about it?"

"We got a tip. What happened, exactly? How many kids are dead? And how did they die?" Ricky had the phone cradled in his shoulder and was frantically typing notes for the managing editor standing over his shoulder. His typing wasn't very good. It looked like "yes kids ded in waverly...ferw minutesago..."

"Listen, kid, I'll tell you what I know and then I gotta hang up because it's chaos around here. The 9-1-1 caller said some clown was shooting up the playground at the Wee Wee Day Care. A whole bunch of kids got shot and most of 'em look dead."

"Any indication of terrorism?" The managing editor smiled at Ricky. The kid was pretty good.

"Why would you say that? It was some jerk in a clown outfit. Look, kid, I gotta go." The officer hung up.

The managing editor slapped Ricky on the back. "Please tell me you recorded that."

"Of course."

"Good work, Ricky. Send me the mp3." The managing editor was already halfway to his desk, loosening his tie. "And get me some coffee!"

At 9:45, CNN broke in with a bulletin about a deadly shooting at the Wee Wee Day Care in Waverly, Iowa. "According to Waverly police," the news anchor said, "someone dressed up as a clown was - quote - shooting up the playground. A whole bunch of kids got shot and most appear to be dead - end quote. Stay tuned to CNN for more on this breaking story."

At about the same time, CNN tweeted a shorter version of the bulletin. Rafi was pleased, but puzzled, too. Why no mention of terrorism? He tweeted again, this time for all to see: "CNN says kids shot dead in Waverly, IA. They should check on Ft. Polk, too. #AllahuAkbar!"

At the time CNN was breaking the news about the Waverly shooting, Allam was in a small farmhouse north of town, where he had slit the throat of an elderly widow. He stripped off the clown outfit, showered, changed into blue jeans and a tee shirt, threw his machine gun and duffel bag into the old lady's car and headed south. He knew his partners were doing pretty much the same thing.

The CNN newsroom was a beehive of activity. Ricky had been assigned to keep track of any tweets with the #AllahuAkbar hash tag. The brain trusts were debating what to do about the allusion to terrorism in the original tweet. Should they report it? Should they call the feds? Opinions were all over the map.

Then Ricky stuck his head in with the news about Ft. Polk. According to police, someone had shot up a Burger King less than an hour ago. Lots of dead soldiers; kids, too.

"And our Twitter friend tipped us off to it, but not just us. Fox News is on it, too."

"Jesus Christ!" exclaimed the news director as he jumped out of his chair. "Let's get busy! Report the potential terrorism connection immediately. Put the fucking tweets on the air! And we better alert the feds."

By ten o'clock, several Waverly parents who had dropped their kids at the Wee Wee that morning were rushing to the scene, having heard about the shooting on CNN or Twitter, or from co-workers. What they found was a grisly scene: lots of little lumps covered with blankets. There were no little children - none - waiting to be picked up by thankful parents.

Rafi tweeted again: "Soldiers of Allah have hit the beast. Infidels dead in IA, LA, WI, KS, MS, IL, FL. Only the beginning. #AllahuAkbar!" Then he called his girlfriend. He wondered if she was free for lunch.

4

By 10:30, it appeared to Rafi that every news network in America was on the story. He flipped from channel to channel, taking immense pride in the reports that a group called "Soldiers of Allah" had taken credit for the killings of dozens of innocent Americans throughout the nation's heartland. Early estimates were 20 dead in Waverly, 18 at the Ft. Polk Burger King, 6 at the drug store in Prairie du Chien, 19 at the Kansas pancake house, 15 at the Tunica casino, only 2 at the library in Metropolis, and 12 at the Clip and Curl in Florida.

The anchor on CNN looked particularly stricken when he said, "Ninety-two dead, so far."

Rafi tweeted: "Not even the children of infidels escape the wrath of Allah. #AllahuAkbar!" He splashed some water on his face, dried it off and winked at his reflection in the mirror. It was time to meet Connie for lunch.

Rafi was dressed pretty much like everyone else, in blue jeans and an open-collared shirt. No turban or any sign of Arab dress, but he still drew a lot of stares as he walked into the restaurant and greeted his darling Connie.

"Here we go again," he said to Connie, as they were seated.

"What do you mean, Rafi?"

"It's just like the days after 9/11, when I was back East. People think everyone who looks like an Arab is a terrorist. It's probably not even safe to be seen with me."

"Don't say that, Rafi. I'm proud to be seen with you. I know how much you love this country." She reached across the table and put one of her fleshy hands over his.

"Thank you, Connie. God, what a horrible day. All those innocent people! And the children! It makes me sick to my stomach." He squeezed her hand. "It's so good to see you."

Connie Baumgartner squeezed back and smiled. God, she was head over heels for this man. They had met a few months earlier at The Rocks. She had been sitting outside, enjoying the sun and a pint of Blue Moon with a girlfriend when Rafi walked up. He inquired as to whether he could scoot an empty chair over to another table. Instead of scooting the chair, though, Rafi stood there talking to Connie.

It was a new experience for Connie. Unlike her friend, Connie was not gorgeous; just the opposite. At least fifty pounds overweight, Connie had pretty much resigned herself to a life without a man, except for the occasional drunk. Rafi, however, seemed genuinely interested in her. And she found his dark looks and fit body attractive.

To her surprise, Rafi called her the next day for a date. They talked for hours. Connie learned that Rafi actually liked bigger women (or so he said). The dating continued and eventually they became intimate. Rafi never once remarked about her weight or even looked at other women while they were together.

Connie had found her soul mate.

Rafi ordered a grilled chicken salad. Connie, it being Wednesday, ordered the meat loaf and mashed potatoes with extra gravy and free pie.

"So," Rafi said, "are you ready for school to start next week?"

"I am! I'm looking forward to it. Just eighteen kids this year. Beats the heck out of 24, like last year."

"But you were the Jefferson City Teacher of the Year last year," Rafi reminded her. "You did alright."

Connie blushed. "Yeah, I had some good kids."

"You're great with kids. Have you ever thought about having some of your own?"

"Well, yes. But not without getting married."

"Yeah, I guess," Rafi said, giving her hand another squeeze as he winked at her. "First things first."

The food arrived, and Connie stuck a forkful of mashed potatoes and gravy into her mouth. But Rafi bringing up the topic of marriage gave her a lump in her throat and was making it hard to swallow.

While Connie and Rafi were enjoying lunch, the confirmed death toll from the day's attacks went up to 97. Also, it was discovered that the crumpled note left behind by Allam at the Wee Wee matched exactly the last anonymous tweet from Rafi: "Not even the children of infidels escape the wrath of Allah."

"My God in heaven," remarked one of the terrorism experts on a CNN panel, not knowing his microphone was hot. "What the fuck is going on?"

5

The White House issued a statement early in the afternoon condemning the "cowardly attacks" and urging Americans to be "alert but not fearful" and warning against "jumping to unfair conclusions." The President, the statement said, was in constant contact with his security team and would be addressing the nation from the Oval Office early in the evening. All of his campaign activities were being suspended.

"The bastard," spat Lucas Washington, chief of staff to Gov. James McHenry and his most trusted advisor. "He's trying to upstage our convention!"

"No, he's not, Lucas," McHenry cautioned. "He's being presidential. The nation needs to hear from him. The whole damn country is scared to death. And announcing a suspension of his re-election campaign is smart, very smart. The question is what do *we* do?"

"Well, we can't act like nothing happened," offered Gunderson from a corner chair. "I can't go out there tonight and give the speech I've been practicing for a fucking week."

"Obviously not," McHenry agreed. He looked expectantly at his chief of staff. "Lucas? Any ideas?"

"Jesus, boss, I don't know." Lucas was pacing his tall, muscular body around the suite. He pointed to the TV, where Fox News was blabbering away about the loss of innocence in the heartland. "We can't have a fucking political convention while the whole damn country is mourning the loss of a hundred Goddamn people!"

"Calm down, Lucas. Calm down. Think. Is there a way we can turn a negative into a positive?"

Lucas stared at the governor for a long five seconds. Then, he snapped his fingers. "What if we turn the convention into a fundraiser? You know, for the families of the victims? Like we did after Katrina?"

"I like it," Gunderson said. "I like it a lot."

McHenry was nodding his head. "Excellent idea, Lucas. And lay it on thick. With the gravity of what happened this morning, I'm betting the public will lap it up like a kitten on cream. Get on it."

Lucas was already on his cell phone. McHenry turned to his running mate. "Gun, get Donna busy on re-writing your speech. Keep it short and stay flexible. Who knows what the hell else is going to happen today?"

"Right on cue," Lucas said, as he was pointing at the television and turning up the volume. "Get a load of this."

Congressman Henry Walters, a liberal war horse who seemed like he was in Congress when Elvis Presley first appeared on the Ed Sullivan Show, was snarling.

"I'm just saying it seems obvious to me," Walters said. "Seven attacks in seven states, all committed with a gun. If guns weren't so damn easy to get in this country, all of these victims would be alive today. It's not the Arabs, dammit, it's the guns!"

Lucas couldn't wipe the smile off his face. "Thank you, Jesus!" he said with his long arms spread wide. Then he turned to McHenry and said, "Stupid sonsabitches! Always blaming the guns!"

An hour later the McHenry campaign issued a statement agreeing with the President to suspend political activities for the time being. The convention would still convene that evening as scheduled, but would become a nationwide fundraiser for the families of the victims. Governor McHenry himself would be among those manning the phones and taking pledges. The campaign donated $1 million on its own.

The news media ate it up. Donations started pouring in immediately on a special website that Lucas had ordered. It appeared the audience for Gunderson's speech would be huge, perhaps the biggest ever for a potential vice president.

At the White House, the mood was glum.

"The sonofabitch is pretty smart, I'll give him that," President Maury Darling said. Darling, at 60 years old, still maintained his slight build and a full head of gray hair. He turned to his own chief of staff, who had been his constant sidekick since he was first elected mayor of Denver twenty-five years ago. "Any ideas, Kennedy?"

Kennedy Jackson looked at his older boss and smirked. "The mind is always churning." But it didn't sound as cocky as he intended.

6

"Make it a Boulevard, Roxy."

Rafi was at The Rocks, chatting with a couple of lobbyists, who also happened to be his clients. Rafi was a private pilot for a flying service that catered to the well-to-do. These particular lobbyists were two of twelve who each owned a fraction of The Screaming Eagle, a luxury jet that was due to arrive from the manufacturer next week. It could seat a dozen adults comfortably, though there would be no reason for all twelve lobbyists to be on the plane at the same time. They wanted it to ferry clients to and from Jefferson City, mostly, and now and then to Washington. And Augusta, Georgia. Pebble Beach.

He was seated at the window, which was actually a garage door that was open, revealing a large screen to the sidewalk.

"Helluva thing," he said for the umpteenth time, shaking his head. The lobbyists agreed it was a helluva thing as they looked at the big screen television behind the bar, reading the scrolling headlines. Hearing the television was impossible.

Roxy brought the pint of Boulevard Pale Ale and pointed to the United States flag on his lapel. "I love the pin."

Rafi smiled. "Gotta be a patriot, especially today." His face darkened. "I get a lot of dirty looks, you know."

"I know," Roxy said. "But don't worry. You're among friends."

"Hey, Roxy, turn up the TV," one of the lobbyists said. "Darling is coming on."

Roxy turned up the sound and the bar got quiet.

"My fellow Americans," President Darling began, "today was a horrible day for all of us. A hundred innocent men, women, and even children, who did nothing more sinister than show up for work or play with their friends, were gunned down by a gang of seven cowardly killers. In one instance, the coward hid behind the makeup of a clown. In all cases, they chose to hide behind one of the world's great religions.

"Tonight, we mourn as one for these victims and their grieving families. And we pray for the lives of dozens more innocent people who at this moment are hurt, hospitalized, or clinging to every precious breath.

"Today's attack was unique in that the killers struck at the very heartland of America, mostly in small towns that had previously been untouched by such horrific brutality and senseless killing. Understandably, all of America is afraid tonight, and angry, especially since these cowards have not yet been caught.

"But make no mistake. All of the capabilities of the federal government have been unfurled in the pursuit of these killers. Along with local and state police in the affected states, we have already developed several promising leads. In Illinois, Wisconsin, and Mississippi, we have obtained footage from security cameras which will help in identifying the perpetrators.

"In every case, the killers left behind spent shell casings. The FBI tells us the weapon was the same in each case - a machine gun that used to be outlawed in the United States before a previous Congress allowed a critical public safety law to expire, effectively creating a dangerous loophole that eventually led to today's multiple massacres.

"We inherited this loophole, but mark my words. We intend to close it and make America safe again. I call on Congress to take this action immediately.

"Obviously, this won't bring today's victims back to life or help us track these killers down and bring them to justice. But we won't look a threat straight in the eye and blink. Not on my watch.

"Finally, I'd like to speak directly to the killers, who I'm certain are somewhere in America, watching this right now."

Rafi flinched, but kept his composure.

"You cowards stand no chance against the United States of America. We will find you and you will spend the rest of your lives in prison. Stop hiding behind the skirt of Islam and show yourselves. Give yourselves up now, or face the consequences.

"My fellow Americans, God bless you, and God bless America."

Rafi quietly tapped out a text message to the other "cowards."

"*We are go for Phase Two.*"

7

The convention center in downtown St. Louis was a bizarre scene. It was all decorated for a political convention, with colorful bunting and balloons everywhere. The usual array of expensive skyboxes had been erected for the major news networks. The floor was full of people in ridiculous hats.

But there was no politics, not in the normal sense, anyway. Speaker after speaker still strode across the podium to the lectern and spoke to the masses, but there was no fiery political rhetoric. Instead, everyone begged for money for the families of the victims. The money was pouring in, too.

Then, shortly before nine o'clock, the delegates nominated Sergeant Major Richard Gunderson to the office of Vice President of the United States by acclimation. A short video played, with scenes from the movie "Gun" spliced together with testimonials about the greatness of the man. The entire convention center hooted when President Darling was seen describing Gunderson as "one of the most courageous Americans who ever lived."

The house went dark. The announcer intoned, "Ladies and gentlemen, the next Vice President of the United States, Sergeant Major Richard Gunderson!"

A spotlight hit the lectern and there he stood, in full dress uniform, as stiff and straight as a hickory tree, the medals practically blinding in their brightness. He stood there, tall and fit, his jaw firmly set, his eyes roaming the crowd as they cheered relentlessly for him. His salt-and-pepper hair was in a strict military cut. Only when the crowd started chanting, "Gun! Gun! Gun!" did he crack a grin and hold up his arms to quiet them.

"My friends," he began quietly, "because I look out tonight and see so much pain and sorrow; and because I believe with all my heart that our fellow Americans deserve better; and because I'm confident that my lifelong experience in the service of this great country has prepared me to help at least a little bit; and because I love this country more than life itself; I humbly accept your nomination to the office of vice president."

This set off another furious round of cheering. Because he had been well-coached, Gun stood erect and let it happen. He panned the crowd and occasionally nodded to those who made eye contact. The news networks cut to scenes of the crowd, where many people, mostly women, were wiping away tears or openly bawling.

"As you know, I've never been in politics, but I understand public service. And service is what I promise.

"Almost exactly twelve hours ago, a bunch of radical Islamic terrorists stuck a bloody dagger into the very heart of this nation. Tonight, we pray for the victims and their families. And we've been raising money for the families, which is a good idea Governor McHenry had, by the way, showing us the kind of leadership he'll offer in the office of president.

"But that's not all we can do. We can, and we must, bring these deadly terrorists to justice. And, make it clear to the world, that the United States of America will not sit back and wait to be attacked. We need to take the fight directly to the enemy.

"I know. I've been behind enemy lines. I have fought the enemy with these very hands. I've seen the evil in their eyes. I've taken shrapnel from the enemy, and I've killed the enemy. And I'm not afraid to do it again!"

This had the crowd in an absolute frenzy. "Gun! Gun! Gun!" they shouted. Some of them started marching around the floor, waving small American flags. The celebration went on for several minutes before Gunderson quieted them down.

"I'm not going to speak for very long tonight, but I want to make something very clear. Earlier this evening, President Darling spoke to the American people and offered the nation's heartfelt sympathy for what happened today. I join him in that.

"But just so we understand each other. I've been around guns all my life. And I've never seen one rise up - on its own - and kill people. To respond to today's terrorist attacks by vowing to get rid of the guns is like wishing George W. Bush had responded to 9/11 by outlawing airplanes!

"And one more thing. Did you notice President Darling never once used the word 'terrorist'? C'mon, Mr. President, you can do it. It starts with a 't', ends with a 't', and has a whole lot of evil in between."

Gunderson was looking straight into the camera, his eyes fierce.

"If you're afraid to say the word, Mr. President, how can we expect you to have the courage to stand and fight? If that's the case, move aside, Mr. President, because

Governor McHenry and I aren't afraid to fight and we're itching for the job!

"Thank you, God bless you, and God bless America!"

At the White House, Kennedy Jackson let loose with a low whistle and said, "That's one tough sonofabitch. One of the bravest men in America."

President Darling looked at his chief of staff and said, "Shut the fuck up."

8

September 1

Allam needed a cigarette. He had made the short trip from Waverly to Cedar Rapids, Iowa, the day before and left the car he had stolen from the dead widow in the parking lot of a city park. He spent the rest of the day riding around the city on the buses, taking in the sights, watching the people. The 'no smoking' signs were everywhere. It appeared the consumption of tobacco was akin to a dangerous felony in the great state of Iowa.

He left his cheap motel room with his heavy black backpack and lit up in the morning sunshine. *Phase Two.* It would be another glorious day for the Soldiers of Allah.

Allam started walking to the nearest bus stop about a block away. It was a busy street; the cars were zipping by. Busy was good. Busy means people, and people mean bodies.

There was a smattering of people waiting to board the bus. One of them was wearing a McDonald's uniform. Another looked like she might be a maid at a Holiday Inn. One old man looked confused, like maybe he wasn't used to catching the bus. What did it matter? Allam already considered them dead.

Allam let everyone else board the bus ahead of him. He even helped one frail old lady, who thanked him for his kindness. Allam took a seat in the middle of the bus. His backpack made it uncomfortable to sit, however, so he slid it off and stuffed it onto the floor of the empty seat next to him. He settled back and waited.

The next stop was only about a mile down the road near a shopping mall. Two people waited to board the bus. Allam stood and walked to the front. The kid in the McDonald's uniform did the same. They exited the bus, one after the other. As Allam stood and watched the bus depart in a cloud of acrid black smoke, he thought about the kid hoofing it to the McDonald's on the corner, and fate.

Free of his heavy backpack, Allam strolled into the mall parking lot, toward the cars parked the furthest away from the building. These would be the cars of the workers; they wouldn't know one was missing for several hours. Allam stole a bland-looking silver one and drove quietly away.

It was 8:30 on a quiet, late-summer morning in Cedar Rapids.

The air was thicker in New Orleans, where Askari was just finishing up his beignets and deep, rich coffee. He wiped the powdered sugar from his lips and beard, threw the paper napkin into a waste can, and walked briskly through the humid air surrounding Jackson Square. His backpack was still in the café.

Basil had found his way to a lovely old church on a university campus in Omaha, Nebraska. He sat for a while, admiring the beautiful stained-glass windows and ornate woodwork. It was an odd choice, he thought, sending him here where there would be no people at this time of the day, but he was a loyal soldier. At the appropriate time, Basil hefted his suitcase along one wall and pushed it under a pew. He left quietly. The church was empty. Outside, an easterly breeze was freshening and it looked like rain. Basil drove away hurriedly.

Hariz was in Tulsa, Oklahoma, where a shopping mall was just coming to life with mall walkers and employees. An overpriced coffee shop called *Latte Da* was doing a brisk business. Hariz ordered a latte, took a seat, and opened his notebook computer. He was just another Internet and coffee addict, paying too much for one so he could get the other for free. After a brief time, Hariz left his latte sitting next to his open computer and wandered away. Five minutes later he was in his car driving leisurely out of the parking lot.

Hasan was standing in line with other gawkers, waiting to get into the Bill Clinton Presidential Library in Little Rock. He struck up a conversation with a retired couple from Eureka Springs, Arkansas. They worked part time selling trinkets at the Passion Play, and they were urging him to visit sometime.

"Lotta good bed and breakfasts up there," the man said with a nod. "Plus, you might learn something about Jesus."

Hasan smiled. "Maybe I'll do that. But first, I'm going to learn about Bill Clinton. You know," Hasan said with a wink, "start at the bottom and work my way up."

They had a little laugh at that, and then Hasan looked stricken. "Oh no! I left my camera in the car! Can you hold this for me?" He handed the old man his backpack. "I need to go get my camera!"

The old man hefted the backpack. "Why sure. Whaddya got in here? Bricks?"

"Just a few!" Hasan joked as he backed away. "I'll be right back. Thanks!" He scurried off in the direction of the parking lot.

"What a nice young man," the lady said. "Kinda restores your faith in young people."

In Nashville, Jasim walked into a post office and slid a heavy box about the size of a briefcase through the slot that said "letters and packages." It didn't have any postage, but what did it matter?

Sayid, after shooting poor Gladys and the other ladies at the Clip and Curl, had driven to Tallahassee, Florida, and spent the night at a downtown hotel. This morning, he walked to the historic original capitol building, where legislators had openly wept upon learning the South had lost the Civil War. Well, Sayid thought, it was time for more weeping.

He carefully placed his backpack near the front entrance and left without looking back.

It was 8:45 on another glorious morning in Jefferson City. Rafi patted Angel on the head and sipped his coffee in the morning sun. He pulled out his smart phone, logged onto the anonymous Twitter account that already had more than 300,000 gruesome followers (including all the important news networks and, he suspected, the Department of Homeland Security) and tweeted: "Shock and Awe at 9:11!

Another mighty blow from the Soldiers of Allah! #AllahuAkbar!"

9

Panic.

Rafi's tweet sailed through the Twitterverse at lightning speed as his followers retweeted it, usually adding their own comments, like OMG or WTF. The major news networks, all of which were discussing the terror attacks of the previous day in some fashion anyway, immediately broke in with bulletins.

"The group claiming credit for yesterday's terror attacks in the heartland has issued a new threat," declared CNN. "Though it hasn't been independently verified, the group is apparently threatening 'shock and awe' at 9:11. But we don't know where, or how."

In cities across the country, people started fleeing the taller office buildings, or tried to. New York City and Washington, D.C., of course were especially nervous, but the panic was everywhere. The killings of the previous day had peeled away the cloak of safety felt by the folks in "flyover country" during and after previous terror attacks. People gathered around televisions. Anyone who looked the least bit like an Arab was shunned.

The White House was in total chaos. In the situation room, President Darling looked at those assembled. "Why can't we find these bastards? Can't we track them through Twitter?"

"It's a totally anonymous account," said the Director of National Intelligence. "As far as we know, he could be tweeting from Bangladesh."

"Bangladesh, my ass! The Soldiers of Allah aren't in Bangladesh. They're *here*. They killed a bunch of innocent people yesterday and it looks like they're going to gun down a bunch more in," the President looked at the clock, "about nine fucking minutes. So tell me. What do we do now?"

The room fell silent. Finally, the DNI cleared his throat. "I guess we wait." It came out sounding like a man waiting to be fired.

The McHenry campaign suite in St. Louis was a beehive of activity. The poll numbers looked good after Gun's speech last night and campaign contributions were rolling in. But there was an electric edge to the air. It wasn't panic; it was more like worry. McHenry and his campaign team felt good about the way they had handled things yesterday and last night, but what would today bring? And now the threat of more attacks in just a few minutes; what then?

The TV was on and the sound was up. The talking heads were having a field day.

"This is an edge of terror we haven't seen before," noted one expert. "We know with absolute certainty that something will happen and people will die. We don't know who or where or how. We look at each other and think, 'Are you next, or am I?' It's dreadful!"

It was 9:05. Rafi was enjoying the last of his coffee. He tweeted: "52401 70112 68101 74101 72201 37201 32301 #AllahuAkbar!"

At 9:10, the Director of National Intelligence snapped his cell phone shut and announced, "They're zip codes. The sonofabitch wants us to know where to look!"

"Shit!" President Darling slammed his left hand on the table. "It's too late to warn anybody. What the fuck are we supposed to do with that information?"

The Secretary of Homeland Security spoke up. "Mr. President, we've notified the first responders in each city listed to be on the alert that any incident could be a terrorist attack, or a prelude to an attack. It's not much, but it's all we got."

Darling started pacing. "Is Washington on the list?"

"No."

"How about St. Louis?"

"No."

"Good. The last thing we need is for McHenry to survive some terrorist attack. The bastard would probably stand on the rubble with a bullhorn."

At precisely 9:11, a bus exploded in peaceful Cedar Rapids, killing 19.

In New Orleans, 15 people doing nothing more threatening than drinking coffee were blown to pieces.

A suitcase in a church in Omaha exploded, killing nobody, but starting an intense and rapidly spreading fire.

At the mall in Tulsa, the only place open with a TV on was the *Latte Da.* A crowd of about 20 was nervously watching the news when the notebook computer Hariz had abandoned buzzed once, then twice. As the people turned to look, it exploded in a shower of roofing nails.

The nice elderly couple in Little Rock had hung back, letting others cut in line ahead of them when the Clinton Library opened at nine. Finally, they went to the admissions desk and the old man hefted the backpack onto the desk.

"Some guy gave..." They were his last words as the backpack exploded with amazing fury, killing him, his wife, and ten other people who were milling around.

Six people died at the Nashville post office when the package without postage exploded. Five of the victims were postal workers sorting the mail. One guy just happened to pick precisely the wrong moment to drop a package through the slot.

And in Tallahassee, only one person was killed - a maintenance worker who had seen the abandoned backpack and was carrying it away. His action saved lives, saved the historic old capitol, but made his wife a widow.

10

Things were not going well in Omaha.

Lloyd Epperson had been fighting fires in Omaha for 30 years. Today was supposed to be an easy last day on the job, complete with a retirement party and a big sheet cake from Hy-Vee. The cake was back at the station, still in the plastic container, sitting on the kitchen table. It was in the shape of a golf hole, with a yellow flag, and said, "Good Luck, Lloyd!"

He thought about that now, because there was something not right about this fire. It was raining, and that helped, but there was something about the smoke. Lloyd wondered what in the heck was in the church that would make such funny-looking smoke.

The rubberneckers were starting to gather, of course, because this church was a landmark of sorts. There was no need to cordon off the area, to keep the onlookers a safe distance away. The heat of the fire was taking care of that. Lloyd was certain it would be nothing but smoldering rubble at the end of the day. He was hoping to save the nearby buildings.

Jesus, the damn smoke. Even with his mask, Lloyd was starting to have trouble catching his breath. His lungs burned, desperate for more oxygen. His eyes started to water, then burn, like they were filling up with heavy sweat. He couldn't see very well, but his heart jumped when he realized Jimmy Bane, the hotshot kid with the killer smile who had only been on the job for about a month, ripped off his mask, fell to his knees and started puking.

"Jimmy! Jimmy!" Lloyd stumbled, then realized that he, too, was about to vomit. "Oh, Jesus!"

Lloyd ripped off the mask, bent over, and let it go. God, it hurt. He looked over at Jimmy, tried to say something, but vomited again, harder this time. Jesus, Jimmy, Lloyd thought, here we are barfing up cinnamon rolls in front of God and everybody.

Lloyd fell to his knees. Somebody was grabbing for him, trying to help him, but he didn't know who. He vomited again, just bile this time, because there was nothing left, and fell to the ground.

Lloyd's thoughts turned to his wife, and suddenly the water in his eyes was from his tears. They were supposed to have thirty more years, dammit! He had promised her. "Thirty years on the job, followed by thirty more years with you, sweetheart," he had said to her, more than once, including this morning. But it was what he didn't say, what he had forgotten to say, that came to him now. With great effort, his lungs searing with pain, Lloyd said it. "I love you, baby doll."

As darkness washed over him, Lloyd also wanted to say he was sorry, but he couldn't get it out. Not that it mattered. He couldn't have said it loud enough for anyone to hear, and besides, everyone within earshot was already dead.

11

"We've got an Omaha problem."

It was Kennedy, the president's chief of staff. They were still in the situation room.

"I thought it was just a church fire," Darling said.

Kennedy cringed, running a hand through his mop of curly black hair. "Please don't use the phrase 'just a church fire' outside this room. And it's not just a church fire, not anymore. There are casualties."

Darling sighed and hung his head. "Go on."

"Thirteen firefighters. The ones who got there first."

Darling looked up sharply. "Are you telling me they're all dead?"

"All but one, and he's in pretty bad shape."

"What the hell happened?"

Kennedy was shaking his head. "We don't know for certain. There was an awful lot of smoke. All of a sudden, this first batch of firefighters just started dropping like flies."

"Mr. President." It was the head of Homeland Security. "We have to consider the possibility that the church bomb was more than just a bomb."

"Meaning?"

"Maybe it was dirty."

Kennedy jumped in, his eyes wide. "Dirty? You mean nuclear?"

She shook her head. "I doubt it. The effects of the fallout you'd get from a bomb packed with nuclear material wouldn't be felt so quickly. I'm thinking some kind of chemical."

"You mean like mustard gas or something?"

She nodded. "Or something."

Darling took a deep breath. "Okay. Let's assume it was dirty, and the bastards have managed to disburse a chemical weapon in the middle of Omaha. What do we do?"

"Evacuate the area immediately, of course. I'd say ten blocks or so, depending on the wind. We need to get a hazmat team in there and figure out what we're dealing with. And we need immediate autopsies on the victims. Activate FEMA."

"What about the fire?" It was Kennedy.

"What about it?"

Kennedy put his hands in the air. "It's still burning! What are we supposed to do? Let Omaha burn to the ground?"

"We can fight it from the air. But we have to act quickly to get the people out of harm's way. Save lives first. Worry about the buildings second."

Kennedy was pacing. "Jesus! I'm having this vision of CNN showing us dropping water on a church fire from the air! And half of Omaha burns to the ground! Then we can send in Janet Reno to finish the job!"

"Calm down, Kennedy." Darling turned to his Homeland Security chief. "Get FEMA moving. Order the evacuation."

"Mr. President." It was the Director of National Intelligence. "The governor of Nebraska is on the phone."

Darling cocked his head in Kennedy's direction. "Who is the governor of Nebraska?"

Kennedy shrugged. "I guess we're about to find out."

Darling put the phone on speaker. "Governor, I know you're dealing with a terrible situation down there. I want you to know we're acting quickly on this end. I've ordered the activation of FEMA and the immediate evacuation of a ten-block radius around the church. We'll have to fight the fire from the air."

"That won't be necessary, Mr. President."

"What do you mean it won't be necessary? We think we're dealing with a chemical weapon down there. We need to get the people out."

"Oh, I agree about the evacuation. In fact, we're already doing it. I mean it won't be necessary to fight the fire from the air. The fire is out."

"It's out? How?"

"Well, it's raining pretty hard, which helped. But we put out a mutual aid call after the first firefighters went down. We made it clear it was a very dangerous fire and any responders would essentially be volunteering to put their lives squarely on the line. More than usual. Almost a suicide mission."

"How many responded?"

There was a pause while the governor gathered himself. "All of 'em. That's why I'm calling, Mr. President. I think you should come to Omaha."

12

"Absolutely out of the question!"

They had been arguing for several minutes after the phone call ended. Anne Scofield, the head of Homeland Security, was hitting the table with light karate chops to emphasize her words. Already a severe looking woman with her black hair pulled back into a tight bun, her face was in a scowl.

"We can't guarantee your safety. We don't know for sure what we're dealing with. This country is under attack. Who knows? This whole thing might have been engineered to draw you in, or at least pull you out of the White House, where you're safe. You cannot, under any circumstances, go to Omaha."

Darling turned to Kennedy. "Didn't you say one of the first responders survived?"

"Yes," Kennedy nodded. "Hospitalized in critical condition."

"Is the Vice President available to command the Situation Room, if necessary?"

"I believe so," Kennedy said. "She's having her annual check-up this morning. She's been bitching about it to her staff, complaining about the mammogram."

"I don't blame her," Scofield interjected. "I hate those damn things, too."

"Get an advance team in the air immediately," Darling decided. "I want to visit the hospital first, then hold a private meeting with the spouses of the dead firefighters, and then publicly thank the many firefighters who responded to the call for mutual aid. We'll take the press pool, but they won't know where we're going until we get there."

"Mr. President!" Scofield was standing now. "You're making a huge mistake! You cannot..."

Darling cut her off. "That's enough, Anne. Your objections are duly noted, but I'm going to Omaha. It's not as good as standing on a crushed fire truck with a bullhorn at Ground Zero, but it ain't bad."

"Mr. President!" Her hands were fisted. "This is not a photo-op!"

Darling smiled. "Anne, like it or not, everything I do is a photo-op, and the imagery is important. In this case, I want the people to know it's the President of the United States who cares enough to visit the critically injured firefighter. It's the President of the United States comforting the grieving spouses. It's the President of the United States thanking the brave firefighters. It's the President of the United States who cares so much about Omaha."

"And it's NOT," Kennedy added with a wide smile, "the Governor of Missouri."

"Bingo!" Darling held up his right palm and Kennedy high-fived it.

Scofield was shaking her head. "Will you at least take extra safety precautions?"

"Of course, Anne. But you don't have to take my word for it. You can see for yourself." Darling smiled at her puzzled expression. "You're coming with me. And afterward, we'll eat Omaha steaks. I hear they're unbelievable."

13

Air Force One landed at Eppley Airfield at 4:45 that afternoon. The press pool was whisked to the hospital first, so they could set up. President Darling, Anne Scofield, and Kennedy Jackson followed behind.

Because there was so little time to prepare, the Secret Service had ordered the airport closed for the duration of the presidential visit. Traffic was stopped for miles. No visitors were permitted within three blocks of the hospital.

"What's the governor's name again?" Darling asked.

"Ribald," Kennedy replied. "Windsor Ribald."

"Doesn't exactly roll off the tongue. Kinda wimpy."

"Yeah, not as manly as Maury Darling."

"Not nearly."

"Might I remind the two of you," Scofield interjected, "that we are about to visit a man who may be dead by the time we get home, and whose wife has probably spent the day crying her eyes out? And the whole damn world will be watching? You said it yourself. Imagery is important."

The motorcade pulled to a stop at the emergency entrance.

"Right you are, Anne. Now pay attention. It's show time."

President Darling instantly recognized the voice of the man who first greeted him and found it interesting that Governor Ribald was, indeed, bald. "Welcome to Omaha, Mr. President."

"Thank you, Governor Ribald. I wish it was under better circumstances. I hear your people did a fantastic job on the evacuation at Ground Zero."

Darling and Kennedy had decided during the flight to call the church site Ground Zero to add gravity to the visit.

"Thank you. Nebraskans are tough people. We get the job done. If you take just one thing with you after this visit, Mr. President, it's the knowledge that Nebraskans are tough - tougher than any terrorist. We'll soldier on."

As they entered the hospital, Darling nodded gravely, patting the governor on the shoulder. "All Americans can draw strength from that, Governor. All of us."

At the Intensive Care Unit, President Darling was greeted by the director of hospital services and the physician treating the firefighter.

"Mr. President," the doctor began, "the patient is in critical condition. He can't communicate, but he might be able to hear you.

"But it's so good that you're here," she added with intensity. Her eyes were on fire. "His wife is here, and she's taking it very hard, of course."

The entourage entered the ICU to the backdrop of the beeping heart monitor and the hissing of the ventilator. The press pool was gaggled into one of the corners.

"Doris," the doctor said to a handsome woman in her fifties with puffy eyes and graying hair who was twisting a Kleenex in her hands. "President Darling is here. Mr. President, I'd like you to meet a very strong woman. Her name is Doris Epperson."

14

"I thought you'd be taller," Doris observed.

Everybody laughed, even the press pool.

"I get that a lot," Darling admitted, chuckling. "Mrs. Epperson, on behalf of the..."

"Oh, please," she said with a wave of the Kleenex. "Call me Doris, Mr. President. Only my students are allowed to call me Mrs. Epperson."

"Okay. And you can call me Maury."

Doris shook her head. "I think I'll stick with Mr. President. I mean, it's an honor to meet the president, and to have you here in Omaha, and every time I call you Mr. President, it reinforces the honor.

"And besides," she added as she leaned closer, "I don't really like the name Maury. Never did."

More laughter. It was hard not to like this woman, Darling thought.

"Well, as I was saying, Doris, the American people are all praying for your husband to pull through. And we're grateful for his courageous service."

"Thank you, Mr. President. Now come over here. I want you to meet my husband."

She took hold of her husband's hand. Beneath the ventilator, with all the wires and beeps, if Lloyd knew what was happening, no one could tell.

"Lloyd, the president is here. President Darling. I know we didn't vote for him." She paused to let the laughter subside. "But it was awfully nice of him to come all this way. Mr. President, this is my husband, Lloyd Epperson."

Darling stepped forward and clasped both of his hands around theirs. "It's an honor to meet you, Lloyd. I'm here with a message from the American people. We want you to be strong and to pull through. We need you to get well. And this wonderful woman you married; she needs you, too. We're all praying for you.

"And I'll promise you this. When you're well enough to travel, you'll get a party at the White House. That's a promise."

Then Darling bowed his head in silent prayer for about five seconds. Kennedy winked at Scofield. His grin was huge.

As they were leaving, Doris grabbed Darling's hand. "Mr. President, I appreciate the promise about the party at the White House, but I need you to make me a promise, too."

"What's that, Doris?"

She leaned in and her eyes were as furious as any Darling had ever seen. "You nail the sonsabitches who did this to my husband!"

15

The mood was grim at the McHenry suite in St. Louis.

McHenry, Gun, Lucas, and the top campaign people had just watched the CNN report from Omaha. It looked like Darling had been in the editing room, directing things and picking the video footage - even writing the script.

"That was a masterful performance," McHenry observed. "And in two hours, I get to go on stage and follow it by looking like a politician. Jesus."

"I think your speech still works, Governor," Lucas insisted. "But we've got to address what the president just did in Omaha. We can't let him own the Epperson story."

"Agreed. Get some talking points put together, something quick, but keep 'em out of the speech. I'll wing it. I want the press to be surprised.

"Now, everybody out. I need to relax before the speech."

Air Force One was back in the air by 7:30 that evening. Anne Scofield was huddled with the traveling press corps at the back of the plane.

"We think it was ricin, and highly weaponized at that. Very sophisticated. It looks like the bomb dispersed the ricin to an area that was breached by the first responders who came in contact with it and became very ill, very fast. As you know, they all died, except for Mr. Epperson."

"What is ricin, exactly?" one reporter wanted to know.

"It comes from castor beans. It's a by-product of making castor oil, which is harmless, as you know."

"Says you," someone wisecracked. There was some laughter.

"But if the mash left behind is then made into a fine powder or a mist, it's possible to poison people through the air, or water, or even food. It usually takes a few hours for the symptoms to kick in, but it was only minutes in this instance, and we're not sure why. Maybe it was combined with something else."

"Is this the first time ricin has been used like this?" the reporters were scribbling furiously.

"Oh, no. In 1978, a journalist was killed in London when someone poked him with an umbrella that injected a small pellet of ricin. Our own military experimented with it in the 1940s. And we suspect Saddam Hussein used it on his own people at one point. But the frightening thing here is that it worked so quickly. And even more worrisome is the knowledge that some very bad people have figured out how to make it even more deadly, how to use it against masses of people, and they're still at large."

16

The major networks started their coverage of the convention from St. Louis at eight o'clock, joining the already continuous coverage of CNN, Fox News, MSNBC, C-SPAN, and the rest. They all opened not with the usual anticipation of the acceptance speech by the presidential candidate, but with the breaking news that it looked like a ricin-laced bomb had been used by terrorists to kill the firefighters in Omaha.

Air Force One was still in the air on its way back to Washington after President Darling's "emotional and uplifting visit with the last surviving first responder," they reported. "First it was machine guns, then bombs, and now the threat of a bunch of marauding terrorists spraying the unsuspecting masses with deadly poisons. America is on the edge of panic. They must be wondering, as we are, what's next? Does it get any worse?"

Meanwhile, the delegates were doing their best to wave the flags and toot the horns and look as excited as possible in their funny hats and scarves, but many of them were also reading about the poison gas on Twitter and elsewhere, and talking among themselves about it.

The campaign manager was on his cell phone, screaming at the network news directors, because none of them were paying the least bit of attention to the introduction of Governor James McHenry. Some of them even ignored the introduction video, which was a slickly produced mini-documentary on the wonderful life of James Madison McHenry.

Most of the networks were busy chattering among themselves about the next steps, and letting Darling surrogates talk about the importance of national unity in the face of terrorism. "This is no time for politics as usual" was a common theme.

Then, finally, McHenry took the stage and hugged his old friend who had introduced him, and this time the roar from the crowd was sincere. The anchor of the most highly-rated network heard the roar, turned to the stage and said, "Well, speaking of politics as usual, Governor McHenry is ready to accept his party's nomination."

The campaign manager wanted to puke, and, if at all possible, puke on the face of the news anchor. Jesus, what a horrible start to the night.

McHenry, for his part, looked remarkably confident and in control. His smile was easy as he waved to supporters and let the applause and the theme song, "God Bless America Again" wash over him.

> *God bless America again*
> *You see all the trouble that she's in*
> *Wash her pretty face, dry her eyes and then*
> *God bless America again*

17

It took almost a full three minutes for McHenry to get the crowd to quiet down, but he wasn't really trying all that hard. He knew a lot of eyeballs were trained on him at this moment, and he knew the number was higher because of the unfolding terrorism that was gripping the country, so he milked it a little. Finally, it was time to begin.

"Thank you for that wonderful welcome. It's good to be home," he said with his trademark smile. "It's good to be home in a city that shouldered the burden of expanding our great nation to the west, and on this night, shoulders the burden of expanding our resolve to stare down and respond to the wave of attacks on our fellow citizens by a gang of cowardly terrorists.

"To those in this country who tuned in looking for leadership and reassurance, and to those across the world who are curious about our response, let there be no mistake. An attack on one of us is an attack on all of us, and all of us are ready, willing and able to respond with force and fury. We will not rest until justice is done, and as far as I'm concerned, justice will be swift, sure, and above all else, final."

This reference to the death penalty for the terrorists earned McHenry a standing ovation.

"This has been a difficult week for America. The very foundation of our republic is built on the notion of a peaceful transfer of power from one administration to the next through free elections." McHenry paused. "Notice I said, from one administration to the *next*," as he pointed to himself. This brought laughter and some applause.

"Our process of free elections is to be celebrated, but the ability to fully celebrate our role in this wonderful process has been taken away as we share in the grief of those whose lives have been ended, ruined or disrupted by the terrorists who call themselves the Soldiers of Allah. We've done some good things this week, like raising millions of dollars for the victims and their families. But it's been difficult to balance the need for grief with the necessities of politics.

"So let's do what Americans do best: let's unite. Let's unite behind the idea that politics has no role to play in this fight against the Soldiers of Allah!"

More applause.

"Earlier today, President Darling flew to Omaha to grieve for the lost firefighters and to pray for the recovery of the only surviving first responder: Lloyd Epperson. It was exactly the right thing for the President to do, and I'm grateful for his leadership today. And I want Lloyd to know, and I want his family to know, that every American, including everyone in this convention hall tonight, is grateful for his courageous service and praying for a full recovery."

McHenry looked into the center camera.

"This is way above politics, Lloyd. This reaches the highest level of patriotism, of God and country. Lloyd, you stand for what sets America apart; what makes her the greatest nation on earth - that courageous men and women are called to serve and protect people they never meet.

People like you, Lloyd, are called to stand up for justice and decency for all, even in the face of evil. Heck, even in the face of people who are beyond evil - who are half past evil, to be sure.

"So tonight, we stand up for you, Lloyd, not as politicians but as Americans. We stand up for you, Lloyd Epperson, united as one against those who are half past evil!"

The delegates rocketed to their feet in wild applause and hooting their agreement. News reports would later indicate that people across America stood in support of Lloyd Epperson and in defiance of the terrorists, many shaking their fists and swearing revenge. It happened in bars and restaurants, in coffee shops and living rooms.

Before the applause could fully end, McHenry raised his voice to talk above it.

"United as one we will hunt down the people responsible. United as one we will drag them to justice. And, united as one, we will see to it that they are executed for their crimes against America!"

This brought down the house again. Strong support for the death penalty was in the party platform, and everyone in the convention hall knew President Darling's party was on record opposing the death penalty, even for terrorists. The noise was thunderous.

Aboard Air Force One, the President, Kennedy Jackson, and Anne Scofield were watching in Darling's office while dining on Omaha steaks.

"Sonofabitch!" Jackson blurted around a mouthful of salad. "He swears off politics, co-opts Epperson, and sticks the death penalty up our ass in the space of five minutes!"

"He's good, Kennedy," Darling acknowledged. "He's very good."

"The press hounds are going to ask you about it, you know. The death penalty thing. What are you going to say?"

Darling savored a bite of his steak before responding. "I'm not going to say anything. Anne is."

Scofield looked dumbstruck, her wine glass poised halfway to her lips. "Me? What am I supposed to tell them?"

"Tell 'em it sounds to you like McHenry has the cart before the horse, that it's too early to talk about executing people who are still on the loose," Darling advised, pointing at her with a forkful of meat. "And, from your perspective, the more immediate concern is the source of the ricin and doing everything we can to protect the American people from another attack. Then tell them every little detail you know or even think you know about castor beans. That'll bore 'em to tears and they'll go away."

Back in St. Louis, McHenry was wrapping up a speech that had wound its way through terrorism to national security and foreign policy, to retirement security and job creation, and, of course, reducing the size and scope of government.

"And, finally, it occurs to me that I have been remiss and not formally done what I came here to do. I accept your nomination to the office of president, because I accept the notion that America is an exceptional place with a higher calling than all the other countries combined;

because I accept the idea that freedom isn't free, and the high price of freedom must be borne by everyone, beginning with the commander-in-chief; because I accept the reality that the person sitting in the Oval Office must also be willing to stand at the gate and keep the barbarians at bay; because I accept the challenge that the future is always unwritten and will be shaped by those unafraid to undertake it; and I accept your premise that the current president is failing to uphold these basic principles.

"And so we venture forth tonight, from this city that nurtured me and this state that educated and enlightened me, to campaign for the joy and privilege of leading a nation that makes me proud to be an American. And we do so hand in hand, united as one.

"God bless you & God bless America!"

The scene was scripted, of course, but impressive nonetheless. As the network cameras scanned the crowd, the delegates were holding hands, lifting them aloft, and singing God Bless America. Then, the balloons started dropping, the confetti cannons erupted, and the theme song - God Bless America Again - blasted out of the speakers.

The perky anchor for one of the highest-rated broadcast networks turned away from the scene on the floor, looked straight into the camera and said, "United as one against those who are half past evil." Then she shook her head in disbelief and said, "I think he might be on to something."

She was fired the next day.

18

September 2

It was a perfect Friday morning in Jefferson City, and Rafi was excited. The new company plane, the *Screaming Eagle*, was going to be delivered today. He could hardly wait to get his hands on it. For now, though, he was trying to be patient as he walked Angel around the Capitol. He looked up at the governor's office.

Rafi noticed the additional security, now that McHenry was officially his party's candidate for president. There were stocky guys in suits pretending to hang out on the portico, even though Rafi knew McHenry was in Texas campaigning, and then Florida, Tennessee, Michigan and some other place. He wondered how thick the security would be if McHenry was actually in town.

Rafi kept walking, not wanting to attract attention, but Angel made him stop while she peed on a car tire. Then they made their way to the coffee shop.

While Rafi was waiting for the barista to prepare his bitterly strong coffee, he watched a talking head on CNN.

"Curiously, there has been no apparent response from the terrorists to McHenry's speech, calling them 'half past evil,'" the talking head said. "In fact, the terrorists have been uncharacteristically silent. 9:11 came and went this morning with nothing unusual happening. Either they've run out of things to do, or they're plotting something even bigger."

Rafi took his coffee outside and rubbed Angel's ears. Then he accessed the anonymous Twitter account.

"What you call deaths, we call victories. And there are many more victories to come! #AllahuAkbar #HalfPastEvil."

Things were humming in the McHenry campaign. The early polls showed a big bump coming out of the convention. He was now leading Darling 55% to 40% with the rest undecided. It was an amazing number against an otherwise personally popular incumbent.

Lucas Washington, McHenry's chief-of-staff, had stayed behind in Jefferson City. There was a lot of work to catch up on, and he wasn't officially on the campaign, anyway. It was his daughter's last weekday before the start of fourth grade next week, and she had begged to join him at the office. He relented.

"Shanique!" he called again. "For the last time, it's time to go!"

"Okay, Daddy!" And down the stairs she came, bouncing around like a ball made of knees and elbows, her grin infectious, and his heart melted.

"Well, well. At long last the princess is ready." Lucas looked quizzically at her hair. "What's that on your head?"

"Duh! It's a butterfly!"

"I can see that. Why do you have a fake butterfly in your hair, Shanique?"

"Because I like it! See, the colors match the beads, and the beads match my outfit!"

"The colors do match. Huh. A monarch butterfly. In your hair. Amazing. Is this your outfit for the first day of school?"

"No, I have something even better for that. It's all pink. But I'm gonna wear the butterfly sometime next week. Maybe Thursday," she said with eyes squinting, as though plotting her outfits for the week ahead.

Lucas laughed. "Maybe Thursday. Are you ready, Butterfly Girl?"

"Let's go, Daddy!" She rushed out the door ahead of him. "We don't want you to be late!"

Lucas watched her go, her beads bouncing and her butterfly flapping, and he thought his heart might just bust wide open.

"She's a real beauty, all right," Rafi agreed as he ran his hands along the fuselage of the *Screaming Eagle*, the private jet owned by the Dirty Dozen, the unofficial handle of the twelve lobbyists who owned her.

"For fourteen million bucks, it oughta be beautiful," the delivery pilot replied. "And the inside is tricked out like a limousine. Amazing. What do these guys do again?"

"They're lobbyists," Rafi said, and he knew what was coming.

"No wonder. Probably a bunch of crooked bastards."

Rafi shrugged. "They pay well."

The delivery pilot looked into the parking lot. "Hey, my ride's here to the Columbia airport. Don't wanna miss my flight. You gonna take her up today?"

"Oh, I think so. Kinda got the itch."

After the delivery pilot was gone, Rafi entered the cabin and was thunderstruck. It seated twelve, all right, but not in seats. There were two long leather sofas facing each other, seating four each, with two leather love seats at each end. There was a refrigerator, a wine cabinet, a liquor cabinet, a sophisticated entertainment system and a 46-inch HDTV.

The flight deck was standard, as Rafi had expected, and that was fine with him. "Well, let's see what this baby'll do," Rafi said to the air, and went into the terminal to file a flight plan for Memphis.

19

Ricky was passing the time at the bar, popping beer nuts into his mouth and nursing a Budweiser. It was his favorite joint - the Tuna Boat - where it got wild at night. It was the kind of place he might have run in his heyday, before the damn feds busted him for trafficking in underage prostitutes at his pride and joy, the Pecker Palace in Brooklyn, Illinois.

All because of that damn underage dancer, he thought as he took another hit of Budweiser. Sure, she was under eighteen, but so what? Of course, Ricky knew she was banging the customers at the Rub-a-Dub Hot Tub Club, but wasn't that her business?

Anyway, she ratted him out and he did some hard time in the federal pen. Then, when he got out, he found her and of course tried to kill her. She got away - the bitch - but a lot of other people died, including his older brother, and now Ricky was on the FBI's Most Wanted List and he couldn't take the chance of running any more strip clubs or sex clubs or condom home-delivery clubs or anything else he was uniquely qualified to do.

Another hit of Bud. Hell, he wasn't even Ricky "The Boner" Barboni anymore, and he missed it. He ached for his old friends to slap him on the back and say, "Hey, Boner, what's up?"

And it shamed him that he couldn't use the name Barboni anymore. There was a time when the Barboni name was feared - FEARED! - in Illinois, almost as much as he feared bats, which was a lot. Now he was Ricky Mather, a mechanic at one of the truck stops in West Memphis, Arkansas who also dabbled in drugs, stole cars, and did other illegal crap that people were too chicken shit to do themselves. Nobody feared Ricky Mather, not even the people he sold drugs to. He was just a dumbass 40-something mechanic with greasy fingernails and greasy hair who got his rocks off by going to sleazy strip clubs.

Ricky drained his Bud and signaled for another. The fuckers, he thought. They'll fear me again, one of these days.

"Hey, Sugar," one of the dancers cooed into his ear. "Ya gonna ride the boat tonight?"

Ricky took a deep breath. He loved the smell of a sweaty dancer with cheap perfume. She was wearing a bright yellow bikini that contrasted sharply against her dark brown skin. It barely covered her heavily subsidized breasts, which were firmly pushed into his ribs.

"I don't know, Squeezy," Ricky replied. He knew all the dancers by name, even the skanky ones. "I gotta talk business with a guy. We'll see how the night goes."

She reached out and lightly brushed his crotch. "Well, if you do, bid on me. I'll make sure you get a good ride." She brushed her full lips against his.

"I know," Ricky said, swallowing hard. "I remember."

She pushed her breasts even harder into him. "Later, then."

"Yeah." His voice was husky. "Maybe later."

Ricky watched her saunter off to another customer, still savoring her sharp scent and the feel of her body against him. The spell was broken when he heard what sounded like a guy from Pakistan who said, "Are you Mr. Mather?"

They found a small round table away from the stages and sat across from each other. It was so dark Ricky could barely see the face of this Arab fellow.

A waitress appeared, bringing Ricky a bottle of Budweiser. She asked Rafi what he wanted.

"Coffee, if you have it."

She rolled her eyes but said, "Sure, honey."

When she left, Rafi said, "You know, Mr. Mather, when we agreed to meet at the Tuna Boat, I thought it would be a restaurant."

"Oh, they serve food here," Ricky assured him, "but I wouldn't really recommend it."

Before the waitress could return with his coffee, a dancer forcibly straddled herself across Rafi's lap, facing him. Her hair was so blonde Rafi thought it might be on fire. "Hey, baby. You gonna ride the boat tonight?"

Rafi's eyes were wide. "Ride the boat? I don't understand."

"You know," the dancer said as she moved slowly up and down, "ride the boat."

Ricky was laughing. "Give him a break, Platinum. He's new here." He reached across the table and slipped a couple of dollars into the back of her thong. "Leave us alone will ya? We gotta talk business."

"Okay, Ricky, but I kinda like him. He's cute."

The waitress arrived with Rafi's coffee and Platinum moved on to her next target. Rafi sipped and nearly gagged. "Good God. This is awful!"

Ricky tipped his Budweiser. "Well, you didn't come here for the coffee. And you obviously didn't come here for the ladies. So why are you here?"

Rafi hesitated, but remembered what he had learned about Ricky Mather: there's nothing he won't do for the right price and he was damned good at it. "I'd like to hire your services," Rafi said. "You know - as a mechanic."

"I'm listening."

Rafi laid out his plan and what Ricky's role would be. As Ricky listened, he realized this Arab fellow was asking him to risk going to prison for the rest of his life. Then he thought: wait a minute. If I get caught doing *anything*, with my record, I'm toast.

"What's it pay?" Ricky asked bluntly.

"A million dollars."

Ricky almost choked on his last swig of beer. He set the bottle down and said, "You just hired yourself a mechanic."

They shook on it, and Rafi left, looking like he couldn't get out fast enough as he stumbled through the darkness. Ricky returned to the bar, swaggering a bit. Hey, maybe it was time for people to start fearing him again. And with a million bucks coming in, he decided he might even hang around and "ride the boat" tonight.

He found Squeezy, put his arms around her stomach from behind and whispered, "Anchors aweigh!"

20

September 3

Ricky awoke with the scent of Squeezy all over him. It had cost him five hundred bucks to "ride the boat" last night, mostly because that drunken trucker kept bidding on that skank who went by the name of Wet.

It was part of her routine with new customers. "Hey, baby, I'm Wet," she would always say, "What's your name?"

Anyway, Ricky and the trucker - his name was Willie something - were the top two bidders so they each got to oil up their dancers. Then Squeezy and Wet competed in something that only vaguely resembled wrestling before another round of bidding was held and Ricky won the right to "ride the boat," meaning he could take Squeezy to a private room with a shower and "clean her up."

Prostitution is illegal in Tennessee, of course, but the law is silent on helping someone shower off a layer of Mazola.

When Rafi awoke, he was in bed with Connie. The flight back from Memphis had been filled with thoughts of the stripper who had straddled him at the Tuna Boat and the way she smelled and moved. It had shocked him at first, but the more he thought about it the more he liked it. He called Connie over and secretly pretended she was Platinum, even though it was one hell of a stretch, and the sex was incredible.

She was snoring. He wondered if Platinum snored when she slept; probably not.

Rafi slipped out of bed and made his way to the kitchen and made coffee. Not as strong as he liked it, because Connie couldn't stomach it that way, and he wanted her to be in a good mood today.

The snoring stopped. The aroma of the coffee was working its magic on Connie. He heard her stirring.

"Rafi?" she called out sleepily. "Where's my lover boy?"

"Coming, darling," Rafi said as he poured her a cup of brew. "I'll be right there!"

He entered the bedroom carrying two cups of steaming coffee, still buck naked, smiling broadly. "Good morning, my love! And thank you for a night I will never forget."

"Nor I," she smiled back, accepting the cup from him. "I didn't know it could be like that."

"Well, now that we know how incredible we are, it can be like that a lot."

"Wow. I like the sound of that."

Rafi took a sip. "What would you like to do today? It's a beautiful day, and it's the start of a holiday weekend. Let's spend it together. Anything you want to do."

"Anything?"

"Anything."

Connie thought for a moment. "Let's go shopping at the lake. You know, the outlet mall. I need some new panties and stuff."

Inwardly, Rafi blanched, but outwardly, he was all smiles. "Wonderful idea! But first I want to show you the new plane. It's amazing."

"We haven't received any new threats, Mr. President."

Anne Scofield was briefing President Darling in the Oval Office. Kennedy Jackson was there, of course. He was always there. Sometimes Anne wondered if they went to the bathroom together. It was just after nine in the morning.

"What about that tweet saying deaths are victories and there are more victories to come?" Kennedy asked, pacing the room as he watched the clock. "That sounds like a threat to me."

"That's too general to be considered a threat. It's more like boasting."

"We'll know soon enough," Darling interjected. "It's almost 9:11."

They were watching a bank of televisions tuned to the cable news channels. All the weekend anchors were openly wondering what would happen, if anything, at 9:11. MSNBC actually had a countdown clock in one corner of the screen. It was almost ghoulish.

"We shouldn't let ourselves get hung up on a specific time of day," Scofield pointed out. "Even though the time of 9:11 obviously holds a great deal of significance to these guys, it could be just a head fake."

Kennedy nodded. "Get us to let down our guard if nothing happens at 9:11, and then smack us upside the head when we're not looking. Good point."

"Well, every government institution is on the highest state of alert, twenty-four seven," Scofield reminded them. "The FBI is sifting through every crime scene for evidence. We're monitoring every form of electronic communications. There's a lot of chatter from suspected terrorists around the world about the Soldiers of Allah. They're pretty excited about what's going on, but nobody seems to know anything about them."

"So maybe they're just a few rogues who don't have the juice to pull off something really big," Darling said, a hint of hope in his voice.

"They could be rogues," Scofield conceded, "but they're rogues who got their hands on highly weaponized ricin, and that scares the hell out of me."

They all fell silent and watched the TV monitors. The countdown clock on MSNBC hit all zeroes, and then started in again from 23:59:59.

"Jesus Christ, that's annoying," Kennedy blurted out. He got no disagreement from anyone in the room.

21

The Jefferson City airport is a tiny place, with most of the traffic coming from small personal aircraft and the state government fleet. The arrival of the *Screaming Eagle* had tongues wagging among the regulars at the popular restaurant inside the terminal. A couple of them walked to the windows to gawk while Rafi led Connie across the tarmac to the shiny new plane.

"No wonder they needed such a big plane if that fat ass is gonna fly in it," one of them observed, his mouth working a toothpick.

"Jesus, Earl, don't be so damn crass," his friend scolded. "She ain't no fatter than your wife."

Earl removed the toothpick and used it to point at his friend. "That's what I'm sayin', Fred. I know a fat ass when I see one."

Outside, Rafi was beaming with pride as he walked Connie around the plane.

"Just wait 'till you see the inside, Connie."

"Okay." She was mostly humoring him, still glowing from last night and anxious to get on with the shopping trip.

Rafi got the door open and folded down the stairs. "After you, my darling."

Connie started up the stairs and Rafi gave her butt a playful slap.

"See there, Earl? The boy likes that big cushion."

Earl shook his head. "Nah. I think he was measuring to make sure it would fit through the door."

"Well, it fits. She's in."

Connie was shocked by the interior of the plane. "Oh, my God! It's like a flying living room. Rafi! I can't believe it."

"I told you. Look at this." Rafi picked up a remote control and turned on the big screen TV. "See? There's a Blu-Ray player and a whole cabinet of movies to watch." He winked at her. "Some of them are kind of dirty."

"Figures," Connie said as she rolled her eyes. "A flying bachelor pad."

"It's designed to entertain, that's for sure. Here, let me show you the cockpit."

Connie was impressed. "Rafi, it takes a smart man to know all this. How did you get into the flying business, anyway?"

Rafi feigned embarrassment. "I guess I've been around it most of my life. When I was just a kid - the fourth grade, I think - a man came to our school and talked about being a pilot. I loved it - the uniform, the stories, the whole thing.

"Then the teacher said some of the kids would be selected to tour the airport and the inside of a passenger jet. I begged and begged the teacher to pick me. She did. And do you know what? Three of the kids who went on that tour are pilots today.

"It's important to expose kids to things like that early in life. It can start a spark, and a spark can start a fire."

Connie was staring at him. "You said the fourth grade."

"Yeah, I think it was. In fact, I'm pretty sure, 'cuz I think the teacher was Mrs. Smith. Why?"

"That's my grade, silly! I teach the fourth grade, remember?"

Rafi slapped his forehead. "Of course! How could I forget! And the Jefferson City Teacher of the Year, too!"

Connie blushed. Suddenly, her eyes sparked. "Hey, would you be willing to come to my class and talk about flying? And wear your uniform? And take some kids on a tour of the airport? And the plane?"

Rafi looked surprised. "Well, I guess so." He looked thoughtful. "You know, it would be like I was repaying Mrs. Smith for picking me all those years ago. The more I think about it, the more I like it. I'll do it, Connie. It'll be an honor to do it."

"Wonderful." They shared a kiss and descended the stairs.

Around his toothpick, Earl said, "Huh. I don't think they were in their long enough to fool around."

Fred agreed. "Not nearly long enough."

The waitress found them at the window, handed them their checks and huffed, "Earl, from what your wife tells me, they were in there plenty long enough."

22

Labor Day

Alpha was clearly agitated as he entered the Westchester Garden Club. Things were not going well, in his opinion. What was supposed to be a big disruption to McHenry's convention had been nimbly turned into a big convention bounce. He was starting to wonder if Zulu was too young, too inexperienced and possibly too incompetent to pull this off.

"Has Beta beaten me to it again, Wilson?" he snarled as he entered and was greeted in the foyer.

"No sign of Beta, sir, but Zulu is here already."

Alpha was taken aback. Zulu was never early. Perhaps she was feeling the heat; preparing her defense.

"Very well, Wilson. Let's go see what she's up to."

As he entered the private library, Alpha barely waited for the door to lock behind him before he started in. Zulu had her back to him, a glass of wine in her hand, staring out a window at a tree outside that was already turning a bright yellow.

"Your plan isn't working," he barked. "That sonofabitch McHenry is way ahead." Alpha stomped his way to the bar and fixed himself a drink.

"Patience, my dear Alpha," Zulu said quietly, still looking out the window. Finally she turned to face him. "Patience is a virtue."

Alpha snorted. "So is winning." He took a sip. "Admit it, Zulu. You didn't see this coming. Your plan did not anticipate these so-called terrorists of yours making McHenry even more popular."

She sipped her wine, sauntered over to a leather wingback chair, sat and languidly crossed her legs, which were sticking out of a tight navy blue dress. She let one of her shoes dangle from her foot. Even at the age of 85, Alpha felt his heartbeat quicken.

"You know, Alpha, you really shouldn't underestimate me."

"That's a non-answer, Zulu. You can't expect me to believe your plan is going exactly as you anticipated. McHenry has a 15-point lead, for God's sake!"

"The higher they are, the further they fall. But you of all people should know polls can be manipulated."

Alpha took a chair across from her. Their eyes locked. "Are the polls being manipulated?"

"Of course," Zulu lied with a smile. "But make no mistake, McHenry is no slouch. I kind of admire the way he has handled the situation, and I understand your concern, Alpha. But the game isn't over. As Clint Eastwood once famously said: It's halftime in America."

The key turned in the lock and Beta and Omega entered together. After the door closed and the deadbolt slid home, Zulu waved a hand at the remaining chairs. "Come on in, gentlemen. Let me bring you up to date on the next steps of our little operation. It's going to be highly entertaining, but I hope you have strong stomachs."

Beta looked like he wanted to flee. After about five minutes, he was actually considering what it would be like to jump out the window.

23

Lydia Wade looked good and she knew it. She worked hard at it, spending hours at the gym every week keeping her attractive body in tip-top condition. At present, her body was tucked into a short, form-fitting dress that showed plenty of cleavage. The men couldn't help but stare, even some of the women, and Lydia liked the attention from both.

She strode confidently into the bar, her heels clacking on the hardwood floor, drawing even more attention. They all wanted her, she knew, or wanted to be her, but tonight she was there for one man: Richie Rollins.

Lydia and Richie had been quite the item for a while, back in high school and one incredibly steamy summer after graduation. Intertwined, both physically and mentally. Inseparable. But then the summer ended and Richie went to college on the East coast and Lydia went to the Midwest. Time and distance cooled things off, as they often do, and Richie had no trouble finding other women; Lydia never lacked for lovers, either.

But then Lydia heard from a friend that Richie had gone to work for the National Security Agency, some kind of on-line spook slithering around on the Internet, and decided it might be good to re-ignite the flame.

"Lydia!"

Richie jumped out of his chair like he had a rocket in his drawers as he saw her. He threw his arms around her, remembering how perfectly she fit into his embrace, the smell and feel of her coal-black hair. Had it really been eight years since that magical summer?

He couldn't take his eyes off her as he guided her to a chair at his table. Her smile, as big and impossible as always, had his heart pounding. Jesus, he should have never let her go.

Lydia studied him. He looked good, she realized. Muscular. Fit. Confident. Sexy.

They had some drinks, caught up on each other, laughed, and enjoyed the strong undercurrent of sexuality that hung in the air between them.

Finally, Lydia finished her wine and said, "Ya know, my hotel is just down the street. How about you walk me to my room?"

His grin was wicked. "I thought you'd never ask."

That had been a couple of months ago. Lydia returned to Washington as often as she could manage, telling Richie her freelance research work required it. They grew closer, and Richie opened up more and more about his work with the NSA.

"The public doesn't know the half of it, hell, not even a tenth of it. There is literally nothing that we either don't know or can't find out," he said to her.

"Nothing?"

"Nothing."

"Then how come you haven't caught the terrorists?"

"The Soldiers of Allah? That's a tough one. When I say there's nothing we can't find out, I don't mean we know everything instantly. But it's there. Every single thing anybody does online leaves a trail. Every phone, every smartphone, every computer or tablet is in our database. The data propagates itself. But somebody has to put it together, to make sense of it."

"Someone like you?"

"Yes, someone like me."

"But you're not working on the terrorists."

"No. Not even close."

"Do you spooks ever look for stuff just for the hell of it? You know, pure curiosity?"

Richie grinned. "We're not supposed to, but, you know. Boredom sets in."

He was looking at her funny. It dawned on her. She punched his shoulder.

"You bastard! You looked me up didn't you? You fuckin' looked me up! Admit it!"

"Don't hit me, again! Yes, I looked you up. It's not like there's a file on you marked 'Lydia Wade' or anything. But I was able to put some things together."

"Why?"

"Because when you got back in touch I was obsessed with you. I couldn't focus on anything else. I wanted to know everything about you. Everything. Like I used to, you know, back then."

Lydia reached up to stroke his face and offered him a smile. "Okay, Spook. What did you find out? Tell me the deepest, darkest secret you found out about me. Am I a serial killer on the side?"

He laughed. "Not that I can tell." Then he grew serious. "Are you sure you want to do this?"

"Yes. Tell me my worst secret and I'll believe in your super-duper spooking prowess," she said, with an I-dare-you look on her face.

Richie hesitated, but then plowed ahead. "About six months ago you bought a home pregnancy test from Amazon. It was positive."

The room went quiet. Lydia was dumbstruck, her mouth agape. She stammered, "No fucking way. No fucking way you would know that! And, and besides, it wasn't positive dumbass. If it was positive I'd be pregnant now! Do I look pregnant to you?"

His eyes roamed her body, lustily. "No, you don't look the least bit pregnant. You look hot."

"So, Spook. Admit it. You were wrong on that one."

Richie hung his head. "I asked you if you were sure you wanted to do this. And you said you wanted me to tell you your deepest, darkest secret."

"So the worst thing you could find was a pregnancy test from Amazon? And you guessed - incorrectly - that it was positive? Some spook you are."

There was a spark of anger somewhere deep inside him from her dismissive tone. And so he said: "No, your deepest-darkest secret is that two weeks after you got the Amazon delivery, your credit card was swiped through a machine registered to a Planned Parenthood affiliate. That's how I knew it was positive."

Lydia stared at him in disbelief. Her cheeks reddened in embarrassment. She hung her head. No one knew about the abortion. No one.

Richie reached out to her but she shrugged him away. "Lydia, God, I'm sorry. Look, I'm not judging you. I don't care. Shit, I should have never looked you up. I should have never admitted that I did. I fucked up, big time."

There was silence for a long time. Then, Richie said: "Look, Lydia, let me make it up to you. I'll do anything, really. Anything at all, please. Just let me bring that smile back. I'm begging you."

Inwardly, Lydia smiled. She had him, right where she wanted him. God, men are so easy.

She looked at him. "Okay, Spook. You have one chance. I want you to find everything you can on this man." She leaned in and whispered the name.

Richie's eyes grew wide. "Christ! You're gonna get my ass fired!"

24

The Labor Day weekend was over and Ricky Mather was back at work at the truck stop, bent over in full concentration on a diesel engine owned by the SOB Willie who made him bid so damn much that night at the Tuna Boat, when he was startled by a tap on the shoulder.

He turned to see a prissy looking fella wearing skinny jeans and a hot pink button down dress shirt. And, oh my God, pink suede shoes.

"I'm so very sorry to bother you, sir," the man began, "but I didn't see anyone else around at the moment. Plus, I think I need a mechanic."

Ricky looked around nervously. What was this guy up to? He was obviously not a trucker. "Whaddya need?"

The man stepped back and pointed. "Over there."

Ricky's eyes followed the finger and he couldn't believe it. It was a stretch limo, sleek and shiny, and every bit as pink as the man's shirt. On the driver's side door, in a fancy, flowing script, was this: *Destiny.*

"There she is," his face beaming, "my pride and joy."

"Destiny," Ricky said.

"Destiny," the man nodded. "Our most popular limo. Have you heard of it?"

"Can't say as I have. What's it for?"

"People rent it. For parties and such. And believe you me," he said with a wink, "some of those parties get pretty wild back there. They don't think I know, but I do." He leaned in closer and whispered, "Cameras." Another wink.

Whoa. Ricky was starting to like this guy. "My name is Ricky. And you are?"

"Roger Best. Best Limos."

"Oh, I've heard of Best Limos, for sure. Just never saw Destiny before. She's a beaut. Cameras, huh?" Ricky couldn't stop grinning.

Roger nodded, matching the grin with one of his own. "You won't tell on me will, you?"

"Tell on you? Hell, I envy you!"

They laughed. Then, Roger got to the point. "Front left wheel is making an awful noise, but not always. I can't afford the hit to our reputation if it goes out while I've got a party going on in there. I need you to fix it."

"Right away? We're kind of backed up in here."

Roger shook his head. "No, no, not right away. But soon."

"Can you leave her for a week or so? Let me test drive her and get her fixed up?"

"Sure, Ricky. That sounds good."

"One more thing, Mr. Best. Why here? Why me? Plenty of mechanics in Memphis."

Roger smiled. "Word gets around, Ricky. About you. I knew you wouldn't rat me out on the cameras."

Another limousine showed up. It was smaller, plainer. Black. Roger Best got in and was driven away.

"Destiny," Ricky said to himself. "Damned if that ain't the truth."

25

President Maury Darling's most loyal supporters were streaming into New Orleans for their own convention. They were determined to out-do that bastard McHenry and get their guy re-elected. And the Vice President, too; don't forget about her.

The atmosphere was festive, from the moment the delegates and alternates and journalists and hangers-on stepped off the plane to live jazz bands, beads, and cocktails. New Orleans knows how to party, by God, so get with it.

Security was there, too, of course, especially after the deadly bombing in the French Quarter, which was awful. All of Jackson Square was still closed off, which was awful, too, and not a good backdrop for the TV folks, that's for sure. But the convention would go on, of course, in the Superdome. It was too late to move it, that's for sure, so party on and by the way there will be no backpacks.

President Darling was nowhere near New Orleans, of course. He was on the campaign trail in Michigan, then Chicago, Denver, and a brief stop in Dallas, just to say he went to Texas, a state he would surely lose by thirty points. He would arrive in New Orleans by steamboat on Wednesday, all decked out, with supporters on the landing yelling the campaign slogan: "Stay the Course! Stay the Course!"

The Secret Service was nervous about it, because the steamboat landing isn't all that far from the bombing site, and they wondered: was there still some lunatic lurking around New Orleans, looking to take a pop at the President?

It was a topic for the talking heads on TV, too. Where were the Soldiers of Allah? Why had they stopped killing people? Would they try to disrupt the President's convention? And this question: is it possible the terrorists are trying to influence the outcome of the presidential election? Do they care?

In Jefferson City, Rafi watched all this with keen interest. His soldiers had gone "dark," to use one of the words tossed around by the terrorism "experts," because they were, at that moment, gathering at a large old farmhouse across the Missouri River. He was sure they were having a great reunion, clapping each other on the back, bragging about their hits on the Great Satan. Rafi would join them in due course. And if everything goes as planned, the reunion will only get better.

Rafi woke up his smartphone and accessed an application that only he had. It was developed especially for him by some geek somewhere who otherwise spent his time writing computer code for an international company. The app allowed him to access his Twitter accounts without leaving the usual digital trail of breadcrumbs. It used servers all over the world, never the same two in a row, and invented phony IP addresses and other digital signatures that would drive investigators nuts if they tried to track him.

He tweeted: "America has a choice to make. This week the choice becomes clear, but first you will know great fear. #AllahuAkbar!"

26

Ricky took a plastic seat cover out to the pink limo and opened the door. Wow. He had never seen such leather, such fabulous, soft, plush leather. He covered the seat, sat down and closed the door. Absolute silence. He smelled the leather. It smelled like money; lots of money.

He turned the key and the car came to life. There was some soft jazz from what appeared to be satellite radio. There was a computer screen, about the size of an iPad, with icons on it. One of the icons looked like a movie camera. He touched it, and the screen came to life with a view of the passenger part of the limo, clear as life. Then the picture changed; another angle. And then another, and another, then back to the original.

Ricky tried to imagine driving the limo around with a bunch of people having sex in the back, right there on the screen. It would be hard to do. Then he saw a red icon at the bottom of the screen and touched it. "Now recording," the screen read.

"Roger Best, you horny bastard," Ricky said with a laugh. "We're two peas in a pod."

Except they weren't, Ricky knew. Roger had money. He probably wasn't a convicted felon on the run. Hadn't killed anybody. But. He had asked around about Ricky, and you don't ask around about Ricky at the public library or chamber of commerce luncheon. You asked about Ricky at the strip joints or where they cook meth or at the payday loan shops. Unsavory places. Plus, here was Roger recording people without their knowledge in a pink limo. And Roger knew that Ricky would figure it out and wouldn't tell. There's more to Roger than meets the eye, Ricky decided. Perhaps they could do business together.

But that's for later. Ricky had another job to do; a big job; a million bucks. He thought about that, too. Why would someone pay him a million dollars for such a simple thing? Simple, yes, but illegal as all hell. He might have to kill someone, the little Arab said. Well? So what? He'd done that before, too. Plenty of times. But no one ever offered that kind of money.

Maybe it's not real. Maybe the little Arab bastard had no intention of paying him the one million. Shit. He should have gotten something up front, he realized. Stupid. Well, if the little shit doesn't come through, I'll just grease his little ass. Then I'll come back here and do business with Roger. Sounds like a plan.

Ricky steered the limo towards the street in front of the truck stop, gingerly, as he had never driven anything with such a long wheelbase. Within just a minute or so, he knew the problem was a bad wheel bearing. Less than an hour later, it was as good as new. And, fortunately for Ricky, Roger didn't need it for a week.

In Jefferson City, the soldier code-named Jasim parked his worn-looking white van on Madison Street and put an orange cone behind it. Air Handler Services was painted on the side, along with a phone number. He walked into the GOB office building in a pair of brown coveralls, carrying a large tool chest.

An hour later, he exited the building with his tools, picked up the orange cone, and drove away. Nobody thought a thing about it.

At precisely 11:30 that morning, a gas canister next to the building's air handler came to life with a little hiss. Not long after that, office workers and visitors started feeling light-headed, then weak. Some couldn't stop coughing. Then, dozens lost consciousness and either fell to the floor in a heap or simply laid their heads on their desks.

Those that could started streaming out of the building, texting friends and family, calling loved ones, and, of course, 911.

Rafi and Angel were watching from down the street. Rafi tweeted: "OMG! They're dropping like flies in the GOB! The Soldiers of Allah are laughing! #AllahuAkbar!"

It was eerily similar to the earlier hostage hoax at the GOB, as the police arrived, then the highway patrol, then the reporters. The speculation was everywhere that the hostage hoax had been some kind of dry run for this, more awful event.

First responders donned gas masks and entered the building. People were lying askew all over the place. They started checking for signs of life. Amazingly, it was the same result every time.

"Still alive here!"

"Here, too!"

"Still breathing!"

Then, remarkably, people started regaining consciousness. They were groggy as hell, and some had hurt themselves falling to the floor or banging a head on a desk, but there were zero fatalities.

The Highway Patrol bomb squad went to the air handler and found the gas canister piped into the system. It was unremarkable in every way, except painted on the side was one word: "Surprise!"

The local police and the troopers argued over who should handle the press conference, since it was mostly good news, and finally agreed to do it jointly. They announced that the Soldiers of Allah, apparently, had tried but failed, obviously, to kill a bunch of folks in the GOB by poisoning the air. Tests were being performed on the gas canister to determine what chemical was used. Yes, the Department of Homeland Security has been notified. No, there were no fingerprints on the canister. No, we don't know why they picked on Jefferson City.

Rafi watched it all. Once the excitement died down, he tweeted: "It was Isoflurane. An anesthetic. Next time it'll be ricin and people will die unless our demands are met. #AllahuAkbar!"

That got the talking heads going on all the news networks doing their shows live from the Superdome in New Orleans in their skyboxes.

"Demands? What demands?"

"Now we're getting down to it. Maybe it's all about money."

"Here's the question: does Darling negotiate with these terrorists? Do we set that kind of precedent?"

"Here's what worries me: who's guarding the air handlers for the Superdome?"

27

President Darling, on Air Force One between campaign stops, turned to his chief of staff and asked, "Who is guarding the air handlers at the Superdome, Kennedy?"

"I'm sure the Secret Service is on it. They're already paranoid as hell about New Orleans. But I'll call and check."

Darling nodded. "What about this reference to demands? And why did they just let it hang there? Should we respond with something?"

"Absolutely not," Kennedy said, forcefully. "The last thing we need to be is an administration negotiating with terrorists over Twitter, for God's sake."

"The press will ask about it, you know."

"That's fine. Let the press people handle it. We haven't seen any demands - which is true - and the United States doesn't negotiate with terrorists - also true. We have better things to do than respond to tweets, which I hope is true."

"Speaking of tweets," Darling said, "can't we shut down the Twitter accounts? That whole Allahu Akbar thing is really annoying."

"Twitter has offered to cooperate in any way they can. But I'm thinking we should leave the Twitter accounts alone. Maybe they'll make a mistake and reveal their location, or an identity, or something. Who knows?"

Governor McHenry was back in Jefferson City, not wanting to campaign against the backdrop of the President's convention in New Orleans. The GOB incident - just across the street from the mansion and a block away from the Capitol - rattled him. Seated around a conference table in his large, oval-shaped office (much bigger than the Oval Office in the White House, by the way) were his chief of staff, the head of the Highway Patrol, the director of the Department of Public Safety, and the leader of his newly expanded Secret Service contingent.

"It bothers the hell out of me," McHenry was saying, "that somebody could simply walk into a government building and contaminate the air supply. Right down the street! Obviously, they're among us, and we have no clue who they are!"

The Secret Service spoke up. "That's why we've updated our security protocols for you, Governor. Before you enter any building, the air supply will be checked and kept secure."

"It's not just me that I'm worried about," McHenry said. "If that canister had been full of that ricin crap from Omaha, we'd have a building full of bodies." He turned to his chief of staff. "Lucas, I want the air handlers in every government building in Missouri checked immediately."

"Yes, sir."

Next he turned to his public safety director. "And we know at least one terrorist either is or was in Jefferson City. I have zero confidence in the Darling administration on this. I want to pull out every trick in the book to find him.

"Nobody - and I mean NOBODY - attacks the State of Missouri and gets away with it."

That night, the news networks were all live from New Orleans, and the talking heads were in full force discussing the Soldiers of Allah. When the most popular network came back from a Viagra commercial, the show host was ashen as he looked into the camera and said: "During the commercial, an envelope was delivered to us by courier. In it was a single sheet of paper. At the top of the page it reads, "The Demands of the Soldiers of Allah." And then: "Read this word-for-word on the air immediately or someone close to you will bleed out."

There was a shake in his voice as he said, "So here goes."

28

"America is the Great Satan. There is no doubt about this. The whole world knows it, except, of course, for Americans themselves. How can they know? They live in the belly of the beast and know only what the beast feeds them.

"We, the Soldiers of Allah - his name be praised - would like nothing more than to witness the total destruction of America. We have killed but a few of you, just enough to get your attention. But know this: we have the means to kill so many more, and we will, unless our demands are met.

"First of all, this is not about money. We want none of your money, for it stinks of the blood of infidels. No. This is about the future course of America and her relationship with the world.

"You have a man running for president - Governor James McHenry - who is promising a return to the Bush Doctrine. This is unacceptable to the world. If you follow this path, you will find yourselves once again bogged down in senseless bloodshed in places like Iraq and Afghanistan. Have you not killed enough innocent people already with your drone strikes?

"Our demands are simple, and easily met. Do not vote for Governor McHenry. If you do, and he wins, the Soldiers of Allah will unleash the fires of hell upon this country. We will not stop until millions are dead and we'll start with the children.

"The other demand is for President Darling. All drone strikes must stop immediately. Any drone strikes between now and Election Day will result in the death of Americans at the hands of the Soldiers of Allah. If you can do this, and you win re-election, the Soldiers of Allah are prepared to sit down and make peace with you.

"It is in your hands, America. We await your decision."

It quickly became the most downloaded document in the history of the Internet, and not just in America. The news spread across the world at the speed of light: a band of terrorists had taken it upon themselves to rig the outcome of a presidential election. It was, the world knew, a seminal moment not just for a superpower like the United States, but for everyone. If terrorists can decide who runs America, who's to stop them from running the world?

Most of the talk radio hosts were indignant. How dare they? Who do they think they are? How did that lousy Maury Darling allow it to come to this? Surely he'll reject what amounts to an endorsement from a band of murderous thugs!

The callers were livid. "We need to find these sonsabitches and burn 'em alive!"

"This is what happens when you come across as weak. Thank you President Darling!"

The TV news shows were less extreme, without callers. The usual panel of experts debated the development, with little to offer but questions. How will McHenry respond? What about President Darling? Is this in fact an endorsement of his campaign by terrorists? Will the drone strikes stop? Does this neuter our global effort to kill or round up the bad guys? And: are they bluffing?

Some within the McHenry campaign were silently gleeful. My God, the terrorists endorsed Darling! This was akin to the Iranian hostage-takers endorsing Jimmy Carter! They're afraid of McHenry! He scares them! Plus, it makes Darling look weak.

Nobody voiced these feelings, however, because it was all very frightening as a whole. The big question: how do we play it?

In the end, the campaign issued a statement: "Gov. James McHenry rejects the very idea that terrorists would even attempt to influence a presidential election. Our founding fathers did not pledge their lives, their fortunes, and their sacred honor so that down the road Americans would cower in the face of such threats. This is our clarion call to defend the cause of liberty, and we will do so."

President Darling had his face in his hands. Through his fingers, he said, "Christ. I'm the first president in history to be endorsed by terrorists. What a legacy."

Kennedy rejected it. "No! They did NOT endorse you! They reminded the world how dangerous McHenry is."

Darling looked at him. "Don't try selling that on Meet the Press."

Now it was Kennedy's turn to bury his face. "Fuck! What do we do?"

"Act presidential," Darling said, "and try very, very hard to change the subject."

29

It was Wednesday morning of convention week, and the world was still abuzz about the demands of the terrorists. There was little else on the news, it seemed, but then this tweet entered the timeline: "BREAKING: Confidential sources confirm VP Olivia Morgan has breast cancer, may drop out."

The staffers for VP Morgan couldn't answer phone calls fast enough. They were caught completely unaware, and had nothing to say. Her closest advisors, of course, were in New Orleans preparing her to accept the nomination that night and give a rousing speech to match that bastard Gunderson. And now this!

Finally, they were called into Morgan's suite. She stood before them: a seemingly healthy 55-year-old mother of three. For 25 years she had been in the political arena, an unabashed liberal. She smiled at them, but there was sadness in her eyes.

"I'm sorry you had to hear it from the press," she began. "So much for health care privacy these days. It's true, though. My own doctor, who I trust with my life, says I have breast cancer. But as you know, I'm a fighter. I intend to beat it.

"I know it won't be easy, though. Which is why I've offered to President Darling to step away from the ticket, to avoid being a distraction, or a weak link in the chain.

Winning a second term for the President is way more important than my health care struggles.

"I haven't heard back from the President about my status on the ticket, but I also offered to go ahead and speak to the convention regardless, and he readily accepted.

"So we have a speech to write, and quickly. It may not be what all of you have worked so hard for, but let's make it a good one anyway."

She paused to gather herself. "I'm sorry about all this. But please know this: I love you all very much."

The steamboat arrived with great fanfare amid the tightest security possible, both visible and invisible. Uniformed officers were everywhere, along with dozens of people who were obviously Secret Service. There were undercover officers all over the place, too, ready to tackle anyone who dared look suspicious. Only fully credentialed convention delegates - and the media, of course - were allowed on the landing.

The delegates cheered loudly as President Darling disembarked, his suit jacket carried languidly over his right shoulder. He smiled and waved, but he addressed the crowd only briefly.

"It's great to be in New Orleans!" Loud cheers. "Look, I don't want to get in the way of a good party." Laughter. "But there's something I want you all to know as we gather in this great city and celebrate our great democratic traditions.

"WE are in charge of our presidential election, not a rag-tag bunch of murderous cowards who dare to call themselves soldiers!

"WE run our foreign policy and our military!

"WE will catch these guys. WE will see to it that justice is done!

"And WE will get back to living our lives as proud Americans! Thank you all; now back to the party!"

A jazz band started playing, mixing with the cheers, as Darling worked a short rope line on his way to the motorcade. Somebody in the press corps shouted, "What about Morgan? Is she off the ticket?"

Darling turned to the reporter and simply said, "Give her some space, Donny. Have some decency." Then he was gone.

"The timing on this is just too damned cute," Lucas fumed as he paced in front of Governor McHenry's desk. "I think they're wagging the dog."

McHenry watched his chief of staff pace back and forth. They had been friends for so long it felt like forever. Lord, the liquor they had consumed back in the day, before he wasn't allowed to have fun anymore. He trusted Lucas with his life; trusted his political instincts, too.

"Even if it is a hoax," McHenry pointed out, "we can't accuse them of it. We'd look like troglodytes."

"I know, I know." Lucas kept pacing. "Can someone else do it?"

McHenry shook his head. "Let's eliminate that entire line of thinking. I don't want there to be a single little thread that some reporter somewhere could pull on that would lead to us suggesting Olivia Morgan is faking breast cancer. Forget about it."

"So what do we do?"

"That's a good question, Lucas."

30

Ricky felt like a big shot. He was tooling up Interstate 55 in the pink limo, listening to classic rock on the satellite radio, and sipping a cold beer. He had been amused, then thrilled, to discover the limo had a refrigerator in the front seat. Hell, every limo had refrigerators for the passengers. This one had a cooler for the driver!

"Roger Best," Ricky said out loud as he raised the bottle in an imaginary toast, "you are one sly little bastard. Even if you do wear pink shoes."

There was no worry that someone passing him or driving nearby would see him drinking; the windows were heavily tinted. He wondered, though, if the six pack would last all the way to Jefferson City. What the hell? He could always buy more!

Ricky had left his crappy old car parked at the truck stop; he had no plans to go back. He either had a big payday waiting in Jefferson City, or he was going to kill the little Arab and get into cahoots with Roger. His days as a truck stop mechanic were over.

"Brown Sugar" by the Rolling Stones came over the radio. Ricky cranked it up and sang along. Life is good!

Everyone filing into the Superdome was handed a pink ribbon. Everyone put it on, of course, including the reporters. The theme for the night was health care. It should be enshrined in the Constitution as a right, one speaker declared. No one should worry about themselves or their loved ones being denied life-saving procedures due to economic circumstances said another. Obamacare didn't go far enough, still another intoned, because the government should provide health care for everyone and pay for it. Period!

Finally, the moment everyone was waiting for arrived. The Superdome darkened. The video screens flickered to life. The crowd roared. It was President Darling smiling at them.

"How ya doin'?" he said with a wave. "Are we having fun yet?"

The crowd was in full throat. The news anchors were in shock. This wasn't in the script.

"Like all of you," Darling said, "I'm wearing my pink ribbon proudly tonight! But it's not about me tonight. It's about Olivia."

The crowd roared its approval.

"Earlier today, we all heard the disturbing news that the Vice President is facing a fight with breast cancer. Frankly, I was shocked that someone would leak such a personal matter to the media, but they did. Olivia, courageously I think, publicly acknowledged her situation and offered to me the choice of removing her from the ticket."

No, the crowd was saying. Some were hissing.

Darling flashed a smile. "I agree with you. We don't cast our friends aside in this country when they are facing challenges. We embrace them. We help them. We draw courage from them.

"And when they win the fight, as I believe the Vice President will, we are inspired by them.

"My friends, I can't think of another American I'd rather have by my side in this campaign than Vice President Olivia Morgan!"

The crowd went wild as the spotlight hit Morgan standing on the podium. She turned to the video screen behind her and saluted the President. He returned the salute and the screen switched to the live shot of Olivia Morgan. She turned to the crowd.

"Mr. President," she began, "thank you for your loyalty. Not just to me, but to the American people. I accept your generous offer to stay on the ticket. Let's get after it!"

This launched the delegates into a long ovation, complete with flag waving and tears and marching around. She let it happen. Never get in the way of a scripted spontaneous display of affection.

"I wish it wasn't like this. I wish I wasn't in this predicament. But I'm lucky in a lot of ways. I'm the Vice President of the United States. I get whatever treatment I need at the snap of my fingers. People dote on me, for pity's sake."

This got a laugh.

"But a lot of Americans aren't so lucky. They get a diagnosis of breast cancer, or prostate cancer, or Alzheimer's, and they don't know what to do or where to turn. They can't snap their fingers and have the best treatments known to man. They are the ones we need to help. I've said this before and I'll say it again here tonight: everyone in America deserves the very best health care available, regardless of circumstances, guaranteed by the

United States of America. Let's finally get it done, once and for all!"

She let the applause die down. "I don't want this campaign to be all about me and a play-by-play of my treatment. So, after tonight, I'll keep pushing the health care fight for everyone but I won't be talking about my personal fight. But tonight, I want to reassure you that I'm lucky in another way. We caught it early. My prognosis is good. And for that, I have my husband to thank. Bill is the one who found the lump."

Bill Morgan appeared on the big screens as he watched from the Vice President's box. His goofy smile and thumbs up to his wife would be on the front page of newspapers across the country the next morning. The crowd roared with laughter.

The Vice President grinned broadly. "Okay. Enough about my private life. Our work isn't done. So let's get on with the business of getting President Darling re-elected!"

Ricky pulled the pink limo to the curb in front of Rafi's apartment in Jefferson City and belched.

"Christ," he muttered. "I got drunk all of a sudden."

He stumbled to the front door and knocked. Rafi opened the door and snorted in disgust. "Good grief. You're shitfaced."

"Yeah? Well, fuck you too. You got the money?"

"Of course."

"Show it to me."

Rafi stepped aside and Ricky stumbled inside and flopped on the sofa.

"It's not in cash, for crying out loud," Rafi said as he shut and locked the door. "It's in a bank and it'll be transferred to you when the job is done. Let me show you to your room so you can sleep this off. We have a big day tomorrow."

But Ricky didn't respond. He was snoring.

31

This Thursday morning, Lucas didn't have to holler after his daughter to make sure she wasn't late. She came bouncing down the stairs and there it was: the butterfly in her hair.

"See, Daddy! I'm your little Butterfly Girl today!"

Lucas laughed. "You are, indeed, Shanique! And the world has never seen a prettier one!"

"Did you sign my permission slip? Today is the field trip. To the airport. We get to see inside a private jet!"

"Oh, so that's why you're ready on time today! Yeah, I signed it. It's on the kitchen counter."

Shanique raced into the kitchen, the butterfly flapping and her hair beads snapping. Lucas smiled and felt his heart swell again. God, she looked more and more like her mother every day. "I wish you could see her, Layla," he whispered to himself. "No, strike that. I hope you can."

In Washington, Lydia Wade and Richie Rollins were having breakfast. He handed her a manila envelope.

"It's all in there," he said.

"Give me the highlights."

Richie sat back in his chair. "What are you going to use this stuff for?"

"None of your business."

"Hey, Lydia, my ass is on the line here. If that stuff somehow goes public, and it gets traced back to the NSA, and then to me, I could go to prison."

"If that happens, I'll come visit you."

"That's not funny."

"Relax, Spook. This stuff is for my use only. It'll never see the light of day. Now: hit the high points."

"Alright. You know the basics. 57 years old, eight years as a state senator, two-term governor, blah, blah, blah. But it's the stuff the public doesn't know about, or doesn't think about, that's the most interesting."

"The divorce?"

Richie waved his hand at that. "Yeah, yeah. He was married for a while and it didn't last. Too much carousing around in Jefferson City while the little wifey was back home in St. Louis, I imagine. It happens. They split up, she got a nice wad of cash and they both agreed to not talk about it. No kids. That's when the interesting stuff starts."

He took a leisurely sip of coffee.

"Like what?"

"Like I said, it's all in there."

"Dammit, Richie! Get to the point!"

Richie smiled. "He likes 'em young."

Lydia's mouth fell open. "How young?"

Now Ritchie was waving both hands. "No, no, no. Not like that. In their twenties. In college, maybe."

Lydia exhaled. "Jesus, Richie. I thought you were going to tell me he's some kind of pervert."

"I'll let you decide that, but he's not a pedophile. He's just a guy in his fifties who really, really, really likes his ladies to be in their twenties."

Lydia huffed. "You know how many fifty-something guys check out my ass when I walk by?"

"All of them?"

"Exactly."

"Yeah, well, not all of them act on it. He has, and probably does, in a rather unique way."

"How so?"

"He joined a website right after the divorce that hooks up young women - 18 and up - with older men. Sugar daddies. He thought his account was anonymous. A lot of people think that. But he used the same laptop to create the sugar daddy account that he used to remotely access his Senate email account, back in the day."

"Okay. So he's a 57-year-old who likes 'em half his age or less. And he hooks up over the Internet. What else?"

"He uses an alias, of course." Richie took a sip of coffee and made sure to swallow it before finishing. "He calls himself Juan Long Johnson." Richie was already laughing before he finished the sentence.

"Oh my God!" Lydia managed around her own laughter. "You men and your preoccupation with your johnsons!"

Richie had to finish laughing before continuing. He was wiping away tears when he said: "And he posted a picture to prove it!" The laughter overwhelmed him once again.

Lydia's eyes went wide. She snatched the manila envelope, opened it, and said: "Sweet Jesus Christ. How do you know it's his?"

"I don't. But he claims it is."

They finally got themselves under control. Lydia said, "My God. This alone could kill his campaign."

"You said it would never become public!"

"I know." Now it was Lydia's turn to sip some coffee. "Is there anything else?"

"Nothing that juicy. His best friend in all the world - apart from his johnson, I suppose - is his chief of staff, Lucas Washington. They're inseparable. Long time drinking buddies. Been together almost twenty years.

"Lucas is black. Like McHenry, he used to be married. But his wife died giving birth to their only child, Shanique. He's raising her alone.

"At about the same time every school day, Lucas gets a 10-second video clip sent to his smartphone confirming Shanique is home safe. It's always the same. She waves at the security camera and says, 'I love you, Daddy.'"

"Nothing funny about that."

32

Ricky woke up on Rafi's couch and at first had no idea where he was. Then he saw Rafi standing there, holding up some kind of uniform.

"Get yourself cleaned up and change into this," Rafi said. "You need to look the part."

Ricky sat up and tasted his mouth. Not good. "My shit's in the car. Toothpaste and stuff."

"I got it already. It's all in the guest bath. And speaking of the car," Rafi shook his head, "couldn't you find something a little less flashy? I mean, seriously? Hot pink?"

"You said you wanted the kids to remember the ride. Trust me; they won't forget riding in Destiny."

Ricky stood up and grabbed the uniform. "Hey, did you show me the money last night?"

"I told you, it's not in cash. It's in a bank. Here." Rafi tapped a file on his smartphone. "This is the account. See? A million dollars. When the job is done, all I have to do is press the 'transfer' button and it'll go to a numbered account in Cozumel that you can access. The password to your account is 'slickface' and the answer to the security question is 'boner'.

Risky looked at him and narrowed his eyes. "The answer is boner? What's the question?"

"What was your favorite childhood nickname?"

"How the hell do you know my favorite nickname?"

Rafi crossed his arms. "Oh, I know everything about you, Ricky Barboni."

Rafi nodded at Ricky's surprised look. "Do you think I picked you for this job by accident? Now, go clean up and put on the uniform. And, by the way, it's your size. I know that, too."

Ricky emerged from the guest bath looking every bit the part of a chauffeur.

"When do we start, boss?"

Rafi shook his head. "The gig isn't until after lunch. This morning, we need to advance the route you'll be taking from the school to the airport, and then from the airport to the farm. No mistakes."

"I don't make mistakes," Ricky replied.

"Did you bring a gun?"

"I always have a gun. That way, if I make a mistake, I can erase it."

Lucas Washington and James McHenry were having their usual cup of coffee. This morning, though, they were standing on the portico outside the Governor's office overlooking the Missouri River and the airport beyond it.

"What a gorgeous morning," McHenry noted. "There's a bald eagle nesting down there, by the river. Sometimes I stand out here and catch it grabbing a fish. Pretty cool."

"Will you miss it?" Lucas asked. "You know, when you're in the White House?"

"Don't jinx me, Lucas! Besides, if I'm there, you're there. We can miss this view together."

Lucas pointed to the airport. "Shanique is going to the airport today. It's a field trip. Says they get to tour the inside of a company jet. She was so excited this morning I thought she might pee her pants."

They laughed. "She's a great girl, Lucas. You're lucky to have her."

"She's my whole world, Jim. My whole world wrapped up in a little nine-year-old kid who's all knees, elbows, and a butterfly in her hair."

"A butterfly?"

"Yeah, it's some kind of pin. She's proud of it. It flaps when she runs!"

They laughed again, took one last look at the river, and got to work.

At two o'clock sharp, Destiny rolled to a stop outside Barker Elementary School. With flair, like he was playing a part in a movie, Ricky emerged and opened the passenger door. Rafi slid out, wearing his pilot's uniform.

"Showtime, Ricky."

Rafi entered the school, went to the office, and announced himself. Connie was already there.

"Rafi! You look so handsome!" She smiled giddily. "The kids are all excited. I'll call for the bus driver."

"No, no, no, my darling. Today, the kids get the full treatment. No bus." He pointed to the window.

Connie looked out and gasped. "A limousine! Rafi! You didn't have to do that!"

"Nothing is too good for you and your students, Connie. Now, fetch the kids and let's teach them about flying in style!"

The kids squealed with delight as they piled in to the back of the limo. They all fit, amazingly enough, even Connie. Rafi rode shotgun.

Ricky couldn't help but grin as he drove smoothly to the airport, watching the kids on the video screen. He hit the record button, just for the hell of it.

At the airport, Ricky drove straight on to the tarmac, parking between the Screaming Eagle and the terminal. He opened Rafi's door first, then the passenger door. The kids piled out; fifteen of them. It reminded Ricky of Shriners falling out of a clown car.

Rafi took them around the outside of the jet first, explaining everything, and most of the kids were actually paying attention. But he knew what they really wanted.

"Who wants to see the inside?" he called out.

Fifteen hands shot in the air. Rafi lowered the stairs and herded them in. He could hear them oohing and aahing.

Connie said, "Please tell me you hid the dirty movies."

Rafi laughed. "No worries, my love. Hey, why don't you go to the café inside and make arrangements for ice cream? Ice cream for everybody, my treat!"

Now it was Connie's turn to squeal. "Oh, Rafi, this is a day the kids will never forget!"

He watched her waddle away and said under his breath, "If you only knew."

Then he turned to Ricky and said, once again, "Showtime."

33

Connie was giddy as she went to the café and made the arrangements for ice cream.

"Fifteen kids and three adults!"

"That's a lot of ice cream," the waitress said.

"My boyfriend is buying," Connie replied, and it made her feel proud to say it. God, she was head over heels in love.

The waitress only nodded, but she was thinking: this cow has a boyfriend? And he buys her ice cream? He's an enabler!

The arrangements made, Connie left the café and saw the pink limo pulling away. Must be going to park it out front, she thought. But, wait. The plane was pulling away, too. That doesn't make sense. Where are the kids?

Oh, no, she thought. Rafi, are you taking the kids for a joy ride? That wasn't on the permission slip! The parents will have a cow!

"Rafi!" she yelled. "Stop!"

But the Screaming Eagle was already at the far end of the runway. Frantic, she waved her arms and shook her head. "Don't take off! It wasn't on the permission slip!"

Rafi could see her, of course, but he didn't care.

"Watch this, Connie!" He gunned the throttle, sped down the runway and lifted off, pretty as you please, into the brilliant blue of the September sky.

Connie couldn't believe it. What was he thinking? She made her way around to the front of the terminal, looking for the pink limo. Please, God, let the kids be in the limo.

But the limo was gone.

Ricky watched as Rafi lifted off, banked to the left, flew low over the Capitol and set a course due east. Ricky snapped open a disposable phone and called 9-1-1.

"What's your emergency?"

"Some crazy bastard just kidnapped the entire fourth grade class at Barker Elementary. He's got them trapped on a plane and he just took off. He said he's going to fly the plane - kids and all - into the first tall building he sees in St. Louis."

Ricky flipped the phone shut, threw it out the window, and kept driving.

The first thing the 9-1-1 operator did was call Barker Elementary. "Where is your fourth grade class?" she asked.

"On a field trip. At the airport."

Ah, Jesus. She dispatched two police cars to the airport and called the local office of the FBI. The FBI called the Department of Homeland Security. The Department of Homeland Security called the White House. The White House called the President, who was rehearsing his acceptance speech in New Orleans.

"We've scrambled two F-16s out of St. Louis," Anne Scofield said. "They'll be intercepting the bogey shortly."

"Intercepting the bogey? Good God, Anne, it's a plane full of fourth-graders! Are you asking me to shoot it out of the sky?"

"Let's hope not, Mr. President, but we need to be ready to give the order. We'll be saving lives on the ground."

Darling wanted to puke. "And go down in history as the man who shot down a bunch of kids? There has to be a better solution!"

Back at the White House, somebody handed Scofield a note. "Hold tight, Mr. President. Police on the ground have interviewed the fourth-grade teacher. She identified the pilot as a man named Rafi Sayahd. We have his mobile number. We're calling it now."

Rafi let it ring three times, and then calmly answered it. "Hello?"

"Mr. Sayahd, my name is Bill Peglow. I'm with the Department of Homeland Security."

"Good afternoon, Mr. Peglow. Why are you calling?"

"We've been told you intend to crash the plane into a building in St. Louis. We can't let you do that."

Rafi chuckled. "If that indeed was my intent, Mr. Peglow, how would you stop me?"

"Are you telling me that is not your intent?"

"I'm telling you nothing. You're the one who called me."

Two F-16s pulled up alongside the Screaming Eagle. They tipped their wings, showing Rafi their missiles.

"So your intent, Mr. Peglow, is to shoot me down? And kill everyone on board? I can't believe President

Darling would want such a legacy. I wish to speak directly to him. Now."

"No."

"I'm hanging up now, Mr. Peglow. When my phone rings again - and it better be soon - the man on the other end better be President Darling. If it's you or some other flunky, we're all going down together."

One of Rafi's accomplices out at the farm saw the plane fly overhead shortly after takeoff. As planned, he started tweeting about it, so the news media was all over it. There was panic in St. Louis, as everyone working in a building they considered "tall" tried desperately to evacuate. People across the country were glued to the news networks. Talking heads openly wondered about a connection to the Soldiers of Allah, though none had been established.

"The world has gone crazy," one of them observed, and nobody could disagree.

Lucas Washington was heartsick. His precious Shanique was on that plane! He was back on the portico, searching the horizon for the plane to come back, to land safely, to disgorge his daughter, and for that bastard pilot to be arrested.

McHenry appeared at his side. "I'm sure the authorities are doing everything they can, Lucas."

Lucas turned to his friend. "What would you do, Jim? Would you shoot the plane down or let it crash into some building? Either way, the kids are dead. My Shanique..." He choked back a sob. "What would you do?"

McHenry sighed heavily. "I don't know, Lucas. Let's hope Darling makes the right call."

"Shit. When has he ever made the right call?"

To the surprise of everyone around him, Darling didn't hesitate. He simply picked up the phone and dialed.

Rafi jumped a little as the phone rang. Yes, he was on edge. The F-16s were practically up his ass.

"Hello?"

"Rafi? It's President Darling, just as you demanded."

Rafi exhaled. "Thank you, Mr. President."

"Now, Rafi, while we're talking, you will do nothing to crash the plane or hurt anybody, okay? Just keep flying."

"Okay."

"And I won't give the order to shoot you down, okay? We'll just be talking."

"Okay."

"Is everyone on board the plane okay?"

"Yes. Everyone on board is okay."

"Good. What did you want to say to me?"

"I'm afraid there has been a terrible mistake, Mr. President. Mr. Peglow accused me of wanting to crash the plane. That's crazy. I never said to anyone that I wanted to crash the plane. And now I have fighter pilots who look like they have itchy fingers."

"They can't shoot you down, Rafi, without my say so."

"Okay."

"So you have no intention of crashing the plane or killing anyone?"

"No! It's all a terrible mistake!"

"Good. Then all you have to do is return to the Jefferson City airport."

"But I'm afraid I'll be arrested, Mr. President! I need your assurance that won't happen. I haven't committed any crimes!"

"Kidnapping is a serious crime, Rafi."

"I haven't kidnapped anyone! It's all a terrible mistake! I'd rather crash the plane than be arrested!"

"Calm down, Rafi. What do you need from me?"

"This plane has a fax machine on board. I want you to fax me a letter, signed by you, that prohibits me from being arrested. I have committed no crimes!"

"Or what?"

"Or I crash the plane!" Rafi was shouting now. "Everyone on board will die! Plus more on the ground! And the blood will be on your hands!"

Darling had to take a breath to keep the edge out of his voice. "No one needs to die today, Rafi. You'll get your letter within five minutes. Turn the plane around and go back to Jefferson City. The F-16s will follow you to make sure you land safely. Are we clear?"

"We're clear." Rafi recited the fax number. "Thank you, Mr. President."

34

The White House leaked word to the national news networks that President Darling himself had convinced the rogue pilot to return safely to the Jefferson City airport. No mention was made of the letter prohibiting Rafi's arrest.

The news bulletins brought a wave of relief to the nation and brought tears to the eyes of Lucas Washington. He headed straight for the airport, ready to wrap his arms around Shanique, his precious little "Butterfly Girl."

The fax machine aboard the Screaming Eagle whirred to life and, sure enough, there was a brief letter, signed by President Darling, prohibiting Rafi's arrest. Rafi especially liked the last line: "This man has committed no crimes."

All three of the local news stations had live cameras ready to catch the landing of the Screaming Eagle. Some other parents had joined Lucas next to the terminal, watchful.

McHenry stood on the portico and watched as the plane arrived over the eastern horizon, banked, and gently drifted to the runway, north to south. The F-16s were close behind, in tight formation, impressive. As soon as the Screaming Eagle touched down, they roared off. McHenry imagined the pilots were breathing easier. They would rest easy tonight, free of the burden of shooting down a plane full of children.

All the national networks picked up the local camera feeds. President Darling was watching from New Orleans, Kennedy by his side, ready to celebrate this great accomplishment. They watched as the plane taxied to a stop and shut down.

Curiously, a pink limousine pulled quickly onto the tarmac, a police officer trying in vain to stop it. The plane's door opened and the steps unfolded. Rafi stepped out and met the police officer. The officer read the short letter and nodded. He had been briefed.

Then, Rafi said: "I have rigged the plane with a bomb. If you try to enter the plane before I am safely away, it will explode. Do you understand?"

"You sonofabitch."

"I said, do you understand?"

"Yes. How long do I wait?"

Rafi handed the officer a pager. "When this beeps, it is safe to enter. Not before. Don't worry. This is only to assure my safe passage away from here. I have no intention of hurting anyone."

With that, Rafi got into the limo, riding shotgun again, and away they went.

"Something isn't right, Kennedy," Darling said, the worry heavy in his voice. "What were they talking about? Why aren't the kids coming out of the plane? Why isn't the officer going in the plane? He's just standing there!"

"Wait," Kennedy said. "There he goes."

Another officer walked toward the plane, the nation watching on television, transfixed by the live drama. They were ready to stand and cheer, but what was happening? Why no kids?

Finally, the original officer scrambled out of the plane. He did not look happy. He looked at the second officer and yelled something.

Darling looked at Kennedy and said, "I'm a pretty good lip reader. Did he just say what I think he said?"

Kennedy looked sick. "Yeah. I think he said, 'The fucking plane is empty.'"

It was only a short drive from the airport to the farmhouse. Ricky pulled the limo into the driveway.

"Are the kids alright?" Rafi asked before getting out.

"They were confused and asking about the teacher," Ricky replied with a shrug. "But, just like we discussed, I said she was buying ice cream for a picnic later. They're locked in the barn, waiting."

Rafi nodded. He pulled out his smart phone, showed it to Ricky, and made a show of transferring the money. "Remember, Ricky. Slickface and boner."

Ricky laughed. "Got it. But why so much money? Seriously. I didn't even have to kill anyone."

"But you would have."

"Absolutely."

"The people paying for all this consider a million dollars a rounding error, Ricky. Enjoy it. You did good."

Rafi got out and headed to the house. Ricky drove off. A six pack sounded good.

The empty plane caused Connie to spring into action. She grabbed the closest police officer.

"They must have been in the limo! The pink limo! And you let it drive right out of here!"

The officer got on his radio immediately. A BOLO was issued for the pink limousine. The media picked it up immediately.

"The authorities are on the lookout for a pink limousine with the word 'desire' on the door. They believe it was used in the abduction of fifteen fourth-graders in Jefferson City, Missouri, earlier today. These are the students initially thought to be in the plane. If you see a vehicle matching this description, call the authorities immediately. Do not approach the vehicle yourself."

In Memphis, Roger Best choked on his coffee and said, "Ricky, what the fuck have you done?"

In Holts Summit, Missouri, a man working the counter of a convenience store picked up the phone and called 9-1-1. "You know that pink limo ya'll are lookin' for? It was just here. I sold the chauffer a six pack."

Trooper Gary Whiteman was racing up Highway 54 toward Interstate 70. He was doing 90. Then 100. Now 110. There it was! The pink limo! He closed fast; too fast. Slowing down, he hit the siren. Pull over you sonofabitch!

Ricky didn't like this one bit. He wasn't speeding, the cruise control was on 70, just a guy out enjoying a cold beer. He calmly put the beer into a cup holder, signaled, and pulled to the side of the road.

Trooper Whiteman approached cautiously, his holster unbuckled, one hand on the butt of his gun. Couldn't see in the car; the windows were too dark. He rapped his knuckles on the glass. "Open up!"

Ricky didn't hesitate, just shot the man right through the glass. The explosion of the window was terrifying. He shot three more times before the trooper hit the pavement.

A truck roared past, but the driver was hitting the brakes hard. Ricky gunned the motor and fled in a hurry, passing the truck, which was pulling over. Ricky was looking, looking, not panicked, but needing new wheels in a hurry. He spotted a farmhouse with a barn. A truck in the driveway.

"Perfect."

He pulled into the property and drove the limo all the way up to the side door. He got out, walked in the door without knocking, and shot the woman working in the kitchen and then the man who apparently had been dozing in the living room. The man managed a confused, "What the hell..." but that was it.

Within three minutes Ricky had the pink limo hidden in the barn - damn, gonna miss that sweet ride - and was pulling out of the property in a three-year-old Ford F-150 that smelled slightly of cow shit. Five minutes after that, he was on Interstate 70, headed east, with no particular destination in mind. Gotta think on that.

Ricky "The Boner" Barboni. On the run again. Damn, it was exhilarating! And he had a million smackaroos in the bank!

He rolled down the window and gulped the fresh air. He yelled, "I'm baaaack, you motherfuckers!"

35

The trucker called it in. Officer down (he was dead). Yes, the trucker saw the pink limo pull away, going fast.

Law enforcement worked fast. Everybody everywhere was looking for the limo. The Callaway County sheriff figured the first thing the limo driver would do was ditch the car. He had his deputies going house to house, in an ever-widening perimeter. After about an hour, a deputy barked on the radio.

"Found it, sheriff. In a barn at Doc Wilson's farm. Doc and his wife are both dead."

"Any sign of the kids?"

"No kids."

Ah, shit. "Is Doc's truck gone?"

"Yep."

They put a BOLO on it, too, and established a perimeter around the barn and the house. Lots to do.

Lucas was back in his office, his head in his hands, when McHenry walked in.

"You keeping it together?"

"Not really," Lucas replied, his voice thick with emotion. "What if they killed them?"

"Don't think like that. Why would they do that?"

"Why do any of it, Jim? It makes no sense. And why did they let the pilot go?"

McHenry frowned. "Apparently, Darling negotiated safe passage for the pilot in return for not crashing the plane, thinking the kids were on board. He looks like an idiot now, of course."

Lucas's eyes turned cold. "He's always been an idiot. You need to kick his ass, Jim. Kick it hard. If anything happens to Shanique..."

"Don't talk that way. Keep hope alive."

For the first time in his life, President Darling felt like shooting himself.

"What the fuck have we done, Kennedy?"

"What's this 'we' shit? I wasn't even in the room when you promised the Red Baron a get out of jail free card."

Darling looked at his watch. "In two hours, I have to march out there and accept the nomination. What the hell am I going to say?"

Kennedy shrugged. "Can we change the subject again?"

"In less than two hours? Who gets cancer this time?"

Kennedy shook his head. "No, cancer only works once."

They looked at each other, and at the walls, and listened to a clock tick, and wondered what the hell to do.

Rafi went to the barn and unlocked it. The kids were in mutiny.

"Where's Miss Baumgartner?"

"Why have we been locked in this stupid barn all afternoon?"

"I'm hungry."

"I'm thirsty."

"I have to pee."

"I think Jimmy Whalen pooped his pants. He's so gross."

Rafi waved them down. "Quiet! All of you! There's been a mix-up. You weren't supposed to be in the barn. I'm moving you to the house. There's food and stuff in there. You'll be comfortable."

"But where's Miss Baumgartner?"

Rafi looked at the little black girl with the butterfly in her hair. "She must have gotten lost. Now, follow me."

The superintendant of the highway patrol was on the horn with McHenry.

"Governor, we caught a break. We had a bird in the air, looking in ever-widening circles for signs of the school kids. It's getting on toward dark, and we were about to quit for the night, when the pilot saw a gaggle of kids being led from a barn to a house, out in the sticks."

"It's gotta be them. Get the SWAT team out there."

"Already in the works, Governor. Should be deployed on site within twenty minutes."

McHenry hung up and just like that his cell phone rang. He disposed of the call as quickly as he could under the circumstances.

"Lucas!" McHenry was up and walking to Lucas's office. "Lucas! A patrol chopper may have spotted the kids. A farmhouse not far from here. Across the river."

Lucas bolted from his chair. "Seriously? Do they look okay?"

"They were walking, so that's a good sign. SWAT is on the way. Wanna go?"

"Oh, hell yes!"

"Get John," McHenry instructed. "I'll meet you at the elevator."

John was the state trooper assigned to drive the Governor wherever he needed to go. When McHenry got to the elevator, John was holding it open. The three of them rode straight to the basement and were hustling out of the elevator car when McHenry bumped hard into Sam Browning, an old school reporter if there ever was one. The young pups joked that Sam Browning filed the first wire story on the invention of dirt.

"What's the hurry, Governor?"

"Nothing, Sam. Just gotta go someplace."

"Bullshit. Lucas here is about to have a stroke his veins are bulging out so bad. C'mon. What gives?"

McHenry looked at Sam and remembered all the times the reporter had found him drunk in his Senate office, or in a bar, and reported nothing. They'd enjoyed drinks and cigars together, back in the day.

"What the hell, Sam. C'mon along. You can file a feel-good story about the rescue of a bunch of fourth-graders."

"No shit? Let's go!"

As they were leaving the Capitol basement garage in the unmarked patrol car, Browning looked around and piped up. "Where's your Secret Service detail?"

"Ditched 'em," McHenry said with a smile. "But I'm sure they'll be along shortly, pissed as hell."

36

On the way, Browning pulled out his smartphone and called his boss, who called his boss, who called the national desk, who called Browning back immediately.

"Use the video feature on your phone and just stream it. We'll handle everything here based on what we see and hear. And please tell me you've got a full battery."

"Pretty good," Browning said. "Of course, the more I talk now the less I'll have later." He hung up.

The SWAT team was on site. They had erected some bright lights around the perimeter of the front of the farmhouse. The SWAT team commander was surprised to see McHenry.

"Governor? What are you doing here? Who knows? This could get rough."

"I wouldn't miss this show for the world, Gus."

"Yeah, well, you stay back here. You ain't getting hurt on my watch."

"Brief me, Gus."

"They're in there, all right. And they were expecting us. You see that sign up there?"

McHenry looked. "Yeah, but I can't read it."

"It says, 'house rigged with explosives, do not touch.' Makes things a little jumpy."

Lucas looked like he was going to be sick. The SWAT commander noticed Browning for the first time. "Jesus Christ, Sam. How did you get out here?"

McHenry interceded. "He's with us, Gus. Somebody has to chronicle your good work."

"Shit. Well, chronicle this, Sam."

The SWAT commander raised a bullhorn to his lips. "You! In the house! You are surrounded by officers of the Missouri Highway Patrol! Come out with your hands up and lay on the ground! Now!"

After about ten seconds, there was a short buzzing sound from an outdoor speaker attached to a tree. Then: "Fuck you!"

Gus looked at McHenry and said, "The negotiations have begun."

The news bulletins hit like wildfire. Darling's national convention might as well have been wallpaper in a truck stop bathroom.

"Missouri state troopers have surrounded a farm house near Jefferson City where they believe the fourth-graders abducted today are being held. They can't storm the house for fear that it may be rigged to explode. Negotiations with the captors are under way."

Gus lifted the bullhorn again. "Give me a phone number I can call so we can discuss the situation like gentlemen."

There was a long wait, and then Rafi was on the speaker again, giving out a number.

"Progress," Gus said, and dialed the number.

"Hello."

"My name us Gus Summers with the Missouri Highway Patrol. And you are?"

"Rafi Sayahd."

"The pilot? Aren't you the pilot for those lobbyists? Does Burley Watson know what you're doing?"

Rafi chuckled. "He fired me about an hour ago. By text message."

"After threatening to crash his plane? I would hope so. What is it you expect to gain here, Mr. Sayahd?"

Lucas looked at McHenry in disbelief. Rafi was doing all this? McHenry said nothing.

"You can call me Rafi, Gus. I have a very precise demand to make in exchange for the lives of the children, but I need a show of good faith from you first."

"I don't think that's how it works, Rafi. I need a show of good faith from you. Let the kids go. Then we'll talk."

"Let me think about it," Rafi said, and hung up.

"Forty minutes, Kennedy! I'm on stage in forty minutes and not a damn soul in America gives a shit!"

"I give a shit."

Darling was in the green room, pacing. "I'm not even sure I give a shit. This morning, we were up in the polls. Olivia Morgan was on everybody's lips. Now, this! And what if those Missouri troopers pull it off and rescue the kids. That damn McHenry will take the credit."

"It could still go bad, you know. Then he'll be taking the blame. Well, except for that get out of jail free card you issued."

"For the hundredth time, Kennedy, just shut the fuck up."

37

Sam Browning's boss's boss's boss decided to offer the video feed from Sam's phone - grainy as it was, and shaky because by this time Sam would ordinarily be into his third cocktail - to any national news network that wanted it. They all did.

In most cases it was superimposed as a small picture-in-picture in the corner as the Darling convention droned on. The producers were listening to the audio, though, and nearly all of them went live at the same time when they could tell something was up.

The phone rang in Gus's hand. "Yes?"

"I'm sending out the children as a show of good faith. Well, all but one. She's my bargaining chip."

"Send them all out, Rafi. Then we'll talk."

"No! This is your chance to save fourteen lives. The chance goes away in five seconds. Will you take it?"

"Yes, I'll take it. Send them out."

"I am opening the door," Rafi said. "They will come out in single file. If anybody out there moves, I shoot."

"Don't shoot anybody, Rafi. Just send them out. Then we'll talk."

Gus said to McHenry and Lucas, "He's sending out all but one of the kids. It's progress."

Lucas held his breath as the kids walked out of the house one by one, across the porch, down the steps, scared as hell, every one, all the way to the end of the yard and into the arms of the SWAT team, who hurried them away. They called for a bus.

People across the country were cheering at their televisions, high-fiving each other. In New Orleans, in the Superdome, several of the delegates were watching on their phones or tablets. In the media suites, the talking heads were trying to explain what was going on in the shaky, grainy video feed.

McHenry's Secret Service detail arrived on the scene, pissed as hell, just as McHenry predicted.

"We're taking you away from here, Governor!" the leader said. But McHenry refused, and told them to shut the hell up and babysit the kids.

The line of scared fourth-graders ended, and the door to the house slammed shut.

"Oh my God, Jim, he still has Shanique!" Lucas could barely breathe. "My little butterfly girl is still in there!"

A flunky stage manager ducked his head into the green room and announced, "Ten minutes, Mr. President. Your tribute video is about to start, and then you're up."

"My tribute video. Shit," Darling grunted. "I wonder how much we spent making it? Nobody will see it. And nobody will hear me speak, either. I'll be the first president ever to accept the nomination for reelection by speaking to an empty room."

"It gets worse," Kennedy said with a shake in his voice. "You heard the audio of the hostage negotiator? He was talking to a guy named Rafi. That's the guy you let go today. He's the kidnapper. He's the one holding on to this 'butterfly girl' the media is so ga-ga about."

Darling stared at his friend. "Maybe I should just walk out there and refuse the nomination. Let Olivia have it."

Kennedy shot out of his chair. "Hell no! The election is two months away! We're gonna fight like hell and win! No giving up!"

"If you say so. Do you know anything about this butterfly girl? Who she is?"

Kennedy looked at the floor. "I recognized the father's voice on the video feed. It was Lucas Washington, McHenry's chief of staff."

Darling wanted to disappear into the sofa. "The butterfly girl is the daughter of McHenry's chief of staff? And she's being held hostage by a man I let go? It just gets worse and worse."

Once again, the phone rang in Gus's hand. "Ready to talk now?"

"Yes, but not with you. Send in McHenry. I know he's out there."

"Out of the question. Who the hell do you think you are?"

"I'm the man holding a gun to the head of a cute little girl with a butterfly in her hair. That's who I am."

Gus wanted to reach into the phone and rip the damn man's head off. "Put the gun down, Rafi. There's no need to put a gun to her head. She's just a little girl."

Lucas heard this, as did the rest of the country, and he couldn't stop shaking. Shanique!

"Send in McHenry within two minutes or I put a bullet through her cute little head."

The line went dead.

Even with all his training, Gus was shaken as he approached McHenry. Lucas was there. And they had all forgotten about old Sam Browning, doing his job, streaming everything to the nation.

"Governor, he says you have to go in there and talk with him. If you don't go inside within two minutes he'll shoo..." Gus glanced at Lucas. "I'm sorry, Lucas. He'll shoot her."

Lucas couldn't stop the sobs this time. McHenry embraced him, then turned to Gus and said, "I'll go."

"The hell you will!" It was the head of the Secret Service detail. "Out of the question!"

McHenry ignored him.

Gus said, "Let's get you fitted with a vest."

McHenry shook his head. "No." He took off his suit jacket and handed it to the shocked and grieving Lucas. "That little butterfly girl has her whole life ahead of her. I love her almost as much as you do, Lucas. It's an easy swap."

With that, Missouri Governor James Madison McHenry stepped into the bright lights. The Secret Service tried to grab his shoulder, but McHenry shrugged it off. His white dress shirt was radiant in the floodlights. With his arms extended outward from his sides, he started walking toward the front porch.

38

"What in the hell are you doing?"

Zulu had been watching the coverage of the hostage standoff, transfixed like the rest of America, glued to the screen, but with more at stake than most. Along with Alpha, Beta, and Omega, tonight's events had been discussed in nauseating detail. Nobody - especially not Zulu - had expected McHenry to accept the demand that he swap himself for the little girl.

How the hell is the Secret Service even allowing this? And why now? Damn it! The timing is all off!

"Oh, McHenry," she said to her empty living room, shaking her head. "I waaaaay underestimated you."

Her phone buzzed. It was a text. Simply: "9am." That would be Alpha, calling a meeting of the Azalea Team. And how would she explain herself?

McHenry could feel a trickle of sweat tracing its way down his back. He could hear the Secret Service trading expletives with Gus. His shoes crunched across a gravel driveway. There were cars - eight of them! - parked haphazardly in the front yard. The license plates were from all over the place.

What was he walking into? Breathe, he reminded himself. Breathe. Stay alert.

He reached the front porch steps. The porch was impressive. Very wide. The kind of porch politicians use to make television ads.

One step. Two steps. Three steps. He was on the porch. Don't look back. Be confident. Three more steps and he was at the front door.

Now what? Do I ring the doorbell? Or knock? As it turned out, the decision was made for him.

The tribute video ended. The stage went dark. Then, the proverbial voice of God: "Ladies and gentlemen, the President of the United States!"

Darling did the best he could, put on his best smile, waved the wave. The delegates did the best they could, too. But it was off. And the network news anchors didn't care. The real news - the incredible news - was being made in an old farmhouse in southern Callaway County, Missouri. If Darling said anything interesting, they could talk about it later.

The Governor of Missouri - a presidential nominee! - was swapping himself for a kidnapped fourth-grader. And damned if a reporter wasn't there with a video camera!

No contest.

The door flew open on its own. There she was, scared as a kitten in a thunderstorm, her eyes red from crying. She jumped at him, hugging him fiercely around the waist, refusing to let go, clinging to him like he was life itself. He was her savior.

"Shanique!" McHenry said. "You need to go to your daddy. He's over there, beyond the lights. You'll be safe. Hurry, Shanique!"

And hurry she did. Shanique ran like the wind, her beaded hair swinging wildly, the butterfly flapping like it might take flight. Lucas stepped forward into the lights and grabbed his little girl, lifting her into his arms in a father-daughter embrace that would be replayed by the news networks over and over and over.

Up at the house, they all heard the front door slam shut. McHenry was inside.

Rafi's voice came over the loudspeaker: "If anyone approaches the house, McHenry is a dead man. We have some things to discuss."

"Gov. McHenry rescues Butterfly Girl" was the graphic splashed all over most of the networks, as the talking heads marveled at McHenry's bravery - or was it stupidity? What was going on in that house? Surely the head of the Secret Service detail would be fired.

Then, even more news came in. Crime scene technicians had lifted fingerprints from the inside of the pink limo and gotten a hit: the driver was none other than Ricky Barboni, he of the FBI Ten Most Wanted List.

Ricky heard about this while he was driving south on Interstate 55. It thrilled him to know that, once again, Ricky Barboni was feared. But it also jolted him into action, taking the next exit and heading west, into the interior of Missouri's mining country. He needed to dump the truck.

Then, in a night of amazing things, the most amazing thing yet happened: McHenry's voice came over the speaker: "We're coming out! Nobody shoot! We're coming out!"

The front door opened, and one after another, out came a line of men, each with their hands behind their heads, looking like deer in the headlights. Seven of them. They lined up on the porch. Then, out came Rafi, his hands in the air, his lips bloodied, and his shirt torn.

Behind him was McHenry, his nose bleeding, his white shirt completely un-tucked and bloody, and he had a revolver to Rafi's head.

39

In New Orleans, President Darling had wrapped up his speech. The confetti cannons fired. The balloons dropped. And most of the delegates were trying to follow what was happening in Missouri. Good God. Who does McHenry think he is? John Wayne? He's irresponsible!

No way would Darling have done that. Not in a million years. See him up there on the stage, smiling and waving? And his lovely wife! McHenry doesn't even have a wife; too much of a cowboy.

And there's the Vice President! She's the brave one! Such a shame, having to face down breast cancer and everybody in the world knows about it. Probably McHenry's people who leaked it. The bastards.

Americans watching TV from their living rooms, or in bars, or at their offices, were cheering McHenry on. Darling was nowhere to be seen. And they could hear it, plain as day, when McHenry shouted: "Hey, Gus! Get your guys over here and handcuff these bastards!"

The response of the viewing public was electric. "Damn straight! Handcuff 'em!"

"Shoot 'em!"

"Book 'em, Dan-o!"

"You rock, McHenry!"

Then, on the screen, all of America could see the "low battery" light flashing. And then, for the first time all night, they heard the voice of old Sam Browning: "Well, shit."

McHenry handed the revolver to Gus. "I took it from Rafi, so it's evidence."

"You look like shit," Gus announced.

"Thanks, Gus." McHenry tested his nose. "I don't think it's broken. Just bloodied."

"What happened in there? It was eight against one!"

McHenry shrugged. "I saw a chance to get the jump on Rafi, so I went for it. We fought for awhile, but I got the gun. The other guys just watched.

"It was weird, you know? I've known Rafi for years; drank with him, played poker with him and Burly Watson and the guys. Can't figure what set him off to be involved in something like this. Kidnapping an entire fourth-grade class? For what?"

"Money," Gus replied bluntly. "If it ain't about sex, it's always about money."

"Maybe both."

"That's sick, Governor. But if it's true, it's a damn good thing we found 'em."

Sam Browning, his dead phone stowed safely in his pocket, was reduced to pen and paper, like the old days. He stepped up on the porch. "Governor, what were you and that Rafi guy talking about in there? What did he want?"

Gus barked at him. "Dammit, Sam! Get off the porch! It's a fuckin' crime scene!"

"We'll talk in the car, Sam," McHenry said.

Sam shuffled away. He couldn't be too upset. What a night!

Gus looked curiously at McHenry. "What *did* you guys talk about?"

McHenry shrugged. "The usual stuff. It was all a big mistake, everybody is okay now, can't we put it behind us? And he claims his seven friends had nothing at all to do with it. He said it was the limo driver's idea."

"The limo driver has been identified. Ricky Barboni. A serious bad-ass on the FBI most wanted list for a series of murders down in Florida. He's already killed three here, that we know of."

McHenry shook his head and tasted blood. "Whatever we know so far isn't the truth, Gus. Maybe not even close."

"Well, we're fixin' to tear this place apart. If the truth is in there somewhere, we'll find it."

Ricky spotted a trailer that was partially hidden behind some trees off a winding road near a town called Silver Lake. He swung in and killed his headlights. The trailer was dark, but he didn't think it was abandoned. There was a satellite dish on a pole in the front yard and a flower pot with some marijuana growing in it on a creaky front porch.

Huh. If the old boy is growing pot, he probably has guns. Better be careful.

Ricky slid out of the truck, gun in hand. He listened. Nothing. There was an old Chevy Blazer parked to the right. He wondered if the keys were in it. He tried the driver's side door, just enough to get the dome light to come on, and jerked up in surprise.

There was a fat guy sitting inside, sound asleep, smelling like a brewery.

40

It was highly unusual for the Azalea Team to be meeting in the morning. But, nonetheless, the loyal staff had everything in order. The booze was replaced with coffee and pastries.

Zulu got there first, nervous. She was up most of the night thinking, rethinking, and then thinking all over again. Round and round. Things hadn't gone according to script. It was time to adapt to the changing conditions on the ground. She finally settled upon a plan of action, but it was the most dangerous plan. For her, especially.

Alpha, Beta, and Omega arrived together. Shit, Zulu thought. They had obviously had a "meeting before the meeting." Not good for her.

Alpha, of course, was impeccably dressed, though his face was lined with worry. He was the chairman of the board of the biggest newspaper conglomerate in the world. Hundreds of editorial writers answered to him. He had spent decades setting the news agenda.

Beta was his usual nervous self, frayed around the edges, looking like he needed to cough up a mouse. He was headed for an early heart attack, surely. He ran the biggest collection of radio and television networks, a tough job in and of itself, without the added stress of *this*.

Omega smiled broadly at Zulu, in his usual jeans and un-tucked shirt, but she could see it in his eyes. The axe was about to fall. Omega's contribution was to manipulate the social media sites. He was the hipster. Get the younger folks moving in the proper direction and keep them going.

Zulu was the ruthless one, the researcher, the strategizer, the one to do the unmentionable things. But she had failed them; it radiated from them in waves. She took a seat in one of the fine leather chairs and crossed her legs. It wasn't quite the usual show, because she was in slacks this morning, though the slacks were impossibly tight. The last time she wore them, Omega had remarked, "It looks like you're showing off your lunchbox."

Men.

"Gentlemen," she said, and simply waited for the verbal beating to begin.

Ricky had spent the night in the trailer, after waking up the fat boy and marching him into the woods. "Don't do this, man, don't do this," the fat boy kept blubbering. But, of course, Ricky shot him in the back of the head.

The trailer proved to be a productive find. Plenty of guns and ammo, and about $3,000 in cash. All would come in handy. He scrounged around and ate some food, hid the pickup behind the trailer, and took off in the old Chevy Blazer, heading back to St. Louis to one of his old haunts. He needed to see a man named Pecker.

"We underestimated McHenry," Alpha began, munching on a pastry. "And we way overestimated you." He was looking straight at Zulu. They all were.

She nodded. "McHenry's move was a complete surprise. I never thought the Secret Service would allow it.

I guess they're not as infallible as people think. The Butterfly Girl was supposed to die, with her blood on McHenry's hands. And the video. I didn't plan on the whole thing being broadcast live. And the timing! The whole thing was supposed to be over with long before President Darling gave his speech, so he could mourn the little girl."

"I don't like mistakes, Zulu. They change the course of history in unpredictable ways."

"I don't like mistakes, either!" she shouted. "But they happen! You said so yourself!"

An uncomfortable silence filled the room at the rebuke. Finally, Zulu relented. "I'm sorry, Alpha."

"You're right, Zulu. Mistakes happen. This organization started because of a mistake: the election of John Kennedy in 1960. He stole the election. It was supposed to be Nixon. So the Azalea Team was formed to take out Kennedy, bamboozle the public, and finally get Nixon elected in 1968.

"And then another mistake: the Watergate burglars were a bunch of clumsy bastards. They changed the course of history by getting Jimmy Carter elected. We changed it back with the help of some radical Iranians and got Reagan elected. I was Zulu back then. The Iranian hostage crisis was my idea and it got me promoted to Alpha. Strange bedfellows and all that.

"Our record over the years isn't perfect, but this," Alpha waived his hands in the air. "This is very bad. Unfixable, possibly."

Beta cleared his throat and spoke up. "Zulu, what will the police find in that farmhouse?" His voice came out shaky, nervous.

Zulu sighed heavily. "They'll find the machine guns that did the original killings, I would guess. Fingerprints. Smartphones full of text messages and emails."

"Connected to us?" Beta's eyes were as big as baseballs.

"Of course not," Zulu snapped. "Give me some credit. I covered our tracks, for God's sake."

"We are murderers," Beta said, looking forlorn. "And all for nothing."

Alpha looked at Omega. "Do you think it was for nothing, Omega? What's your take?"

Omega nodded. "My analysis of the social media trend is that Darling doesn't stand a chance. McHenry is John Wayne reborn. And once they analyze the evidence in the farmhouse, it'll become clear that not only did McHenry rescue the Butterfly Girl, but he also caught the Soldiers of Allah, all in one brave little walk up that porch on live TV. It's over."

There was a long silence as they all contemplated the current reality of things. Finally, Zulu said, "Maybe McHenry deserves to win, if he's that brave. Maybe my biggest mistake was my initial research that convinced us Darling deserved another term."

"Oh, God," Beta was nearly weeping. "We killed all those people."

"Shut up, Beta," Alpha said sharply. "Enough with the guilt trip. What's done is done. And, if it turns out that McHenry really is the best man for the job, then everything we've done has led us to this moment. Our job right now is to think clearly, act rationally, and worm our way into the McHenry administration. So we can control him."

"Actually," Zulu said as she crossed her legs again, "I have a plan for that."

41

Ricky parked the Blazer in front of the sleaziest strip joint in Brooklyn, Illinois. It was barely noon, so business was sparse. Just inside the door was the biggest, meanest-looking black man Ricky had ever seen, and he'd seen plenty.

"Twenty bucks," the bouncer said.

"I ain't here for the ladies. I wanna see Pecker."

The bouncer scowled at him. "Wrong joint. We show girls here, not peckers. Scram."

"No, not like that. I mean I need to talk to the owner. You know, Pecker."

"Nobody calls him Pecker anymore, not for awhile. Who are you?"

"Tell him it's Boner."

The bouncer lit up a smile. "You're the Boner? Shit. He talks about you all the time! You were runnin' brothers, back in the day. C'mon back."

The bouncer led Ricky through the joint. It was dark as midnight inside, and once Ricky banged a knee on a chair. A stripper, looking bored, was trying, but failing, to get the attention of two guys deep in conversation near the stage. The bouncer opened a door in the back, leaned his head in and announced: "Hey, Bud! It's Boner!"

Ricky walked into the office. Bud lit up when he saw him. "Boner! Sure as hell! I never thought I'd see you again!"

They hugged. Ricky said, "What's this 'Bud' shit? How come nobody calls you Pecker anymore?"

Bud rolled his eyes and pointed Ricky to a chair. "Fuckin' lawyers. After you got busted, and a few others, my lawyers said I needed to start running a more respectable place. So now it's 'Bud's Place' instead of 'Pecker's Place.' You can see where it gets me. Business sucks."

"Business would be better if the girls sucked."

Bud laughed heartily. "God damn, Boner! You ain't changed a bit!" Then he darkened. "You do know the whole fuckin' world is looking for you, right? You are public enemy number one, dude. They're saying you might have been the mastermind behind all that terrorist shit. What the fuck, man?"

"That's horse shit, Pecker. All I did was help kidnap a bunch of fourth-graders for some Arab guy. Paid me a bundle, too. I got nothing to do with that other shit."

"Killed some people. A trooper, even."

Ricky waived it away. "Fuckers got in my way."

"So," Bud said as he leaned back in his chair, "you're here to get a new identity from your old buddy Pecker."

"Yup."

"Who are you these days, Boner?"

Ricky tossed his driver's license across the desk. "Ricky Mather, Memphis. But that's blown."

"Alright. We'll shave your head. Give you some cheap fucking glasses. Take a picture. Make you a new license."

"Passport, too."

Bud shook his head. "That's a lot tougher."

"It doesn't need to be good enough to fool the best," Ricky said. "Just good enough to fool some jack leg in Cozumel."

Bud raised his eyebrows.

"Gotta get my money," Ricky said. "My allowance for stealing those snot-nosed kids."

"There's no way we can win."

It was Kennedy delivering the body blow to his boss. "The polls are ridiculous. McHenry is a hero, a god. He couldn't lose to Jesus Christ."

"Kennedy," Darling said, "back when you were still pissing in your diapers, President George H. W. Bush had a 91% approval rating. He went on to lose to the Governor with the Golden Zipper. Shit happens."

"Bush didn't single-handedly rescue a little black girl AND round up a bunch of killers on live fucking TV!"

"Right. But McHenry didn't catch Ricky Barboni, either. He's the mastermind. We get Barboni, we're back in the game."

"Is Barboni really the mastermind?"

"He is if we say he is, Kennedy. And we say he is. Every chance we get."

42

The weekend did not go well for the Darling reelection campaign. By the time the Sunday morning news shows rolled around, an avalanche of evidence had been disclosed connecting the men arrested in the Missouri farmhouse with the shootings and bombings of the previous two weeks.

Rafi Sayahd lawyered up immediately. His only statement to police was that the whole thing had been planned and executed at the behest of Ricky Barboni, who for reasons not fully understood was trying to rig the election for Darling. He had said so, Rafi's lawyer disclosed.

All of Rafi's accomplices were staying absolutely mute, as they had been instructed to do. All were being kept in separate cells across several counties in Missouri, awaiting transfer into the state and federal courts. They couldn't even talk to each other.

The machine guns used in the original killings had indeed been found in the farmhouse, along with more than a hundred boxes of ammunition. No bombs were found; that threat had apparently been empty. Also found in the farmhouse: the original fax of the letter from President Darling protecting Rafi from arrest, boldly declaring he had "committed no crimes."

The cars parked haphazardly all over the farmhouse yard had all been stolen from across the Midwest.

An edited version of the grainy, live video feed from Sam Browning's phone was playing incessantly on all the news networks and had millions of views on YouTube. Several folks were taking it a step further, splicing in images and lines from John Wayne and dubbing in heroic-sounding western music. Governor McHenry was larger than life. His running mate, Sgt. Major Gunderson, kicked it up another notch by saying, "The Governor's bravery tops anything I've ever witnessed on the battlefield."

The Darling Administration sent their minions to the news shows with instructions to talk about Olivia Morgan's cancer struggle, health care in general, and Darling's new program designed to lift people out of poverty. He had planned to unveil it with great fanfare during his acceptance speech, before everything went to shit.

Darling called it "Fulfilling America's Promise: A Living Wage for Every Worker." Repeal the minimum wage laws and replace them with the new Federally Mandated Living Wage: every employer would be required to pay every worker at least 75% of the average wage in the county where the job is performed, plus at least 75% of government-approved health insurance, dental insurance, vision insurance, car insurance, homeowner's insurance, and life insurance.

"It's time for the working folks to get what they deserve," the talking points went. "It's the working class that keeps this country moving, not the privileged few. Yes, this might increase the cost of labor in some instances, but it'll make sure the rewards of work end up in the calloused hands of the people who earned it."

When the questioners inevitably got to "the heroic turn of events that led to the arrest of the terrorists," the minions were instructed to turn the tables: "We caught the field hands, or allegedly so, but let's not forget that the mastermind of the entire conspiracy is still at large. Until we have Ricky Barboni in custody, we can't really feel safe, or understand the full scale of the conspiracy, or believe that justice has actually been done. President Darling has made it clear that he will leave no stone unturned in the hunt for Barboni.

"It's our job now to close this disturbing chapter in American life. Governor McHenry's rather clumsy role in all of this is over now. Luckily, his cavalier behavior didn't result in the deaths of some of those children. But let's not forget: Barboni, the mastermind, slipped away almost literally right under his nose."

For his part, McHenry played it low-key. He sent Gunderson out to do the Sunday talk shows, in full uniform with medals a-blazing. At one point, he was asked, "What about this threat from the Soldiers of Allah that a McHenry victory in November will lead to the deaths of millions of Americans?"

"Americans should ignore it. It would be a sad day indeed when a gaggle of terrorists are allowed to scare the people into voting a certain way. I've watched friends of mine fight and die against these people to preserve our way of life. The voters don't have to die for the cause of freedom, just go vote the way you want to vote. And then tell the damn terrorists to kiss off."

43

Ricky Barboni, now carrying a driver's license, passport, and credit card in the name of Brian Cove, arrived in New Orleans in plenty of time. He was going to hop a cruise ship that had, as one of its many stopovers, Cozumel. There, he would show up at the bank that little Arab fella had chosen to park Ricky's money and figure out his next move from there. Maybe he'd just stay in Cozumel for awhile. He wondered if the whores were any good.

He parked the stolen Blazer in long-term Seaport parking and debated trying to sneak a gun on board. No, he decided, not worth the risk. Besides, the likelihood of confronting someone on the cruise ship who needed to be shot was next to nil. He also knew, strictly from hearing others talk about it, that Mexico had no tolerance for guns. So: no guns. He would feel naked.

Ricky locked up the Blazer and caught the shuttle to the Seaport. He'd never been on a cruise, but Pecker had assured him the security requirements were a little more lax than getting on a plane, and his best option for using the fake passport. He studied the ship as the line of passengers moved along. It was massive.

Now it was Ricky's turn at security. He had to admit it: he was nervous. He was the most wanted man in America, the Mastermind. He liked the term, but it pissed him off that he was being blamed for things he didn't do.

He didn't mind being blamed for killing people, but he didn't like being labeled a terrorist. That went too far.

Ricky's newly shaved head reflected the afternoon sun. He smiled at the woman wearing the security uniform, handing her his boarding pass and passport, and said, "It's my first cruise. I'm pretty excited."

She took the passport and boarding pass in her hands, which were protected with vinyl gloves, like maybe Ricky would give her a disease or something. She looked at the picture on the passport, then quickly at Ricky, made a mark on the boarding pass, and said, "Next."

Is that it? For a moment Ricky hesitated. Could it be that easy?

She looked at him with irritation as he stood there. "Right up that ramp, sir. Next?"

Ricky finally got moving, relief flooding over him. He did it! The Mastermind was about to flee the country! "I hope there's plenty of Budweiser on board," he said jovially, to anyone paying attention.

No one was.

Lydia Wade was dressed in what she considered her most drop-dead, sexiest outfit, at least the sexiest thing she could wear in public. Every dress she owned was form-fitting, and with the perfect form, every dress was a killer. This little number, in perfect black that matched her flowing hair, offered up a little more cleavage than average and was by far her shortest. Add in her matching stiletto heels and a diamond necklace, and she was certain that 99% of the men and even some of the women who saw her tonight would want her desperately.

That was fine with Lydia, but she really was only interested in catching the fancy of one person tonight: Governor James McHenry. She was in St. Louis, on her way to a fundraiser at the rural estate of a local industrialist. She had donated the maximum amount to McHenry's campaign, plus another $50,000 to the national political party to reserve her spot in "McHenry's Inner Circle," sort of a fundraiser before the fundraiser, where only the well-heeled few would be admitted.

The thought of seducing a sitting governor - a presidential candidate! - had her nerves hitting on all cylinders. She needed to remind herself that above all else, he was a man, and perhaps a lonely one at that, who "likes them young" in Richie's words. Young, as in Lydia. Pretty, as in Lydia. Sexy, as in Lydia. Easy, as in Lydia.

Yep, she was certain; she would get him into bed. If not tonight, then soon. And she would get a good look at that "johnson" he's so proud of.

She pulled to the front of the estate and was greeted by a young man in a red vest. Valet parking; very nice. She gave the kid a good show getting her legs out of the car and a big smile.

"Wow," he said, bug-eyed. "That dress is a killer."

"Thanks! Uh, where's the Inner Circle event?"

"The Inner Circle is inside the house. The main event is over there," he pointed, "in the pavilion."

"Thanks, again," she said with her best smile, and took off up the walk to the impressive house. The valet watched her go, and thought, *wow.*

Inside the house, Lydia was greeted by a man in his thirties who identified himself as the political director of the national party, thanking her profusely for her generous contribution.

"The Governor is already here," he said, "and he is very interested in meeting you, to thank you himself."

"Well, I'm anxious to meet him, as well. I'm a big fan."

"Follow me."

The political director led Lydia deeper into the house, pausing at one point to say, "This is where the Inner Circle event will be, in a few minutes. But right now, McHenry is relaxing in the study."

When they arrived at the study, there was a Secret Service agent guarding the door. The political director said, "The Governor has requested a meeting with her." Then he opened the door and announced, "Governor, it's Lydia Wade."

Lydia walked into the study. The door closed behind her. To her amazement, they were alone.

McHenry was holding a cocktail glass. When he first saw Lydia, he nearly dropped it.

"Miss Wade! How wonderful to meet you!" he put the glass down and walked to her, his right hand extended, trying desperately to keep his gaze on her eyes, but losing the battle.

"Please, Governor" she said, grasping his hand in a firm grip, "call me Lydia."

She didn't let go. Neither did he.

"Only if you call me Jim, Lydia."

"Deal."

He seemed to realize they were still locked in a handshake, and let go. Stepping back, he gave her an obvious appraisal.

"Wow, Lydia. When they told me a woman previously unknown as a political contributor had given over fifty grand, I never thought I'd be standing here saying thank you to someone so....so..."

"Young?"

He grinned. "Yes, young, but also beautiful. I mean, my God, that dress is a killer."

Lydia laughed. "I seem to be getting that a lot tonight."

"And for good reason. Tell me, Lydia. What is it that you do?"

She shrugged. "I get things done."

Now McHenry laughed. "Okay, you get things done. What kind of things?"

"Anything."

McHenry gave her a puzzled look.

"And I mean anything," she continued. "I have clients who need certain things to happen a certain way, like a product launch or something, and I make it happen, even if it's difficult."

"How do you do that?" McHenry was openly curious.

"Knowledge. Knowledge is power, Governor. I mean, Jim. I'm the best there is at research. I know every single detail about whatever subject I'm researching before anything is set in motion. Everything."

"Everything? About everything?"

Lydia grinned. "Only everything about the things I need to know. You know, to make something happen." She reached out and touched her fingers lightly to his face.

McHenry's breathing quickened. "Tell me, Lydia. Did you come here tonight to make something happen?"

"Indeed I did."

McHenry felt the current between them. He looked deeply into her eyes. He wondered: how much does she know about me? Everything?

"Will it be difficult, Jim, getting this done? Getting you to make sweet love to me tonight?"

There was a sharp intake of breath before he answered. "No, Lydia. I don't think it will be difficult at all."

44

Three days later

After two full days and nights at sea, Ricky was glad to see land. He wasn't sea sick, just stir crazy. The first night he got so drunk in one of the bars that he couldn't remember how to get back to his cabin and simply slept it off on one of the deck chairs. The second night he thought he was going to get lucky with a woman at the bar, but when he got back from taking a piss she was gone.

He left the ship and walked straight into downtown San Miguel, Cozumel. It was bustling with activity. There were little shops wedged between bigger shops and all manner of bars and restaurants. He would have time to check them out later. First, he wanted to find the bank and lay his hands on the million dollars.

Ricky walked through an old town square, where there were more shops, more bars, more restaurants. There was also a lady coated with what looked like mud, pretending to be a statue, and there were at least a dozen pigeons standing on her arms and head. Tourists took pictures and dropped dollars in her bucket.

There it was: the bank. He couldn't pronounce the long name, but to Ricky it simply said, "Come here to get your money!"

There was an armed guard at the doorway. Ricky nodded and was about to walk past him when the guard reached out to stop him. *"¿me excusas, señor, tienes negocio aquí?"*

"Sorry, there, *amigo*. Do you speak English?"

"Yes, of course. I asked if you have business here?"

"Yes, sir, I do. I have money in this bank. A lot of money."

"I see. And what is your name?"

Ricky hesitated, trying to remember. "Brian Cove. But it's not under my name. It is a numbered account."

"I see, Mr. Cove. All such accounts are handled by the manager personally. Follow me."

The guard led Ricky through the small bank lobby to an office in the back. The guard leaned in and said, *"Este estadounidense dice que él tiene una cuenta numerada con mucho dinero."*

Ricky understood part of that. *"Si! Mucho dinero!"*

The bank manager looked at Ricky and smiled. He said to the guard, *"Gracias, Ricardo. Lo dirigiré de aquí. Pero no vayas a lejos."*

The guard nodded. *"Guardaré un ojo cercano."*

The guard closed the door, but Ricky could tell the guard was standing just outside the office. The manager stood and shook hands with Ricky. "I am the bank manager, Roberto Campinel. And you are?"

"Brian Cove. I'm an American."

"Yes, of course. How can I help you?"

"Well, I have an account here. A large amount of money was transferred into it a few days ago as payment for services rendered. I'd like to withdraw some of it in cash and make arrangements for accessing the rest of it later. Like with an ATM card."

"How much money is in the account?"

"One million dollars."

"Mierda!" Roberto said in surprise. "That is indeed *mucho dinero*. Do you have the account number?"

Ricky recited it from memory. Roberto typed it into a computer terminal. "Yes, I see the account exists." He slid the keyboard across the desk to face Ricky. "You need to type in the password."

Ricky typed "slickface."

Roberto nodded. "Now it is asking a security question. What was your favorite childhood nickname?"

Ricky smiled as he typed "boner."

Roberto saw only asterisks on the screen. Then, he said, "We're in."

"Excellent," Ricky said, relieved. Up to that point he had worried if somehow the little Arab had faked everything.

"But I am very sorry, Mr. Cove. There has been a misunderstanding."

Shit. "What do you mean?"

"You do not have one million dollars. You have one million *pesos.*" Roberto turned the screen so Ricky could see it.

"That looks like a dollar sign to me."

Roberto nodded. "It is a common mistake for Americans to make. But I'm telling you the truth, Mr. Cove. This is pesos."

"Rafi, you sonofabitch."

"Excuse me?"

"Sorry," Ricky said, trying to control his anger. "So how much is one million pesos in real money?"

Roberto chuckled. "If by real money you mean American dollars," he said as he punched an adding machine, "at today's exchange rate it would be seventy-three thousand dollars."

Ricky was too stunned to speak. Finally: "I guess I'll take it in cash."

"Oh, no, Mr. Cove. That is not possible."

"What the hell are you talking about? It's my money and I want it."

"You're an American in Mexico. You cannot take that much money. You can have ten thousand in cash, plus an ATM card. Of course, once you're back in the states, you can have all of it transferred to your bank up there. It's the best I can do."

Ricky cracked his knuckles and seethed, "I'm gonna kill that motherfucker."

"¡Ricardo! ¡Podemos tener una situación!"

The door swung open and there was the guard, his gun drawn.

Ricky put his hands up. "Whoa, whoa, whoa. I'm pissed but not at you guys. It's not your fault. Just give me my cash and I'll be on my way."

"Very well, Mr. Cove. I need to see your passport and I'll take care of this right away." To the guard he said, *"No dejes este bastardo loco fuera de tu vista."*

Ricky wasn't sure, but he was thinking the bank manager had just called him a crazy bastard. Well, Ricky thought, you got that right.

45

Gov. James Madison McHenry was full-on smitten with Lydia Wade, and what 57-year-old man wouldn't be? She was half his age (or thereabouts; he didn't dare ask), had the body of a goddess, the legs of an Olympic hurdler, and her sexual hunger for him seemed beyond description. Talk about getting lucky; lottery winners weren't this lucky. When they were alone together, McHenry couldn't get enough. When he was on the campaign trail, he couldn't stop thinking about her, seeing her in his mind's eye, wanting her.

He had returned to the Governor's Mansion in Jefferson City for a brief stopover before heading back out on the campaign; 12 states in the next 7 days. They were intertwined on his bed, enjoying the warmth of their recent tryst, and he couldn't bear the thought of travelling without her.

"I'm going to have you pinned," he announced.

"You're going to have me what?"

"Pinned."

"You pinned me pretty good just awhile ago."

He laughed. "No, it's a Secret Service thing. You get to wear the pin of the day. The color changes every day. It tells the security guys that you get special access to me."

She reached over and cupped his testicles. "I have pretty good access already."

Her touch sent a shiver up his spine. "Yes, here you do. But I want you to travel with the campaign. At the end of the day, I want to know that you're there for me. Can you do that? Can you travel with me?"

"You're asking a lot, Jim. Am I supposed to drop everything and just tag along?"

"I know what I'm asking, Lydia. But I'm having the time of my life. I think I'm going to win, Lydia. The presidency! I want you to share this experience. Please."

"It does sound like fun. But if I agree to do this - to drop everything I'm working on just for you - I want to share more than the experience. I want to share the spoils, too."

"The spoils? You mean a job in my administration?"

"No," she said, giving his testicles a harder squeeze. "The White House."

A sharp intake of breath, partly from pain, partly from pleasure, and partly from surprise. "I've already promised the chief of staff job to Lucas."

Lydia shook her head. "I don't want anything as high profile as that, Jim. Just an advisor job, down the hall somewhere. But at your beck and call."

"Tell me something, Lydia. Is this what you meant when you said you make things happen?"

McHenry looked down at the top of her head. Lydia didn't answer. She couldn't; her mouth was full. He moaned as he leaned back into the bed, eying the ceiling. She was definitely making things happen.

Ricky was relaxing on the sun deck, a cold Budweiser at his side, contemplating the grisly death of a little Arab bastard he knew only as Rafi. They were back at sea and would reach New Orleans that night. But then what?

Ricky knew Rafi had been arrested, along with the others, and also knew they were blaming him as the Mastermind. So how do I get to Rafi? How do I pull it off? How do I hang that little fucker on a meat hook?

After two more Budweisers, Ricky decided he didn't know enough about the little guy, and that was a mistake. Never go into business with a mystery. He had been blinded by the promise of a million bucks; too thrilled to be in the hunt again.

Ricky shook his head. In truth, if Rafi had been honest and offered a million pesos, Ricky would have taken it. Who knew the peso was so fucking worthless? Hell, if he had offered $75,000, or even $50,000, Ricky would have jumped at it.

But he had clearly promised *dollars* and delivered *pesos.* The account needed to be settled, with Rafi hanging from a meat hook, screaming as he bled out. Business was business.

After another three Budweisers, it dawned on Ricky that the people who knew Rafi best were all back in Jefferson City. Dangerous, going back into the belly of the beast, but necessary. And, quite possibly, fun.

46

Bobby Rinds was playing Angry Birds on his iPad, with the sound on, when the bank of computer monitors in front of him pinged and put a blinking alarm on one of the screens, so he didn't hear it or notice it. Finally, after managing for the first time to lob one of the birds just right to go down a chimney and hit a box of dynamite, blowing everything all to hell, he did a fist pump.

"Fuckin' A!" he blurted, and then looked around sheepishly, wondering if anyone saw him. They didn't, of course. He was in a secure room. It was his job to see other people.

Bobby glanced over the monitors, one by one, and was startled to see the blinking alarm. It was triggered by one of the new-fangled passport readers. One of the passengers coming off the ship from Cozumel had triggered it. The new equipment snapped a photograph of every passport holder as the passport was mechanically screened. Fewer people on the payroll that way, plus the line moved faster.

What most people didn't know was that the camera was tied in to a biometric facial recognition database. In this particular instance, a man named Brian Cove had placed his passport on the scanner, but the computer recognized the snapshot taken by the machine as Ricky Barboni, the most wanted man in America, and sent Bobby an alarm, as it was programmed to do.

That was twenty minutes ago.

"Ah, shit," Bobby cussed. "They're gonna fire my ass sure as hell."

Bobby called his supervisor and told him the computer identified Ricky Barboni reentering the country on a passport issued to Brian Cove. "That was twenty minutes ago," Bobby confessed, "But I missed it 'cuz I was taking a dump."

The tongue-lashing was intense but brief, as the supervisor knew they had to get moving, but Bobby knew he was in deep shit.

The TSA was notified immediately, and the Port of New Orleans was locked down - nobody in or out. Ricky, though, had already gotten into the stolen Blazer, grateful it hadn't been stolen from him, and that all the guns and ammo were intact. He had hurried out of the parking area, because the machine taking the picture had spooked him.

So he was driving smoothly out of New Orleans, heading south, into the swamps. Every warning bell he had, honed over a lifetime of crime and mayhem, was telling him to go underground and lay low. Revenge on Rafi would have to wait.

"We got a lead on Barboni!"

Kennedy was excited. They were on Air Force One, between campaign stops, when DHS Secretary Anne Scofield had called with the news.

"The fucker went on a cruise!" Kennedy spouted. "Can you believe that? He whacks a bunch of people and goes to Cozumel!"

"Slow down, Kennedy," Darling said. "What do we know for sure?"

"He apparently got his hands on a fake passport by the name of Brian Cove. Apparently, it was good enough to fool security in New Orleans and get on the ship." Kennedy paused. "You know, every time I hear about the TSA fucking up it makes me wonder."

Darling nodded. "Go on."

"We're still trying to piece together what he did in Cozumel, if anything. There are no reports of anyone being killed while the ship was there, so that's progress, I guess. The Mexicans aren't happy with us, by the way."

"Nothing new, Kennedy. Go on."

"So the ship pulls into the Port of New Orleans, and our new automated passport screener recognizes Brian Cove as Ricky Barboni, and issues an alert. But the guy on duty misses the alert for twenty minutes because he was sitting on the fucking can! The TSA again."

"So you're telling me he slipped away while some guy was wiping his ass?" Darling asked in disbelief.

"Exactly. A security camera snapped a shot of a Chevy Blazer leaving a parking garage with Missouri plates. Probably stolen. Gotta be him."

"And the dragnet is under way."

"Absolutely. His phony passport photo is out there, in the media. He shaved his head and put on some dumbass glasses. Not much of a disguise."

"Well, it was good enough to make us look like the Keystone Cops." Darling shook his head in disgust. "We need to get him, Kennedy. This shit has gone on long enough."

"You're tellin' me!"

One would think that Ricky Barboni was tired of looking over his shoulder, being on the run, always one wrong move from arrest or death. Wrong. This was his juice. Every nerve ending was on fire. This was livin', by God.

He knew he needed to dump the Blazer, the passport, the driver's license, and the credit card. All were worthless to him now; blown. He also needed to find a place to hide for awhile; maybe a long while.

Life on the run isn't easy.

He passed a trailer court. On his right was some kind of body of water, which was promising, but the trailers were too close together, and too exposed. He kept going. A short time later, he hung a left. The road turned to dirt, then threatened to peter out entirely and there it was: literally, the last house on the left, surrounded by swamp.

Perfect.

47

There was a fat man in overalls sitting on a wraparound front porch eyeing Ricky as he drove onto the lawn, which was mostly weeds and bare dirt. He was in a rocking chair, smoking a pipe. He looked to be in his forties, though it was hard to tell because he was pretty heavy.

Ricky stuck a snub-nosed .38 revolver in the back of his pants and untucked his shirt. He got out of the car with a big smile.

"Howdy!" Ricky said with a wave. "You look mighty comfortable up there."

The old boy blew smoke. "I am."

Ricky looked around. "Nice and quiet out here."

"It is." More smoke.

"I was wondering if you could help me out. I saw a 'land for sale' sign down the road aways but couldn't read the number 'cuz it was faded. You know anything about that?"

"The old Cooper place. Coop died here awhile back. Kids got the land but they don't want it. Trying to sell it. Ain't nothin' but swamp." More smoke.

"Is there a house on it?"

More smoke. "There is. About like this, but run down. Not a bad fishin' shack, I reckon."

"Sounds perfect," Ricky lied. "Can you give me directions to it? Maybe I'll swing by and take a look."

The old boy was looking at the Blazer. "That a four-wheel drive?"

"Yeah."

"Good." The old boy leaned over and spit. "You'll need it." Then he looked at the Blazer again and said, "You're a long way from home, boy. What brings a guy from Missourah all the way down here to the end of the road?"

Ricky shrugged. "Some people like to get away to the beach. I prefer the swamp. Quieter."

The old boy tapped his pipe on the side of his chair. "It is that. Say, I was just fixin' to pour a couple fingers of whiskey. C'mon up and join me. I'll tell ya how to get out to old Coop's place."

"Sounds mighty fine," Ricky said, climbing up on the porch. Then he stuck his hand out and said, "And by the way, you can call me Sugar."

"Sugar? What kind of name is that for a man?"

Ricky shrugged as they shook hands. "My old man was a sugar beet farmer, way back when. Folks called us Big Sugar and Little Sugar. Now it's just Sugar."

"Alrighty," he said as he got out of the chair. "And folks around here call me Booger. So who am I to judge?" He laughed as he went in the screen door. "Be right back with the whiskey."

Nice guy, Ricky thought. Be a shame to kill him. Maybe he wouldn't need to.

"Here you go, Sugar," Booger said, handing him a glass. "Let's drink a toast to old Coop. He was a helluva guy."

"To Coop," Ricky said as they clinked glasses. They drank, and Ricky thought the whiskey was mighty fine. Then his blood turned cold as he heard someone come out through the screen door and rack a shotgun.

It was a woman, a big woman, about fifty years old, droopy jowls, bad teeth, in an ill-fitting house dress. And damn if she didn't have a twelve-gauge shotgun pointed straight at Ricky.

"Booger?" Ricky managed. "Why does your wife have a shotgun pointed at my head?"

"What?" he seemed genuinely puzzled. Then he laughed. "Shit, Sugar, that ain't my wife! That's my sister!" He laughed some more. "Holy shit, Sugar. That's funny!"

"You live here with your sister?"

"Ain't nothin' wrong with it. I don't sleep with her, for the love of God. Her name's Delores, but everybody calls her Snot. See? We're Booger and Snot, like peas in a pod."

"Okay, then, Booger. Why is your *sister* holding a shotgun on me?"

"Oh, that. Well, we don't get many visitors out here, as you can imagine. Especially strangers. So when we do, we like to take advantage." Then Booger winked.

"Take advantage? You're gonna rob me?"

"Oh, hell no, Sugar. Ya see, if you was a woman, I'd be the one holding the gun so Snot could take advantage. But since you're a man - and a good lookin' one at that - I get to take advantage."

Ricky didn't like where this was going.

Booger leaned over, licked his lips and said, "Tell me, Sugar, you ever had your mouth around a big old piece of Louisiana sausage?"

Ricky burst out laughing. "Ah, Booger, nobody has ever had to put a gun to my head to have sex. For crying out loud, all you had to do was ask! C'mon over here. Drop those drawers and give Sugar a taste."

"Ya hear that, Snot! Hot damn! Got us a live one!"

Booger stood up, undid the overalls, and they dropped around his ankles. Ricky dropped to his knees, made like he was going to get after it, but then used all his strength to shove Booger back into Snot. Then he whipped out the snub nose .38 and started firing. He emptied it, then picked up the shotgun and blew both of their heads off.

Ricky dragged both of the bodies into the swamp behind the house. Alligators were swarming almost immediately. He figured that whenever Booger and Snot "took advantage" of a stranger, the poor soul ended up back here. Gator food.

Then he pulled the Blazer around back, as well, hidden completely from the road. Not that he expected much traffic. It was a dead end. The nearest neighbor, Ricky guessed, was the Cooper place, and it was vacant.

Ricky went inside and took stock. Plenty of provisions. Running water. Guns and ammo. He was building up quite a stockpile of weaponry. Satellite television.

Yup, Ricky decided. Home sweet home.

48

A week later

Jurisdiction over the Soldiers of Allah was turning out to be a sticky wicket. The states where the original shootings occurred all were clamoring to charge the shooters with multiple counts of murder. But there was a problem: which shooter pulled the trigger in which state? Nobody was talking. They had found the machine guns, of course, but no prints. So even though ballistics could match which gun fired which cartridges, they couldn't put the individual gun into an individual hand. Early on, President Darling had said there was video evidence, but that had been a lie, an attempt to spook the shooters into making a mistake.

The states where the bombings occurred all wanted to file charges, too. But the problem was the same.

Missouri was ready to file charges of unlawful restraint for the incident with the school kids. A search of the pink limousine had turned up video of the kids all sitting in the back, but they were all excited kids, enjoying the ride. They had plenty of fingerprints matching Ricky Barboni, but the evidence implicating Rafi Sayahd was dubious.

Finally, the feds decided that federal terrorism, murder, and conspiracy charges would be filed against the whole bunch, with Ricky Barboni implicated as the Mastermind. The Soldiers of Allah were transferred to federal custody, but kept apart. Nobody was talking, except for Rafi who insisted, through his attorney, that everything was Barboni's idea.

"They should be named as enemy combatants," Gov. McHenry declared to the gaggle of reporters following him on the campaign. "They were waging war on the United States. They should be executed. Just give the order and get it done."

"But, Governor," one of the reporters asked, "What about due process?"

"They gave up the right to due process when they mowed down innocent men, women, and children in the name of jihad," McHenry replied. "They even made a rather pathetic attempt to frighten voters and rig the election. If I was president, they'd be dead already."

"I thought we had grown beyond the notion of cowboy justice," President Darling countered when he was asked about it on the campaign trail.

"These guys will have their day in court, and if found guilty will face whatever punishment the court deems appropriate, including the possibility of the death penalty, which is still on the books."

"But, Mr. President," a reporter interjected. "Under that scenario, it could take decades before they're executed, what with all the appeals and such."

"It is what it is, Donna. We have a system of justice in this country, and we're not going to throw it out the window under my watch.

"And one more thing. Everybody in America needs to be on the lookout for the Mastermind, Ricky Barboni. Until we get him, the job isn't finished."

Ricky watched the exchange with interest from the living room of the former Booger and Snot. It seemed pretty clear that if McHenry wins the election, he'll order Rafi executed, along with the others. Would that satisfy his need for revenge? Ricky didn't think so. It would deny him the opportunity to watch Rafi die, slowly, with the full knowledge that it was Ricky Barboni doing the killing.

Still, though, he'd be dead, and that was something. Unless some limp-wristed judge stepped in and stopped it, which was always possible.

Under Darling's scenario, Rafi might very well outlive Ricky, with appeals and what-not. That would be a total miscarriage of justice. Unless, of course, Ricky found a way to get to Rafi and kill him.

And being declared public enemy number one by the President was certainly a complicating factor. It was a lofty title, something he relished, but it layered certain degrees of difficulty on everything. Like his current situation: the Booger and Snot Bed and Breakfast was running out of food, and was already out of whiskey.

It was time to move on, but how, exactly? Booger's car was a piece of shit Oldsmobile. Worse yet, the license plate said BOOGER. Too memorable. Ricky had discovered that little gem when he went to switch license plates with the Blazer. Plus, Ricky had to assume that by now, surely, somebody had missed that fat fuck from Silver Lake, Missouri, and gone looking for him, finding the

Blazer missing and the pick-up he had stolen from the farm couple he shot.

The Blazer was blown. He had already burned the passport, license, and credit card belonging to Brian Cove. Booger had a credit card, in the name of Buford Boggins, that should be good for awhile, at least for gas.

Then there was the telephone. It had been ringing a lot today. There was no answering machine, so it would ring 10, 15, even 20 times before the caller gave up. Somebody was missing Booger. Or Snot. Either way, somebody was bound to come looking. Given the situation, it was something Ricky needed to have happen.

And then he heard it, the unmistakable deep-throated growl of a Harley, slowing down, pulling into the driveway.

Ricky grabbed the shotgun, which was always nearby, and waited.

The growling stopped. "Booger! You in there? What's goin' on, man? You okay? Booger!"

Ricky listened as the man climbed onto the porch.

"Booger! You sonofabitch! Where's the fuckin' rent? Booger!"

The man waited, listening. He heard footsteps inside.

"God damn it, Booger. I know you're in there. You're late with the rent and I'm here to collect!"

"Here's the fucking rent, asshole," Ricky said as he shot the man right through the screen door. The blast knocked him all the way back off the porch, onto the bare dirt in front of the steps.

"Did you hear that shot, gators?" Ricky shouted, laughing. "More food on the way!"

He pushed open what was left of the door and stood on the porch, looking out at the Harley. Man, did it look sweet. Ricky stepped over the man's body and went to inspect it. It was a Road King, pretty new, all black. There was a black helmet attached to the back with a darkly-tinted visor.

"Oh, man, just what the doctor ordered."

Ricky checked the man's pockets, found almost three grand in cash, two credit cards and a driver's license in the name of Brent Cooper. Cooper, huh? Ricky found that interesting. He dragged the body back to the gators, who were waiting, and hurled the shotgun as far into the swamp as he could.

Then he jammed the saddlebags on the Harley with guns and ammo, and roared off, heading north. It was the only direction available.

49

It was one of the London tabloids that broke the story first, but it went viral in the United States in a hurry. The headline was unforgiving: "Gunderson a Hero. But is Wife a Schmuck?"

The full page picture was that of Molly Gunderson, a cocktail in one hand, a boy toy in the other, quite obviously drunk, in a nightclub somewhere. The story went on to point out that according to e-mail and text messages compiled in a top secret file by the National Security Agency, but somehow obtained by the tabloid, Molly Gunderson had carried on numerous tawdry affairs with other men while "the bravest man in America" was off fighting for God and country.

The NSA had apparently also logged all of Molly's phone conversations. She talked to her lovers at least ten times as often as she talked to her husband. The reporter used one of the oldest tricks in a journalist's book when he ended the story with this line: "Some are now speculating about the wisdom of having such a woman so close to the White House - even as First Lady."

"Who the hell are *'some*?'" McHenry roared as he flung the pages, printed off the Internet, into the air. "What a crock of horse shit!

"And why in the living hell is the NSA compiling a top secret file on Molly Gunderson! Tell me that!"

His campaign team stayed quiet, fearful of reaching into the rotating blades of McHenry's fury. Finally, Lawson Forbes, the campaign manager, adjusted his thick, circular glasses and said, "I think we can use this."

McHenry turned to him in disbelief. "Use it? Use it? Jesus Christ, I'm sitting here feeling horrible about Gun and Molly and you're thinking of ways it can help us? You really are a heartless bastard."

Lawson adjusted his glasses again. "Yes, Governor. Yes, I am. That's why you hired me. Look, everybody knows the NSA polls really bad. Everybody hates them. They stick their noses where they don't belong.

"And, in this case, not only did they pry into the private life of Molly Gunderson, but then they couldn't keep the dirty laundry from flapping around in public.

"This will not play well with the voters, Governor; trust me on this. They will blame the NSA, feel sorry for Gun and possibly Molly if we play it right, and if we can tie the leak to the Darling campaign, he is done."

"I thought you told me Darling is already done," McHenry said.

"Yes, well, he'll be even more done."

"Where did the picture come from?"

It was Gun, inquiring of Molly, who was across the kitchen table from him, sobbing.

"I don't know, Richard," she sobbed. "I've never seen it before."

Gun nodded. Somebody probably had it in their files and sold it to the tabloid. In fact, it might have been the spark that ignited the story.

"And the young man? Who is he?"

More sobbing. "Jesus, Richard. Do we have to do this?"

"Molly, I'm not running for Vice President of a PTA somewhere. I'm going to have to deal with this. *We're* going to have to deal with this. Who is he?"

"I don't know!" she wailed. "He was just one of many! Are you happy now! One of MANY!" Now she was all-out bawling.

He waited and said nothing, thinking back on all the good times they'd had through the years, how intensely they had loved each other, before Afghanistan. Things had been different since then, he now realized.

Finally, when the bawling subsided, he asked, "So it's all true?"

Molly's voice was barely a hoarse whisper. "Yes."

Gun leaned back, closed his eyes, and took several deep breaths. He needed to compartmentalize this; deal with it fully later. But he couldn't let it derail the election.

Then he reached across the table, took Molly's hands in his, and asked, "Are you sorry, Molly?"

Her eyes were pleading. "Yes, Richard. Oh, God, I'm so sorry. If I could take it all back, I would."

"Okay, then. I forgive you."

More tears from Molly.

"It's okay, Molly. We'll get through it. Lord knows it can't be easy for a young wife to be alone with her husband halfway around the world. Some handle it better than others, but war is hell for everybody."

50

"Did we do this?"

President Darling was looking expectantly at Kennedy Jackson for an answer.

"Okay, I'm gonna pretend I didn't hear that," Kennedy said sternly. "Don't ask questions you don't want to know the answer to."

"But maybe I do want to know the answer."

"No, you don't, Mr. President. Some reporter is going to ask you if we leaked the Molly Gunderson story, and you're going to get irritated and say you have no knowledge of that, never signed off on anything like that and would never condone such a thing. Got it?"

"Got it."

"That said," Kennedy continued, "The contrast is accidentally beneficial. You're a caring husband and loving father and grandfather. The First Lady volunteers her time teaching reading to kids with disabilities. Olivia Morgan and her husband are a Hollywood romance come to life, and she's staring down breast cancer with his help.

"McHenry is a divorced skirt-chaser with a history of public drunkenness. Gunderson may be the 'bravest man in America,' as you so indelicately put it, but he had the bad judgment to marry a skank."

Darling nodded.

"Oh, and one other thing. McHenry has a girlfriend."

"Good for him," Darling said. "I mean, being a divorced skirt-chaser and all that."

"Yeah, really good for him. She's half his age."

Darling's eyebrows shot up. "No shit?"

Kennedy smiled. "We haven't gotten a full handle on her yet, but she's a looker."

"Well," Darling shrugged, "if you're gonna have a girlfriend, she might as well be a looker."

Lawson Forbes had it mapped out.

"Governor, you're going to have a press availability and denounce the NSA in the strongest possible terms. Then you're going to come out squarely in favor of the American people being able to live their private lives without fear of an intrusive government agency logging their every move. And once you're in the White House, you plan to clip the ears of the NSA and make Americans safe in their private affairs."

"Uh," the press secretary spoke up. "Probably shouldn't use the term 'private affairs.'"

Lawson nodded to her. "Good catch. Private lives, then, not affairs." He cleared his throat and adjusted his glasses. "I've spoken to Gun. He and Molly have come to terms with this. They're okay with going on one of the TV talk shows and doing the 'stand by your man' thing, except this time it's 'stand by your woman.' She'll cry, he'll forgive her, yada, yada, yada. At the end of the day, it'll add to his street cred of a loyal soldier unafraid of anything."

McHenry spoke up. "Do we accuse Darling of leaking it? I gotta believe his people did this."

Lawson shook his head. "I've thought about that. We can't prove it, and it'll just give Darling a chance to huff and puff and deny it. Our target here is the NSA. The people will appreciate it and give us credit for not trying to politicize it."

"But we are politicizing it."

Lawson smiled and adjusted his glasses. "Of course. It just doesn't look like we are."

The McHenry campaign was in Dallas. He finished up a speech to a local business gathering skewering Darling's "ridiculous attempt at micro-managing the employment decisions of job creators" with his living wage proposal.

"There is no logical benefit," McHenry told them, "to having the all-powerful federal government dictating terms of compensation and benefits for employees.

"It's a job-killer and it will wreck the American economy," he concluded.

The press was gathered in a room backstage.

"Governor! What do you make of the story about your running mate's wife?"

McHenry scowled like he didn't appreciate the question. "I feel horrible for Gun and Molly, to have their private lives drug through the gutter like this. But, more than that, I'm horrified to learn that the National Security Agency was tapping the private life of an American citizen. Worse yet, they couldn't keep their ill-gotten secrets secret!

"America is about liberty, about the freedom to pursue our dreams without an all-too-powerful federal government poking around in our private lives. It's unconscionable!

"The real meat of the Molly Gunderson story isn't what she did or didn't do in her private life. The meat is that the NSA is out of control. I will make it my business to clip their wings when I'm in the White House.

"And to make damn sure it gets done, I'll put Sergeant Major Richard Gunderson in charge of getting it done!"

That was the clincher. The headlines were all about the same: "McHenry says Gunderson to Lead Effort to Clip NSA."

That night, in a wonderful suite at the Hotel Palomar, Lydia traced her right index finger around one of McHenry's nipples.

"I'm not so sure going after the NSA is such a hot idea," she said.

McHenry looked surprised. "Really? Lawson says it polls through the roof."

"I'm sure it does, with the public. But how does it poll with the people at the NSA?"

"Who cares what they think? The NSA is out of control."

"Oh, I agree. But I read an old quote somewhere that said, 'Don't get in a war of words with people who buy ink by the barrel.'"

McHenry smiled. "Ah, yes. Back when newspapers mattered. When you were but a child."

Lydia smiled back. "Yes, well, I'm thinking it's not a good idea to declare war against someone who knows all your secrets."

McHenry grunted. "My secrets? You think the NSA will come after me? They can't possibly have anything on me."

Lydia thought about the dick picture, but held her tongue. "It just worries me, is all."

51

"Hey, Spook."

It was several days later, and the McHenry campaign was in Northern Virginia for a fundraiser. There would also be a press availability to continue hammering home the effort to clip the wings of the NSA. Lydia had used the opportunity to meet Richie Rollins for a drink.

"How are you and gramps getting along?" There was ice in Richie's voice.

Lydia scoffed. "He's not old enough to be my grandfather, Richie."

Richie just stared into his drink.

"Look, Richie, I'm sorry. I never meant to hurt you."

"So what the hell are you doing, fucking a man twice your age? Do you know how that makes me feel?"

Lydia looked away. "I'm doing what I have to do."

"Why?"

"Richie, I can't tell you."

"Christ, Lydia. You had me dig up all that dirt on McHenry, just so you could blackmail him with it and get into his pants?"

"No! I didn't blackmail him! I seduced him."

"By showing him a picture of his own dick?"

Lydia shook her head. "He doesn't know about the picture. He doesn't know about any of it. But, knowing how much he likes younger women, I used that to get to him. That's all."

"What for?"

"I told you, Richie. I can't tell you."

Richie snorted. "Yeah. You told me you can't tell me. So why are we having this drink? Am I your pinch hitter for the night?"

Lydia smiled. "Sounds wonderful, but not for the night." She looked at her watch. "How about just for the seventh inning?"

He watched them go, the NSA geek and the sexy young woman. He could have followed them - they would never know - but he already knew where they were going. In a little bit, if he wanted, he could reach for his smartphone, fire up a neat little app and watch the action live, courtesy of the tiny little video cameras he had planted in the geek's apartment. But, he didn't need to. Everything would be recorded automatically, stored on a special server, and made available to the chosen few who had the password for whatever purposes were deemed necessary.

He congratulated himself on a job well done. He was smart enough to know the woman would want to meet the geek while she was in the area. After all, she might need the geek's services again. He was smart enough to know the geek would relent - who wouldn't? And he was smart enough to have installed the tiny video cameras in plenty of time.

Yes, he thought, I am Smart Man.

It was blustery in Omaha, with a cold rain lashing the hospital windows. Doris Epperson was there, of course, as reliable as the guards at Buckingham Palace, day after day, the same routine. Reading the paper out loud to Lloyd, not knowing if he could hear or comprehend anything. Then she would sit and simply listen to the beeps of the machinery and watch her husband's chest rise and fall gently with each breath, wondering if it would stop, worried sick it might, but deathly afraid to look away.

Wait a minute. Was that...? Did his head just move? Just a little bit?

"Lloyd? Honey?" Doris was standing over him now, gently shaking one of his hands. "Lloyd, can you hear me?"

Then, like some movie miracle, Lloyd opened his eyes and tried to speak, but it was all gibberish.

Doris stuck her head out into the hall. "He's awake! My husband is awake. Get the doctor!" Then she returned to his bedside. She was fighting back tears. "It's okay, Lloyd. The doctor will be here soon."

Lloyd nodded, his own eyes wet. He was whispering something. Doris leaned in close.

"I forgot to tell you something this morning," he whispered.

"What?" Doris was confused. "This morning?"

"Before the fire, Doris. I forgot to tell you I love you."

52

The hospital administrators figured it was such a feel-good story that they should schedule a press conference to update America on Lloyd's condition. Good PR, that's for sure. As a courtesy, they notified the White House, since President Darling had been good enough to visit when things looked bleak.

The White House managed to convince the hospital to wait until they could get somebody there. Not the President, that was impossible on such short notice. But they managed to get Vice President Olivia Morgan to divert from a planned campaign event in Minneapolis.

The White House was almost giddy with the symbolism: Olivia, fighting her own heroic battle against breast cancer along with her strong, loving husband; Lloyd Epperson, heroic firefighter, climbing his way out of a coma to tell his wife that he loved her.

Olivia was greeted warmly by Doris Epperson, who by now was absolutely jubilant with her husband's progress. She led the Vice President to Lloyd, who was sitting up in bed, fully alert. He was gaunt, and needed some serious nourishment before the doctors would release him, but he managed to grasp Olivia's hand and thank her profusely for coming.

The reporters were eating it up.

"You're a real American hero, Lloyd," Olivia assured him.

"Nonsense," Lloyd managed, his voice still a bit weak. "All I did was throw up and pass out."

She smiled. "Well, the entire country has been pulling for you, praying for you. We're thrilled you're going to make it. We've arrested the people responsible and they'll be prosecuted."

Lloyd nodded. "There needs to be justice done. For the firefighters who didn't make it. They were my friends."

"We'll see to it."

"Um, Madam Vice President? I've been a little out of touch," Lloyd said to laughter all around. "And I don't want to be impolite. But Doris told me you're fighting breast cancer?"

"That's right, Lloyd. It's okay. The whole country knows about it."

"Well, I was just thinking, all those people who were praying for me? Maybe it's time they start praying for you, too. I know I will."

Olivia felt a surge of tears from the simple sincerity of what he said. She fought through it and said, "God bless you, Lloyd. Thank you."

"That was PERFECT!"

Kennedy had his hands in the air, like he had just witnessed a last-second, winning touchdown. He and Darling had watched the touching network story of the Vice President visiting Lloyd in the hospital.

"Oh my God! Not a dry eye in any house in America!" Kennedy shouted. "I'm telling you, there's no way we lose the women vote with Olivia out there! No way!"

Darling nodded. He had to admit, it was compelling. "And women are 53% of the vote. So..."

"We're back in the game!" Kennedy said with a fist pump. "We are back in the fucking game!"

McHenry whistled. "Damn. That Olivia Morgan is good at this."

"And kinda hot," Lawson Forbes added.

McHenry squinted at his campaign manager. "You think she's hot?"

"Well, kinda. I mean, there's the breast cancer thing. So the first thing everybody does is check out her boobs. More than usual, I mean. And, I don't know, it seemed like they were...standing at attention."

McHenry laughed. "Jesus, Lawson. And you were over there saluting."

"Well, yeah."

"Lawson, how old are you?"

"Thirty-eight."

"And the Vice President is what? Fifty-five?"

"So?"

"So she's old enough to be your mother. Stop saluting her boobs."

Lawson guffawed. "Right. Like you're one to talk. Does Lydia salute?"

McHenry had a lascivious grin on his face. "Of course, Lawson. Because when Lydia is in the room, everything stands at attention."

53

Zulu listened to the news in disbelief. This couldn't be happening.

The newscaster was appropriately somber as he said "The sudden death of H. Robert Camden has shocked the media world. Mr. Camden was the chairman of the board of the world's largest media conglomerate. Reportedly, a longtime co-worker went to check on him and found him dead this morning after an apparent fall down a flight of stairs in his New York home. Mr. H. Robert Camden, dead at the age of 85."

Oh, God, Zulu thought. Alpha was dead. Now what? She supposed Beta would take over, and that was a disaster.

Her phone buzzed. It was a text. It said, simply, "noon." So the Azalea Team would gather at noon. That made sense. But then a chill went up her spine. What the hell? The text was from Alpha's number.

It was a crisp October day in New York as Zulu climbed the steps into the Westchester Garden Club. As she entered, the man who greeted her was not someone she recognized. He had a Spanish look about him. Cuban, maybe. Handsome, with a wide smile. He greeted her professionally and led her to the third floor library.

He unlocked the door and held it open for her with a nod.

Zulu was the first to arrive, even though it was a few minutes past noon. She headed straight for the bar to pour herself a glass of wine. She heard the door close and lock behind her. But when she turned, wine in hand, she saw the man was in the room with her, staring.

"What the hell is this about?" she demanded.

"You should have a seat, Zulu."

"Who are you?"

"You can call me Smart. But you need to sit down."

Zulu barked out a laugh. "Smart? How about I call you Stupid, instead? Because this is a very stupid stunt you're pulling. You're breaking protocol. I'll have you fired."

"You can call me what you wish. But in a few moments you will discover that I am indeed the smartest one in the room." He pulled out a smart phone and touched the screen, then held it out for Zulu to see. "Watch closely."

Zulu watched, her mouth agape. She almost dropped her wine. Finally, rather clumsily, she managed to sit down.

"Stop it," she pleaded. "Just turn it off."

"You have seen enough already? But you and your lover were just getting started. It gets really good here in a couple of minutes."

"Just turn the damn thing off!"

"Very well." He put the phone back inside his suit pocket. "The others aren't coming, by the way. It's just the two of us having a friendly chat. Lydia."

"Don't call me that."

"But it's your name!"

"Not here. In this room I am Zulu."

The man chuckled. "Very well." He sat across from her.

She looked him in the eyes, hard. "How? Why?"

"Ah," he said, leaning back. "Two very simple questions, but with complicated answers."

"I'm listening."

The man nodded. "When you reached out to your friend Rollins you landed on our radar screen. So we started monitoring your cell phone and using it to track your whereabouts."

"What?"

The man held up a hand in a stop gesture. "This is when you need to listen, not talk. Trust me on this."

Zulu nodded, but inside she was fuming.

"We weren't listening to your phone calls, just gathering the metadata and analyzing the matrix. You got a text on the night McHenry rescued the school kids. So we started analyzing the metadata from the originating phone, and we noticed the same text message went to two other cell phones. And so on.

"The next day, all four cell phones arrived at this very building. A meeting, obviously. From there, it was easy to identify the players. And here we are."

Zulu stared at him. "So you're NSA."

"I didn't say that."

"You bastard. You obviously planted cameras in Richie's bedroom. To catch us in the act. Buy why?"

"Why, indeed?" he said with a grin. "You're a smart woman. Why would a smart man do such a thing?"

"Blackmail."

"Such an ugly word," he said with a shake of the head. "I prefer to think of it as motivation."

She closed her eyes. "Motivation to do what?"

"Cooperate, of course. Such a simple thing."

"Or what?"

"Oh!" he exclaimed, "I almost forgot! Did I tell you there's audio, too? Wonderful audio!"

He pulled his smart phone back out and hit play. "Oh, God! Richie! Ohhhh! It's so hard! Oh, God, how I've wanted this. I've needed this! After all those nights with that fucking geezer! Harder, Richie! Harder!"

"Shut it off, you sonofabitch."

"Very well. Where were we? Oh, right. You asked, 'Or what?' I can't imagine McHenry would be pleased to receive this little video. Or, better yet, see it on YouTube."

She felt like the world was about to swallow her up. It was all coming apart. She had her head in her hands, trying not to cry. She was too strong to cry. Think! Stay alert!

"Zulu," he said gently, quietly. "Open your eyes."

She did. And when she saw what he was holding out for her to see, the world did, indeed, swallow her whole.

"It looks pretty much like the lapel pin you're wearing, Zulu, but a little bigger. You recognize it, of course. Alpha wore it proudly."

"Oh, my God," Zulu muttered through her hands. "You murdered him."

He shook his head. "Murder is such an ugly word. We had a conversation, although not a very pleasant one.

He likes to keep his secrets. And for such an old fart, he held up pretty well. But, eventually, he spilled the beans. They all do."

"You tortured him?"

"You are so fond of ugly words, Zulu. I convinced him. But here's the important part. I know everything, Zulu. Everything."

Zulu was wide-eyed. "Everything about what?"

"The Azalea Team. Your arrangement with Rafi Sayahd. The conspiracy, Zulu. Gunning down kids. Blowing up people. Creating a terrorism scare. Trying to rig the election. It all adds up to treason, Zulu. All of you are facing the death penalty. No question."

"I'm confused," Zulu said. "Are you here to blackmail me, or arrest me?"

The man laughed. "This is when you find out I really am the smartest person in the room, Zulu. You see, we don't really care who the president is. All we care about is that we have full control over him. Or her. Whatever.

"But, you see, Zulu, you quite literally have McHenry by the balls! And you must understand by now that we own you lock, stock, and barrel. Just keep doing what you're doing. Stay tight with McHenry. We'll tell you what to do, and when."

Zulu let out a long sigh. "And by 'we,' you mean the NSA."

"Ah, there you go again. The NSA is another ugly word."

Then the man pinned the azalea blossom to his lapel and said, "From now on, in this room, you can call me Alpha."

54

The Smart Man was sitting in the Director's office, feeling very pleased with himself. Not just anybody could have so skillfully "recruited" such a highly placed mole within the McHenry camp, while at the same time assuming command of a secretive, egocentric organization that for decades has been trying to manipulate presidential elections. Now who gets to crown the kings in this high-stakes game of political checkers?

"So we have this Lydia Wade completely over a barrel, and she has agreed to be our inside connection to McHenry?" the director asked, his fingers forming a steeple.

"Yes, sir."

"Can we trust her?"

"Of course not," the Smart Man replied with a dismissive wave. "But, like you said, we have her over a barrel. She wants nothing more than to be in the White House, so she will do it."

The Director nodded. "Damn. That's good work."

"Thank you, sir!"

"So. If McHenry wins, we have our mole just down the hall from the Oval Office, with a direct line to the President's ear. Obviously, it behooves us to have McHenry win."

"Yes, sir."

The Director thought for a moment. "Okay. We should encourage McHenry to keep whipping away at the NSA, invasions of privacy, freedom, liberty, and all that. It's a winning issue. Have you seen the polls?"

"Yes, sir. Very convincing. Americans hate the NSA."

"So tell the girl to tell McHenry to keep it up. All the way to Election Day."

"Yes, sir."

"Then that shit stops."

"Of course."

The Director took off his glasses and rubbed at his eyes. He was a man of many secrets, and the years were weighing on him. "To be safe, we need to clear the field of any opportunity for Darling to throw a Hail Mary."

"And what would that be?"

"This so-called Mastermind. What's his name? Barbery?"

"Barboni, sir. Ricky Barboni."

"Yes, that's it. Barboni. Public Enemy Number One. We can't let Darling get him and risk the PR bounce."

"That's a difficult assignment, sir. The guy is an expert at living off the grid. He leaves his fingerprints and bodies all over the damn place but by the time law enforcement finds anything, he's long gone. Right now, we have no idea where he is or what kind of vehicle he's driving or even where he was last. Once he left the Port of New Orleans, he just disappeared."

"Could he be dead?"

The Smart Man shrugged. "Who knows? It's not like anyone would report him missing."

The Director drummed his fingers on his desk. "Okay. The best way to keep Darling from catching Barboni and taking the credit, is for us to catch him first and lock him away somewhere until after the election."

The Smart Man nodded. "And maybe a diversion or two? You know, to keep Darling occupied?"

"I like the way you think, Smart Man. So dream up some diversions, and while you're at it, bring me the Mastermind."

Lydia was drawing circles around one of McHenry's nipples again. "You were right about the NSA. I've seen the polling. The people are eating it up. You need to stick with it."

McHenry couldn't help but laugh. "So, my little down-the-hall advisor is catching up with the times?"

She pinched the nipple, hard, and McHenry uttered something between a grunt and a moan. "The NSA is evil, Jim. Dead fucking evil. Hell, they're the ones who are half past evil, like you said about the terrorists. I was worried they might retaliate. But, at this point, even if they do I still think the people will eat it up. Maybe more."

"So we double down?"

"Double down." Then, amazingly, she had her mouth full again.

55

Sometimes the Smart Man liked to whistle while he worked, but not tonight. He had managed to get copies of Barboni's fingerprints and palm prints. At that moment, he was applying them in strategic places at a storage facility in West Memphis, Arkansas. Satisfied, he retreated to a truck stop parking lot, pulled out a throw-away phone and called the number listed for information about renting a storage garage.

"Hello, this is Sock It Away," a rough voice answered.

"Um, yes. Um, I was just out at your place? Over by the truck stop? Kind of looking around? I mean, I might want to a rent some space, you know, to store stuff?"

"You should have called first. I don't like people just poking around."

"Yes, I guess that's right. But, I just thought you should know that I saw someone kinda suspicious loading stuff out of one of the garages into a truck? Kinda sneaky like? And I saw him drop a box and it looked like a bunch of bullets went everywhere. Man, he looked spooked."

"Huh. You know what the unit number was?"

"Yes, I memorized it so I could call you. It was number 33."

"Is he still there?"

"No. He grabbed up the bullets and got the hell out of there."

The police cordoned off the area around storage unit 33 and started working the grid for evidence. They found a couple of stray cartridges that had apparently rolled far enough away to escape the suspect's attention. They also lifted some very good prints from the garage door handle. The only item left in the storage garage was a five-pound sack of castor beans.

The discovery of the castor beans jiggled something in the brain of Officer Brian Wand, who had a history with Ricky Barboni, except he thought he was Ricky Mather at the time. Officer Wand suspected Mather was dirty, but could never prove it. Then, the news broke about Ricky Barboni being the Mastermind of the terror attacks, and Officer Wand was startled and disgusted to discover he'd had the Mastermind under his nose the whole time.

Officer Wand had also paid attention to the news about the ricin attack in Omaha, and how ricin is made from castor beans. So the discovery of the castor beans convinced Officer Wand to compare the prints lifted from the garage door handle to those on file for Barboni. Bingo!

So the phone calls started, hot and heavy, with the FBI and Homeland Security and the White House. The NSA chimed in with the rather unsettling news that they had just at that moment been analyzing intelligence indicating that the terrorists might have stored ricin gas in the West Memphis area, near where Ricky Barboni had been living, but hadn't been confident enough in the intelligence to release it to the other agencies.

Then the news arrived that the cartridges found at the scene generally matched those used in the first terrorist attack, with the machine guns.

It certainly appeared the authorities had stumbled upon the armory of the Soldiers of Allah, and the Mastermind had somehow returned and run off with whatever was left. One gruff, pessimistic talking head on MSNBC said, "Hell, folks, they might have lots of armories out there. Did you ever think of that?"

Ricky was watching all this in amazement, eating peanut butter straight from the jar with his fingers, and wondered how his fingerprints had gotten on that storage door. He knew the storage facility. He used to drive by it every day on his way to work, but had never set foot in it.

It's obviously a set-up, but why? And who did it?

The Mastermind had no idea.

Lydia watched the news with equal amazement and curiosity. She knew where the ricin gas was stored, and a various assortment of weapons and ammo, and it was nowhere near West Memphis, Arkansas. So the feds were obviously lying; but why?

Something to ponder.

"Jesus Christ! The bastard keeps giving us the slip! It's maddening!"

Kennedy was pacing furiously in the hotel Presidential Suite. "And I'll tell you something else! The damn talking heads are openly speculating that the Mastermind is preparing for another attack! And with God knows what? Ricin, again? Bombs? Cannonballs? Who the fuck knows?"

"Should we up the threat level?" Darling asked, watching his chief of staff wear a whole in the rug.

"Jesus, I don't know. If we don't, and something happens, we're screwed. If we do, and nothing happens, we look foolish."

Darling felt he had no choice. "Notify all local authorities, through Homeland Security, to be aware that Barboni may be armed with a weapon of mass destruction - the ricin - and go on full alert."

Kennedy looked like he needed to puke. "Jesus, I hope we don't end up looking foolish."

"Kennedy, are you saying you hope something happens?"

"What? Oh, no, shit no. Not what I mean. What I mean is, ah, hell, I don't know. I'm just tired of all this shit."

"Agreed. But there's something else we need to focus on, Kennedy. The debate. We really need to kick McHenry's ass in the debate."

McHenry waited for the media gaggle to settle in and said, "Here we have a total failure of the NSA. They get intelligence that could perhaps have been useful in finding a weapons cache and maybe even arresting Ricky Barboni, and they're apparently too busy sitting on their thumbs or reading everybody's love notes to each other to pay attention.

"I'm telling you, the NSA is incompetent. But because these goons appear to have unlimited resources under our current president, the NSA is also dangerous to the very cornerstones of a free society.

"This has to stop, and under my administration, it will."

56

The debate

It was a crowd of dignitaries who gathered in Richmond, Virginia, for the one and only presidential debate between President Maury Darling and Governor James McHenry. It was an invitation-only event, a spectacle, not only because it was the only debate of the election. This one was different: no moderator, no media. Just Darling and McHenry, seated across from each other at a shiny table, eye to eye, having a conversation. The atmosphere in the hall was electric.

The crowd was split evenly between the candidates, and they had been given strict instructions to behave themselves. Sit quietly and watch history be made.

The lights dimmed. The table and two chairs were brightly lit. There were two glasses and two pitchers of ice water. Then, over the speakers, came a booming voice: "Ladies and gentlemen, President Maury Darling and Governor James McHenry."

The crowd stood and applauded as the two men entered from opposite sides and greeted each other with a firm handshake and smiles. Then they acknowledged the crowd with a wave and took their seats. The people took their seats, too, and soon the hall was silent, except for some guy in the back trying to cough up some phlegm. He finally succeeded.

McHenry spoke up first. "Mr. President, as the incumbent, I think you've earned the right to go first."

"Thank you, Governor. And thank you, too, for agreeing to this historic debate format. This is the way all debates should be, in my opinion."

"I agree."

Darling nodded, then turned to face "his" camera. "And thank you, my fellow Americans, for watching tonight. This is a very important evening. It's your best chance to take the measure of each of us, not packaged into a thirty second ad or filtered by the media. Tonight, I hope you'll listen carefully as we talk about our vision for America. I hope you agree that the choice is very clear. My administration has worked very hard to create an atmosphere of equality and justice in America, and we've made great progress. But there's more to do. There are still too many people who struggle in this country. They don't get paid enough, but their bosses get paid too much. There are still too many people who fear sickness, not only for themselves, but for their children. They don't have adequate health insurance, but their bosses all have Cadillac plans. And there are too many people out there who are victims of gun violence, or trapped in their homes because they're too afraid to walk their own neighborhoods. They dread the sound of every shot, wondering if one of their own children got caught in the crosshairs.

"This is my vision for America: a land where everyone earns at least a living wage, where no one fears that a trip to the doctor means bankruptcy, and our neighborhoods are places to learn and grow, not duck and die."

With that, Darling turned to McHenry and nodded.

McHenry nodded back and looked into "his" camera. "I certainly agree with much of what the President just said. The choice certainly is clear. And who can argue with an America where everyone is making plenty of money, nobody gets sick, and nobody gets hurt? But that's a pretty simplistic view of the challenges we face. I look forward to a detailed discussion tonight as we debate the President's misguided living wage proposal, health care promises, and his efforts to confiscate guns. But there are other issues out there, like the NSA. The National Security Agency is completely out of control. These goons are snooping into every aspect of your life. Reading your text messages. Logging your phone calls. Tracking your movements through the GPS device in your cell phone. My fellow Americans, think right now about your deepest secret, and realize this: the NSA already knows it.

"It is unconscionable that a sitting president would allow this to go on. All he has to do is pick up the phone and tell them to stop it! If you elect me as your president, on my first day in office, I will pick up the phone and this stuff will stop."

Some of the McHenry supporters started to applaud, but they were quickly shushed into silence by the Darling crowd.

Darling looked directly at McHenry. "Governor, you called my vision for America simplistic. But there's nothing more simplistic than thinking I should pick up the phone and tell the NSA to stop gathering intelligence on potential threats to American citizens. The work they do is important. The American people expect their government to keep them safe."

"Then why did the NSA fail so miserably with the Soldiers of Allah?" McHenry countered. "A lot of good Americans - including children - are dead because the NSA was clueless the attacks were coming, and did absolutely nothing to catch the terrorists. It was the good folks of Missouri who got that done."

Darling's eyes flared at McHenry. There it was. The first body blow.

"We're still investigating the Soldiers of Allah, Governor. And the NSA is playing an important role in that. As of now, the people can rest assured that the Soldiers of Allah are in federal custody, and will face the federal justice system. Justice will be done."

McHenry shook his head. "Mr. President, under your scenario, some of the children who survived the terror attacks will be old men by the time justice is finally delivered, if it ever is. These people aren't criminals, they're terrorists. They tried to influence the outcome of this very election through the use of terror. I won't stand for it. On my first day in office, I'll sign an executive order labeling the Soldiers of Allah as enemy combatants and they will be summarily executed. That, Mr. President, is the delivery of justice."

Darling cocked his head to one side. "And will you also find time on your first day to shred the Constitution?"

"That's nonsense. The Constitution is there to protect Americans, not terrorists."

"But the Soldiers of Allah are Americans, Governor. Every one of them."

McHenry couldn't hide the surprise on his face.

"Oh, you didn't know that? Yeah, that's one of the things the NSA tells me they turned up in our investigation. So take a breath, Governor, before you continue to advocate for the immediate execution of Americans."

McHenry was thinking: something is clearly off here. The President knows more than I do. Time to move on.

"Mr. President, let's move on to your economic policy. The so-called living wage."

"Certainly, Governor. As you know, we would repeal the minimum wage and require that all employers pay all employees at least 75% of the average wage in the county where they work. That way, people who live and work in high-cost areas would earn more money to help pay the bills."

"But what business is it of the federal government to mandate the value of labor?" McHenry demanded. "Mr. President, all your proposal will do is kill jobs. For many employers, the cost of hiring someone will simply be too high and they'll take a pass. No growth, no jobs. Plus, your plan mandates that employers pick up the lion's share of all kinds of insurance products, even life insurance. They can't afford it."

Darling waved it away. "Almost half the wealth in the entire world, Governor, is owned or controlled by 85 people. 85! I know your supporters hate it when we talk about spreading the wealth around, but c'mon, man! 85 people controlling half of everything? There's plenty of room to share at least a little bit."

McHenry chuckled. Gotcha. "I'm sure you enjoyed reading that story when it was published, Mr. President, but you should have also read about it being retracted. It's false. But, in any event, when it comes to wealth distribution, it shouldn't be the government mandating it!

"Let me tell you something," McHenry continued, pointing at Darling. "Every time the federal government tries to insert itself into the natural creation and distribution of wealth, it backfires.

"In fact, the federal government is far too big and way too intrusive. I blame it all on that moment in 1913 when the states rather stupidly ratified the 17th Amendment."

There was audible gasp from some in the audience.

Darling leaned in. "I'm sorry, Governor. Did I understand you to say that allowing the people to elect their United States senators is stupid?"

"Absolutely. The framers of the Constitution understood the importance of keeping a strong hand on the federal government. The states created the federal government and they feared it would expand and gobble them up. So the senators were supposed to represent the states, not the people, and keep the federal government in check. The senators were chosen by the legislatures to represent the states. But now, the senators answer directly to the voters, and they see the federal government as a fat Santa Claus that can hand out the goodies to get them re-elected."

Darling could barely restrain his smile. "So, what would you do, Governor? Repeal the 17th Amendment?"

McHenry shook his head in disgust. "I doubt it'll ever happen, but I'd sure support it."

57

"What in the name of God were you thinking, Governor?" It was Lawson, the campaign manager, and he was livid. "We never once discussed you bringing up the 17th Amendment!"

They were riding together in the back of a Suburban, on their way to a Richmond hotel.

"I thought the little shit needed a history lesson."

"Do you know what your history lesson is being called on Twitter? And Facebook? And most of the news networks?"

"I have a feeling you're going to tell me."

"They're calling it your 'Todd Akin moment'! That's shorthand for saying something so incredibly bizarre that it could cost you the election!" Lawson was actually red in the face and his hands were shaking.

"Jesus, Lawson, calm down before you have a stroke. It can't possibly be that bad."

"They're saying there must be something in Missouri's water!"

"C'mon, Lawson. Our polling is solid. You said yourself we're on our way to 300 electoral votes."

"That was yesterday! I have a feeling tomorrow will be different!"

"So let's see what tomorrow brings, Lawson. The election is a week away. If we're bleeding as bad as you think, we'll need some fancy footwork to get me across the finish line."

"I wanted to jump onstage and kiss him on the fucking lips!"

Kennedy couldn't even stand still, he was so giddy with excitement. "We're gonna run that clip until every voter in America can recite it by heart! The election is as good as over!"

Darling smiled. "It was like he had a brain fart or something. All of a sudden, he's talking about something that happened more than a century ago. Bizarre. His campaign must be freaking out."

Kennedy's smile was almost wicked. "Do you think they'll panic and do something even more stupid?"

"What could possibly be more stupid than this?"

The Smart Man was sitting in the director's office. The director was behind his massive desk. Behind him, several televisions were tuned to a variety of news networks, the sound muted. All were blathering on about McHenry's abysmal debate performance.

"We may have to do something drastic," the director said. "Darling is too weak on terrorism and national security. Plus, I badly want McHenry in there with our cute little mole down the hall."

"Yes, sir. What are you thinking?"

The director sighed heavily. "We have evidence that shows the cancer diagnosis on the Vice President was faked."

The Smart Man was aghast. "Faked? How did you....never mind. I know better than to ask how you got the evidence. But, what is the evidence?"

"Text messages exchanged between Darling's chief of staff and Olivia Morgan's personal physician."

"Good God. Her own doctor agreed to cook this up?"

The director nodded. "I suspect the White House made him an offer he couldn't refuse."

The Smart Man shook his head in disbelief. Then: "My God, does the Vice President know it's fake?"

"We have no evidence to indicate she was in on it. She might very well believe she has cancer. Wouldn't you believe it? If your doctor said you have cancer?"

"But what about that story she told at the convention? You know, that her husband was the one who found the lump?"

"Stagecraft, obviously," the director responded. "To make the story more personal to people. And, it worked."

They sat in silence for a few seconds. Then the Smart Man spoke up. "What are we going to do with this evidence?"

"Leak it, obviously. We'll use our usual London connections. Blame the leak on the NSA again."

"Jesus, the people will go wild thinking the NSA is reading their text messages."

The director smiled. "Yeah, it's like a three-fer. They'll be pissed at Darling for lying about the Vice President having breast cancer. They'll hate the NSA for reading text messages and leaking all that shit to newspapers. And they'll like McHenry again when he calls for the NSA to be disbanded, which he needs to do right after the story breaks."

"I'll see to it."

The director shook his head and sighed. "I feel sorry for the Vice President. This could devastate her emotionally. But," he looked across his desk at the Smart Man, "all in a day's work."

58

WHITE HOUSE FAKES CANCER DIAGNOSIS!

The headline screamed across the London tabloid over the top of a picture of Vice President Olivia Morgan at the convention, saluting the image of President Darling on the big screen. The story pulled no punches.

In what we now know was a shameless maneuver by the Darling Administration to change the subject after a terrorist group demanded Americans vote to reelect him, the White House teamed up with the personal physician of VP Olivia Morgan to concoct a phony diagnosis of breast cancer for her that was then leaked to the public as genuine.

Worse yet, the evidence provided to this newspaper by the National Security Agency appears to indicate the fake diagnosis was cooked up without Mrs. Morgan's knowledge. When told by her own doctor that she had breast cancer, she believed it. Her story was sold to Americans as one of courage, and from her perspective it certainly was. Now we know it was all a fraud.

The evidence is damning. It all started with this text message from President Darling's chief of staff Kennedy Jackson to Mrs. Morgan's doctor: "We need to wag the dog big time. Are leaking to press the VP has cancer. You will confirm." The doctor responded: "Hell no. R U crazy?" Mr. Jackson: "You will do it. IRS." After several minutes, the doctor responded: "K."

The White House refused to comment for this story. Efforts to contact Mrs. Morgan or her personal physician were unsuccessful.

The news hit Vice President Olivia Morgan like a thunderclap. Dr. Vincent Spark - Vinnie to her for more than twenty years - had looked her in the eye, held her hand, and delivered the devastating news that she had breast cancer. He had cut into one of her breasts to remove what was apparently a non-existent tumor. He had radiated her chest. He had provided oral chemotherapy pills. Were they sugar pills? And he did all this because the White House threatened him with the IRS?

No. It couldn't be true. She had cancer. She was beating it. Sure, she had agreed to tell the little white lie about her husband finding the lump. Where was the harm in that?

Vinnie wasn't answering his cell phone. She had tried a dozen times. It was odd, but she needed him to tell her it's not true, that she really does have cancer; the London tabloid is full of shit.

She closed her eyes, fighting back the tears, the headache, the rage. She heard someone enter the room, quietly. Part of her Secret Service detail.

"Madam Vice President?"

Agent Connor. He was a good one. Professional. She nodded, her eyes still closed.

"I'm sorry. We sent a couple of agents to Dr. Spark's home. When he didn't respond, they entered."

Oh, God. She could feel it coming. It closed around her like a dark mist.

"He was dead. He shot himself."

And then there was no holding back. Not the tears, not the pain, not the anguish. She had faced death and thought she was beating it. Now, she felt like she would welcome it.

Kennedy and Darling were alone in the Oval Office, staring out the windows. Kennedy broke the silence first.

"This is bad."

"It's worse than bad, Kennedy. You could go to prison."

Kennedy looked at him sharply. "You can't let that happen."

"We've talked about this, my friend. The officeholder never takes the fall. It's always the staff."

Kennedy tried to swallow the rising nausea. "You're right, Mr. President. I just never thought it would happen."

Kennedy turned to leave, stopped, and looked around the Oval Office. "I'm gonna miss this."

"Yeah," Darling replied. "Me, too."

McHenry stepped to the lectern covered with microphones.

"I am heartbroken over this. It sickens me that people in the White House could be so consumed by their own thirst for power that they would throw one of their own to the wolves. And I'm devastated over how this will impact Vice President Morgan and her family. She's a good woman and doesn't deserve any of this. My thoughts and prayers are with her as she copes with this latest development in her life.

"But I'm also angry that we have further evidence of abuse by the NSA. Reading text messages? And leaking what they know to foreign news organizations? It's preposterous! It borders on treason!

"That is why today I am announcing my plan to completely disband the National Security Agency should I be elected next Tuesday. Surely we can structure a way to gather intelligence important to our national security without snooping on our citizens like some kid with an ant farm."

59

Ordinarily, the initial response by any presidential administration to a scandal - true or false - is to deny, deny, deny. Not this time.

It was the Friday before the election, and President Maury Darling strode to the lectern in the briefing room.

"It is with a great deal of personal regret and sadness that I accept the resignation of my good friend and chief of staff, Kennedy Jackson. You'll be receiving a copy of his resignation letter shortly. As you will see, he takes full responsibility for conspiring with the Vice President's personal physician to leak a false diagnosis of cancer to the public. It was a horrible thing to do. Kennedy also makes clear I had no knowledge of any of it. If I had, I would have stopped it immediately, of course.

"Kennedy also makes it clear he'll cooperate with investigators and accept whatever consequences come his way.

"I've been in touch with the Vice President and expressed my anger and regret over Kennedy's actions. I frankly found it very difficult to express in words the full depth of my sorrow. But she's still a courageous woman and she'll get through this. My hope is that she'll continue to serve her country, because we need her."

Darling paused before continuing. "This is a sad moment in American politics. How can we allow ourselves to be so caught up in winning and losing, in name-calling and finger-pointing, and in trying to make our dirty tricks dirtier than the other guy? I think we all have a great deal of soul-searching to do.

"I wish none of this had ever happened. But it did, and on my watch. The American people will deliver a verdict on my administration on Tuesday. I hope they'll weigh the evidence in its totality, and not just this horrible event that resulted from the overzealous actions of a good friend.

"These past two months have been like a whipsaw. From the murders of innocent children in Waverly, Iowa, to the ricin attack that took so many lives in Omaha to the kidnapping of children in Missouri and the maddening reality that the Mastermind of all this craziness is still at large.

"Without question, this is the most bizarre presidential election in history. Regardless of the outcome on Tuesday, I'm thinking a lot of people agree with me when I say: let's get it over with."

Olivia didn't believe for a second that the President was blameless. But she was a team player, so she stored her anger deep within her for later use. Getting Darling re-elected put her closer to occupying the White House herself one day. She took a deep cleansing breath and nodded to the network reporter. She was ready.

And she did a remarkable job. Amazing, really. Just the right amount of tears, but not too much. Anger, of course. But a heavy dose of determination. The health care issue is still critical to America, she maintained. Her passion for public service still burned strong. The choice on

Tuesday is still clear. Don't let her unfortunate situation cloud your judgment, she insisted.

Her message was clear: she lost a lot because of this. She doesn't want to lose the election, too.

60

Election Eve

The BREAKING NEWS logo flashed across the screen. The news anchor looked excited.

"We are getting reports that federal agents in Omaha have taken custody of Ricky Barboni, the so-called Mastermind of the terror attacks of two months ago that took so many lives across America. Our initial reports indicate the man was acting suspiciously near the home of Lloyd Epperson, the firefighter who famously survived the ricin attack in Omaha. There is some speculation that perhaps Barboni was planning to kidnap Mr. Epperson, or harm him somehow, in his continued attempts to sway tomorrow's presidential election. Stay tuned for more on this breaking story."

The network talking heads, who had been talking about the last pre-election poll showing the race too close to call because of a surge of female support for the Darling-Morgan ticket, suddenly had new material.

"Well, this is interesting," one of them noted. "If this Barboni character was trying to influence the election in Darling's favor, his arrest might just do the trick. I can see the headlines now: Darling gets the Mastermind."

"Sonofabitch!"

McHenry was in the Governor's Mansion, enjoying cocktails with Lawson, Lucas, and a few others within his inner circle. "Couldn't that dumb fuck stay away from the cops for at least one more day?"

Lawson looked thoughtful. "It's hard to tell how much Barboni's arrest will move the numbers. Remember: a lot of people have voted already. It might hurt our big lead with male voters. But we still have the ad showing you marching the terrorists out of the farm house at gunpoint on ESPN and other male-dominated networks."

Lucas looked pissed. "I bet that fucking Darling will take a victory lap on this. You watch."

Lucas was right. Darling arranged for an Oval Office address to the nation at 9 p.m. on the east coast.

"My fellow Americans, at my direction this evening, federal agents in Omaha took custody of a man acting suspiciously near the home of national hero Lloyd Epperson. This man turned out to be Ricky Barboni - the Mastermind. I'm happy to report that he has confessed and is currently cooperating with authorities. We expect that very soon we'll be able to provide a full accounting of what was actually behind his murderous conspiracy.

"While the capture of this madman will not bring back the many victims he left in his violent wake, we can all breathe a sigh of relief that this man is in federal custody and will face justice.

"Tomorrow is a very important day in America. I'm happy to say that with the capture of the Mastermind tonight, tomorrow you can exercise your glorious right to vote without fear of violence. Sleep easy tonight, my friends, and we'll see you tomorrow."

In Marco Island, Florida, a man named Rip Snyder jumped to his feet and cheered.

"They caught the bastard!" he yelled to his wife. "They caught that sonofabitch!"

Rip had once been hip-deep in Republican politics in Florida, skewering Democrats regularly with his blog *The Ripper*, until the Democrats ran him off as a discredited racist due to comments he made to Carrie, his girlfriend at the time, that showed up in her diary. A sleazy fellow reporter had stumbled across her diary and leaked it to the Democrats.

In her teenage years, Carrie had run away from her unhappy home near Henley, Missouri, and went to work for Ricky Barboni as an underage stripper at his beloved Pecker Palace in Brooklyn, Illinois. It was her testimony that put Barboni away in the federal pen.

Upon his release, Barboni stumbled across Carrie and tried to kill her. Rip and Carrie escaped and had set up shop in Marco Island writing a harmless, slick magazine for the island's upper crust.

Now, Carrie heard him yelling and found him in the den. "Who caught what?"

"The feds!" Rip said with a fist pump. "They caught that fucking Barboni!"

Carrie put a hand to her mouth. "Oh, my God! It's about fucking time!"

Inside a dilapidated, nearly abandoned trailer home on the far outskirts of Miami, Oklahoma, the television flickered with the news. It was the most remarkable news story the viewer had ever seen. President Darling had pulled off the impossible: arresting the Mastermind in Omaha while the real Ricky Barboni was sitting in this worthless trailer, eating Doritos and scratching himself.

"What the fuck is going on?" he said, sniffing his fingers.

61

Election Night

The McHenry camp was holed up in the Presidential Suite of a downtown St. Louis hotel. Laptops were open, the keys clacking. Cell phones were buzzing. The air was alive with a mixture of excitement, stress, and worry.

It was going to be close; everyone knew it.

Downstairs, in the ballroom, supporters were gathering for what they hoped would be a triumphant evening. The drinks were flowing freely. They watched as a big screen TV was tuned to Fox News.

"The Decision Desk is making its first call of the evening," the anchor said. "The polls have closed along most of the East Coast. We're calling Maine for Darling."

Maine turned blue, and the four electoral votes went into Darling's column. A short time later, New Hampshire went red: four votes for McHenry. A cheer went up. Then: Vermont and Rhode Island went red at the same time: McHenry 11, Darling 4. The cheering got louder. Then: Connecticut went blue: tied again.

The crowd groaned. They sought out more drinks. Gonna be a long night.

Darling and his entourage took up the entire top floor of the Hay Adams Hotel near the White House.

Darling had invited his old friend Kennedy Jackson to join him. It was a bittersweet, emotional night for both of them. Darling was fearful he might lose, and knew if he won that he was facing four years without Kennedy at his side. Kennedy already felt like an outsider, almost a leper. Plus, he worried about going to prison. But he accepted the invitation because he damned sure wanted to be there to watch his old friend win, and would be there to console him if he lost.

"The suspense is killing me," Kennedy said, after taking a long pull on a rum and coke.

"Tell me about it," Darling replied. "They're telling me New York is in play. New York! It's not a good sign."

"Hang in there, buddy."

They watched as Massachusetts, Delaware, Maryland, and the District of Columbia went for Darling. Darling 38, McHenry 11.

Kennedy's former assistant, the acting chief of staff, approached them, looking sick.

"We have a problem."

"Ah, shit," Darling said. "Is it New York?"

She shook her head. "The guy we arrested as the Mastermind - who insisted he was Barboni and confessed to everything - is a nut job. His name is Leo Snyder."

"Ah, Jesus." Darling was looking around like he wanted to find a place to puke. "So the working theory that this guy was Barboni trying to kill Lloyd Epperson was fucked up?"

"Major league fucked up. Snyder admitted after they checked his fingerprints that he wanted to be Barboni, wanted the fame and attention of being the Mastermind.

But all he wanted from Epperson was his autograph. Straight from the loony bin."

"Mr. President?" Kennedy was being cautious, unsure. "If I might suggest something?"

"By all means, Kennedy. You know I value your advice."

"You can't let this get out. Lots of other states are still voting. The news that all we did was finger some nut job instead of the Mastermind could be devastating."

Darling turned to his acting chief of staff. "Put a lid on it, Sarah. As far as the world knows, the Mastermind is still behind bars."

"Got it."

"One other thing, Mr. President," Kennedy injected. "You need to have the Secret Service hold this Snyder guy as a potential security threat. They can do that, indefinitely, on your order. Who knows how long this election is going to take? It could be Bush-Gore all over again."

Darling rolled his eyes. "God help us. Prepare the order, Sarah. I'll sign it."

Downstairs, a roar went up as New Jersey went blue. Darling 52, McHenry 11.

"Damn," Lawson muttered. "I thought we might take New Jersey." He was clacking away on his laptop.

"How about New York?" McHenry wondered.

Lawson shrugged. "It's really close. Our message of standing tall against the terrorists really resonated. If we take New York, it's over. We're gonna do really well throughout the south, the Great Plains, the mountain states.

The only way Darling pulls it out without New York is if he wins Florida, and I don't see it happening."

The Decision Desk at Fox News broke in again. Virginia, North Carolina, and South Carolina all went for McHenry. It was the biggest cheer so far; Virginia and North Carolina had been considered swing states. Darling 52, McHenry 48.

"I'm telling you, Governor McHenry might just pull this off," one of the Fox News analysts said. "And it'll be the first time a sitting president was defeated since Bill Clinton blindsided Bush 41. And just think of what we've been through. Dozens of innocent Americans slaughtered by the Soldiers of Allah. A threat by the terrorists to kill millions more if McHenry wins. The kidnapping of fourth-graders. The rescue of those children - on live TV - by McHenry! We're told Vice President Olivia Morgan has cancer, and then we're told it was fake! McHenry's running mate has to endure the public shame of finding out his wife is unfaithful by reading about it in the news! And McHenry fumbles the ball in the only debate by coming across as a deranged descendant of Ben Franklin!

"At some point, the election will be over and we'll have to figure out which of these bizarre events played the biggest role. It makes my head hurt."

Another analyst leaned in. "And remember this: the threat to kill millions if McHenry wins is still out there."

"But they're all in custody," yet another chimed in. "Including the Mastermind."

"How do we know for sure there aren't more out there?"

On that note, a cheer went up at the Hay Adams. Darling took New York with 51.1%. Darling 81, McHenry 48.

"Sonofabitch!" Lawson blurted. "It's the women. We're not getting enough of the damn women!"

He was crunching exit polls. "The women love Olivia Morgan, and they feel the pain of her fake cancer diagnosis." Lawson looked at McHenry. "Plus, they're skeptical about putting a fifty-something divorced guy with a hottie on his arm in the White House."

"Is it hurting us in Florida?" McHenry asked.

"Damn right it is. We're losing in the Eastern Time zone. We need to seriously kick Darling's ass in the Panhandle."

The Decision Desk broke in again. Georgia and West Virginia were called for McHenry. Darling 81, McHenry 69.

The night wore on. Darling took Wisconsin, Illinois, Minnesota, Iowa, and, in a squeaker, Louisiana. McHenry got Ohio, Kentucky, Tennessee, and Alabama. Darling 135, McHenry 115.

The revelers were caught up in it, getting drunk, and placing bets. One poor fool who had been drinking since mid-afternoon bet one of his friends a hundred bucks that the election would end in a tie, and got ten-to-one odds.

To the consternation of the Darling side, the next bulletin hit like a lightning strike: Indiana, Mississippi, Missouri (of course), and Arkansas went red. McHenry 148, Darling 135.

"He's killing us with men," Kennedy observed. "They like the cowboy swagger, the tough talk about executing the terrorists, and Gunderson. He's like a God to them. You know, the bravest American..."

"Don't say it, Kennedy," Darling interrupted.

Kennedy tossed him a smile. "Right. And the men don't mind a bit that McHenry has a little hottie with a body. Shit, they're probably drooling on the ballots."

In a bit of a surprise, Kansas went for Darling, along with his home state of Colorado. But McHenry took the Dakotas, Nebraska, Oklahoma and, in a landslide, the big prize of Texas. McHenry 204, Darling 150.

As the numbers rolled in, the networks started digging up footage from the 2000 election, with the hanging chads.

"Once again, this whole thing could come down to Florida," one analyst said. "And we might be in for more than a long night. I hear both campaigns have lawyers in the air, headed for Tallahassee."

"What the hell is going on with Michigan and Pennsylvania?" Darling asked. "I thought we had them in the bag."

"Some irregularities in the counts in Michigan, so it's taking a long time," Kennedy noted. "But the folks on the ground are confident. Pennsylvania is a lot closer than expected. You're not doing so good in Pittsburgh."

"Maybe we should have gone to Pittsburgh."

"You hate Pittsburgh."

New Mexico went blue, but Montana, Wyoming, Idaho, Utah, and Arizona all went red. The McHenry camp was excited; they could smell it. Or maybe it was the liquor. McHenry 231, Darling 155.

Then the dam broke out west. Washington, Oregon, and the biggest prize of all, California, went for Darling. The Hay Adams was rocking. Then Michigan finally clocked in for Darling. Darling 245, McHenry 231.

Pittsburgh notwithstanding, Pennsylvania finally went blue. Darling 265, McHenry 231. The networks were frantic. Then the Florida count was finished. McHenry did, indeed, kick Darling's ass in the Panhandle, winning Florida by some 5,000 votes. Darling 265, McHenry 260.

The lawyers in Tallahassee all realized they were in the wrong spot. The real showdown would be in Carson City, Nevada.

Hawaii went blue; Alaska went red. Darling 269, McHenry 263. The nation was poised at the point of impossible. If McHenry took Nevada - and he was leading in a tight count - the election would indeed end in a tie.

In the wee hours of the morning, after the final Decision Desk call of the night, a drunk McHenry supporter stumbled over to his friend, who was scooping out the last of the popcorn, and with boozy breath said: "You owe me a thoushand bucksh!"

62

As the sun rose over the nation's capital, President Maury Darling and Kennedy Jackson were still at it, disheveled, bleary-eyed, and exhausted. A tie in the Electoral College. It seemed impossible, but there it was.

The first thing they had done was dig deeper into the numbers in Maine and Nebraska. In those two states, electors are chosen by congressional district, plus two additional electors to the statewide winner. But nothing changed there.

The way forward was obvious.

"We need a faithless elector," Kennedy said. "Maybe two or three, just to be safe. It's like a whole new campaign. Out of the 269 electors pledged to McHenry, we need to find a few who are willing to switch."

"I assume that won't be easy," Darling noted. "Electors are the most loyal people the party can find. It's a huge honor, bestowed only on the privileged few. A faithless elector would be publicly scorned. In some states, they can face fines for violating their loyalty oath. Who would do such a thing?"

"Somebody who wants to be the ambassador to Monaco."

Darling's eyes widened. "But the ambassador to Monaco is J. Roger Turnbull! Have you forgotten what he did for us?"

"Of course not. He raised over ten million bucks back in the day. But that was back in the day, Mr. President. What can he do for you now?"

Darling looked disgusted. "And I'm supposed to trust some faithless elector who pledged to defeat me as my ambassador to Monaco?"

"It's not like Monaco is important. It's just a plum. Plus, you can find something else for Turnbull to do."

"But he loves it so."

"And if you lose he's gone anyway. Look; all I'm saying is we have a lot of plums to hand out. Cash even. I don't care. The campaign was like a world war, but this is hand-to-hand combat. We need to do whatever is necessary."

Darling sighed. "Can you handle it, Kennedy? I'll put you on the campaign team as an advisor, but I need to be as far away from this shit as possible."

"Yes, I'll do it. Any restrictions?"

Darling turned to leave. "Like you said. Whatever is necessary. I'm going to bed."

"We need a faithless elector."

It was Lawson Forbes, the campaign manager. "It happens very rarely, usually as some kind of protest vote. But it has never changed the outcome of an election."

McHenry nodded. "And Darling needs the same thing."

"Correct."

"So while we're trying to convince one of his people to be a disloyal bastard, we also have to protect our flank."

"Also correct."

"Okay, Lawson. Print out a list of our 269 electors and their phone numbers. I'll start calling them personally later today. Boost their loyalty."

Lawson adjusted his glasses. "You'll have to do more than that, Governor. This is going to be a messy business. You need to tell them to avoid having any contact with Darling's people. If anyone gets an offer of anything of value to switch, they need to report that to us immediately. And you need to beat whatever the offer is."

McHenry shook his head. "Sounds like a bribery contest."

Lawson nodded. "The Super Bowl of bribery. And the best man wins."

The Smart Man was sitting across from the director, who was not happy.

"It was the capture of Barboni that did it for him. The bastard would have lost Louisiana but for that," the director lectured.

"I agree."

"Under no circumstances can we let Darling get re-elected. If our national security gets any weaker, we'll be vulnerable to fucking France."

"I agree."

"Obviously, both sides will be looking for faithless electors. I want every one of the electors flagged, all 538 of them. Full metadata - calls, texts, GPS tracking, web searches, the works."

"Of course."

"Have our best geeks pull together an algorithm to sift through the data and help us predict which electors might switch."

"Yes, sir."

"And tell Lydia Wade that we are going to move heaven and earth to put her in the White House, and she better by God be grateful."

"Done." The Smart Man hesitated. "May I ask you something?"

"Certainly."

"Aren't you worried McHenry will replace you? With his own guy?"

The director stared for a moment and burst out laughing. Finally, he said, "I have so much shit on that man, he wouldn't dare fart in my presence!"

Then they were both laughing.

63

Two weeks later

"Based on the data we have so far," the Smart Man reported, "the geeks down in the basement have identified five electors who seem vulnerable to switching."

The director was surprised. "Only five out of 538? Pretty loyal bunch."

"I agree. Of course, there's still time before the electors meet in each state capital to cast their votes. But the data the geeks have put together looks compelling."

"So let's go over the list. The Faithless Five."

The Smart Man smiled at that. "Okay. They are ranked one through five, with one being 'most likely' and five being 'least likely.' Number five is a lady named Betsy Lopes. Arkansas. She got a phone call from a cell phone we have identified as belonging to Kennedy Jackson."

"Kennedy? I thought that sonofabitch got fired!"

"He's on the campaign payroll. Obviously heading up the bribery operation."

The director shook his head. "Go on. Tell me about Betsy Lopes."

"Her phone call from Jackson lasted just over six minutes. That's one of the major data points. Calls from him that terminate quickly are pretty much ignored. Anyway, since that phone call, she has been Googling the words 'France' and 'ambassador.'"

"These fuckers are so predictable."

"Yes, sir."

"Who's number four?"

"A guy named Sean O'Connor. West Virginia."

"Let me guess. Ireland."

"Bingo."

"It's almost laughable."

"Yes, sir. Number three is Richard Bahl in Texas. He has some pretty sizable gambling debts, plus he's been Googling the price of silver. We assume he has been offered money."

The director nodded. "That's easy enough. Thirty pieces of silver and he's ours."

"Yes, sir. Number two is a young gun from Georgia named Julio Mendez. First generation American. He's been on the phone with Jackson three separate times for a total of 53 minutes. He wants Mexico."

The director looked thoughtful. "Interesting. None of these are insurmountable. All McHenry has to do is match the offers on ambassadorships. We pay off the deadbeat gambler. Who's number one?"

"A lady named Melissa Cooper. Louisiana."

The director leaned in. "Louisiana? Wouldn't she be pledged to Darling?"

"Yes, sir. She has been on the phone with McHenry. There is a long paper trail concerning the disappearance of her husband around the time Barboni was thought to be on the loose in the New Orleans area. She's convinced Barboni had something to do with it. When Darling announced that Barboni had been arrested, she started calling and emailing the White House to have the Justice Department look into the Barboni connection. She has basically been ignored.

"We're assuming McHenry has promised her he'll order Justice to investigate. All she has to do is switch and become number 270."

The director whistled. "Hell hath no fury. Wow. Melissa Cooper, you are about to become the only one in America to personally pick a president."

64

A blustery, cold November wind whipped at Zulu's short black dress as she hurried from the taxi to the door of the Westchester Garden Club. Winter was on the way, and America was still wondering who would be giving the Inauguration Address on January 20.

When she was escorted into the upstairs library, her new Alpha was already there, dressed impeccably, sitting in one of the leather wingback chairs, a glass of bourbon in hand, his smile wide and brilliant. He openly admired her impossible legs as she strutted to the bar and poured some wine. She was glad to notice his admiration; people who lusted for her legs could be manipulated.

"Have a seat, my dear Zulu."

"Where are the others?"

"We don't need them; not today."

"You should know it's highly irregular for the Azalea Team to meet without all four of us present."

"But I don't trust them."

She sipped her wine. "I doubt they trust you, either. Have they even met you yet?"

"Oh, yes. We've had...discussions."

Zulu rolled her eyes. "Like we had a discussion?"

Alpha flashed his smile. "Exactly! But I don't need their trust. All I need is their loyalty, and that has been assured."

"Spare me the ugly details."

"Very well." He handed her a list of five names. "These are what we call the Faithless Five. You'll see a brief explanation below each name. All McHenry has to do is match the ambassadorship offers to names two, four, and five. Maybe even sweeten the offers with a little cash or something. People you don't need to know will pay off number three. Are you familiar with number one?"

Zulu nodded. "I've heard Jim talk about her."

"Very well. We have arranged for all attempts to contact her by the Darling campaign or his people in Louisiana to fail. Only her closest friends will get through, and McHenry of course, and those contacts will be monitored. A security detail is already watching her house and tailing her for her own protection. She has the weight of the world on her shoulders right now."

Zulu leaned back, sipped her wine, and crossed her impossible legs. "You're missing something, Alpha. It's so not like you."

Alpha took his eyes off her legs and frowned. "What?"

"We need to have numbers two through five tell Darling they'll accept his offer. Hands down, end of story. That's what the extra cash they'll be getting is for: lying to the President."

Alpha smiled wide. "So they'll stop bribing people. Brilliant."

"Absolutely *fucking* brilliant, in my opinion," she said, letting one of her stiletto heels dangle from her foot. She was glad to see he noticed that, too.

Leo Snyder was yelling through the bars of his cell like it mattered. He was in the middle of a concrete building in the middle of a Secret Service detention facility that didn't officially exist.

"I want a lawyer, God damn it! I'm entitled to a fucking lawyer!"

Finally, a jailer stuck his head in the hallway and said, "Shut the fuck up down there!"

"I want a lawyer!"

"You ain't gettin' no lawyer."

"Everybody gets a lawyer!"

"Not you, dickhead. You threaten to kill the President, on top of treason, so you get a lawyer when we say so."

"I never threatened to kill anybody!"

"The boss says you did, so sit down and shut up or I'll spit in your dinner. Again."

65

The First Monday after the Second Wednesday in
December

C-SPAN was in its element.

"This is the day the Presidential Electors gather in their respective state capitals, and here in the District of Columbia, to cast their votes for President and Vice President of the United States," the anchor intoned. "And if all goes normally, it'll end in a tie.

"That throws the election of the President to the newly elected House of Representatives, where each state delegation will get one vote. They must pick from among the top three candidates in the popular vote: President Darling, who finished first; Governor McHenry, who finished second, and Lawrence Kittering, who finished a distant third. The house will cast ballots until one candidate gets 26 votes and is declared President of the United States.

"Wouldn't that be a spectacle!

"The election of the Vice President goes to the Senate if today's Electoral College vote ends in a tie.

"It's also important to remember that the electors today will vote separately for President and Vice President. So it's possible that at the end of the day we could have tie votes for both offices, or if there are electors who switch loyalties, we could even have a President of one party and a Vice President of a different party!

"And people say democracy can sometimes get messy," he said with a chuckle.

C-SPAN humor.

It was a surprisingly warm day in Baton Rouge as eight very important people gathered under the watchful eye of Louisiana Secretary of State Henslowe Frappe.

Their credentials were carefully checked against the list of Darling's electors. They were seated and greeted warmly by Frappe. Instructions were read. A few politicos took the opportunity to give self-serving speeches.

The crowd was fairly chatty. They all knew each other from years of party politics. Darling had not been expected to win Louisiana, so the list of electors was not made up of officeholders and dignitaries. These were the foot soldiers of the party. So they chatted away and waited excitedly for the big moment.

Except for one. Melissa Cooper was unusually quiet. When the time came to mark her ballot for President, she closed her eyes, said a prayer for her husband, Brent, and cast her ballot for McHenry. For Vice President, Gunderson.

Melissa was tempted to vote for Olivia Morgan, the poor woman. But in the end, she worried McHenry would be pissed. Plus, she knew Brent really liked Gunderson.

"We're kindred spirits," he said once.

Secretary of State Frappe couldn't believe his eyes. He had endorsed McHenry and campaigned for him. Election Night had hit him like a shot put to the gut when Darling carried the state by a slim margin.

Frappe looked up and caught Melissa's eyes. He could see they were wet.

"As you may or may not know, each of you must complete six Certificates of Vote, and sign them and certify them. I have them prepared. Mrs. Cooper, please approach. You may sign and certify first."

At first she looked confused, but then understood. He was getting her away from the mob.

"Thank you, Mr. Secretary." Her heart was hammering away as she quickly signed her name on each document.

Frappe leaned in as though she were whispering to him. Then he said to everyone, "Oh, yes. Good question. The restrooms are down the hall and to the right."

"Thank you," Melissa said. "Please proceed. I won't be long."

Melissa hurried through the door, out of the building, into the sunshine. She couldn't stop the tears.

"Mrs. Ditzler," Frappe said. "Please approach."

Wanda Ditzler, from New Orleans, looked at the first document, raised her voice and said, "I *knew* we couldn't trust that crazy bitch!"

66

Melissa Cooper checked out of her Baton Rouge hotel and drove to another, checking in as Lizzy Hargrove.

The front desk clerk smiled pleasantly and said, "All your costs are being covered, Miss Hargrove, including incidentals. I hope you enjoy your stay."

"I've had a tough day, Mister...."

"Wilson."

"Thank you. I'd appreciate it if you would see that I am not disturbed in any way, Mr. Wilson."

"Certainly. Would you like me to put a block on your phone?"

"That would be great. Thank you."

She rode the elevator to her floor, emotionally exhausted. When she opened the door and flipped on the light, she nearly screamed.

There was a man sitting in a chair next to the window. He looked Cuban. Handsome. He smiled widely.

"Don't be afraid, Mrs. Cooper. I'm on your side. I'm here to protect you."

"But, how did you know what room I'd be in?"

He waved it away. "Arrangements were made, of course. But don't worry. No one in the hotel but me knows who you really are. But I'm sure your picture will be all over the national news very soon."

"Who are you?"

"I'm your friend, Mrs. Cooper. Call me Mr. Friend."

"Okay, Mr. Friend. You can go now. I'm here, safe and sound."

He nodded. "I have the connecting room. Do not answer the door for anyone. There are people in this town who would like to harm you. I can think of seven off the top of my head. Not to mention some very powerful people in Washington."

She shuddered. "I just want to get some sleep and go home."

He shook his head. "Not for awhile you don't. The media will be all over your home like buzzards on a corpse."

She stared at him. "So I'm a prisoner in this fucking room?"

"Just for a few hours. Then we'll move you again to a safe place until everything dies down."

He stood and opened the connecting door. "Get some rest, Mrs. Cooper. I'll let you know when it's time to leave."

"What the hell do you mean we lost one?"

Darling was livid. "I thought all of our people were solid!"

Kennedy rubbed his face. "That was our thinking. Nobody saw it coming."

"Who is it?"

"Melissa Cooper from Louisiana. McHenry must have gotten to her."

"Cooper?" Darling sat down in a heap. "Ah, shit. Cooper."

"What? You know her?"

"I know of her." Darling said, suddenly very tired. "After we announced the arrest of the Mastermind, she started badgering us, insisting he was responsible for her husband disappearing. But we couldn't do anything about it because we didn't have Barboni. We had that fucking nutcase instead."

"So you ignored her."

Darling nodded.

"Sonofabitch! All you had to do was fake it! Just tell her you were investigating! Jesus!"

Darling looked at Kennedy. "Sarah isn't you, Kennedy. She doesn't think that way."

Kennedy started pacing. "Okay, what's done is done. We should still be okay, if our flips from Arkansas, West Virginia, Georgia, and Texas hold strong. They all assured me they were solid. And you know the best thing?"

"What?"

"We didn't even have to kick Turnbull out of Monaco! None of them had ever heard of it."

67

But Kennedy Jackson was wrong. Betsy Lopes, Sean O'Connor, Richard Bahl, and Julio Mendez stayed true to McHenry.

"What we have here is an incredible moment in American history," noted the CNN anchor. "For the first time ever, a faithless elector has altered the outcome of the presidential election. She has, with her own hand, altered the course of the most powerful nation on earth.

"Her name is Melissa Cooper," the anchor said, as a smiling picture of Melissa filled the screen. "She is from Happy Jack, Louisiana. That's south of New Orleans. In the swamps.

"What you're looking at now is a live picture of her modest home in those swamps. We don't know why Melissa Cooper took it upon herself to violate her pledge to the President and, effectively, throw him out of office. She isn't home, and all attempts to contact her have failed.

"But she has her own hashtag on Twitter. As you can imagine, Darling supporters are not happy with her."

On the CNN screen, big as life: Melissa's smiling picture. Below it: #SwampMonster.

"I want to change my mind," Melissa said to the Smart Man when he came to get her.

"Impossible."

"But I don't want to go through life as the Swamp Monster! I'm changing my vote."

"You can't. The vote has been cast. It's over."

Melissa sat on the bed and looked around. "So this is my life? Going from hiding spot to hiding spot in the middle of the night? Hated by half the country?"

"But loved by the other half."

"I didn't think it through. I was pissed at the President, so I violated my pledge. I didn't think it would make me a monster."

"You're not a monster, Mrs. Cooper. You're a hero."

Melissa looked at him. "What's your real name? It's obviously not Mr. Friend."

"I don't have a real name. Mr. Friend works just fine. Now, it's time to go."

He handed her a large, floppy hat and sunglasses.

"Sunglasses?" she asked. "In the middle of the night?"

"It's fashionable," he said, putting on a pair of his own. "Let's go."

"Get the lawyers in the air!" Kennedy barked into his cell phone. "We're going to Baton Rouge."

Kennedy clicked off and looked at Darling. "It isn't over. Not by a long shot."

"What good will the lawyers do?"

"We're gonna sue that sonofabitch Frappe. He was in the tank for McHenry all along. We're gonna claim he coerced Melissa Cooper to change her vote."

"Do we have any evidence?" Darling asked, worried about the answer.

"We have one of the other electors, her name is Wanda Ditzler, who will testify that Frappe allowed Cooper to leave the room before anyone knew how she voted. They obviously were coordinating."

"So what's the path forward?"

"We convince a judge to throw out the Louisiana electoral vote," Kennedy declared, hands on his hips. "Then we move to remove Cooper for violating her pledge, replace her with someone we trust, and have a do-over."

Darling put his hands behind his head. "All that does is get us back to even, which throws the election to the House. Don't we lose there?"

Kennedy spread his arms wide. "We'll have to crank up the bribery machine again. And, in my experience, congressmen are easier to bribe than presidential electors."

Darling grinned. "So old Turnbull may not be safe after all."

68

Secretary of State Henslowe Frappe had meticulously prepared all six Certificates of Vote for their final destinations. He was fully aware of the gravity of the roll he was playing in the nation's history. He had studied history all his life, preferring to spend his childhood poking through dusty books instead of running around on dusty playgrounds. He chalked it up to his parents having stuck him with the name Henslowe.

He set his glasses on the desk and thought about Melissa Cooper. What a courageous woman! How would the history books treat her? Not well, in all likelihood. She'll be blamed for everything President McHenry does wrong, and get little or no credit if, in fact, anything goes right.

She was facing some very bad times.

He put his glasses back on and checked the envelopes again. The first, and most important, was addressed to Vice President Olivia Morgan, in her capacity as President of the Senate. Her office would assemble all the votes and announce them to a joint session of Congress. Only then would the election be official.

Two copies would go to the national archives. Two copies were kept in Frappe's office. The final copy would go to an old friend: federal judge Sylvester Sly, who presided over the 5th Circuit that included Louisiana, Mississippi, and Texas.

Frappe smiled as he held the envelope addressed to Vesty, as Frappe knew him. They had somehow managed to graduate from LSU together, despite having consumed enough beer to drain half the swamps. Vesty went to law school, and Frappe went to work in this very building, helping to archive the history of the great state of Louisiana.

A long time ago, but the friendship had lasted, and deepened, over the years.

"Here's your little piece of history, Vesty," Frappe said, rising from his desk to mail the envelopes himself. He wasn't about to let some meager staffer handle such an historic moment.

There was a knock on his door jam. Frappe looked up to see one of the clerks from the federal courthouse.

"Mr. Secretary," the clerk said as she handed him a document. "You're being sued."

"What?"

"I'm here to collect the Certificates of Vote," she said with her hand out. "They're evidence."

"You and I shouldn't be talking about this, Henslowe."

The first thing Frappe had done after the clerk left was call Judge Sly on his cell phone.

"No one has to know, Vesty."

"Well, by God, nobody better know."

"Have you read the lawsuit?"

"Yes."

"I didn't do what they said, Vesty. It's all a lie."

"I don't care, Henslowe."

Frappe pulled up. "What do you mean you don't care? Vesty, I'm the chief elections official. I can't be accused of throwing an election!"

"Well, apparently you can be accused, because you are," Sly said in his usual drawl. "But I'll be damned if I'm gonna let some Harvard snob come down here and think he can prove it."

Frappe swallowed. "What are you saying?"

"I'm not saying anything, dammit, 'cuz we're not even talking about it! Just make sure you got all your ducks in a row. If your story matches this Cooper woman, then I'd say they lose. And don't talk to her either, by the way."

"I don't even know her! Never saw her before yesterday."

"That's a good story. Stick with it."

"It's the truth, Vesty!"

"Even better. Golf Saturday?"

"Of course."

"Melissa Cooper has to testify," the director told the Smart Man. "No question."

The director and the Smart Man were in their usual spots. Melissa Cooper was in an agency safe house in rural Virginia.

"She has to testify that she changed her allegiance because President Darling refused to investigate the disappearance of her husband in connection with the arrest of Barboni" the director ordered. "No coercion. Nothing."

"Of course."

"She needs to deny any kind of promise from McHenry, but she can say it is her *belief* that McHenry will be more diligent in following up. All she wants is justice."

"Of course."

"In exchange for her cooperation, she gets a new identity, a wonderful home that beats the hell out of that shack in the swamps, and a pile of cash."

"Of course," the Smart Man said. "But she'll want something else."

"What else could she possibly want?" the director said, exasperated.

"She wants a real investigation."

"Well, then, by God, let's promise her one."

"I'll see to it."

Melissa Cooper was horrified.

"Testify? In court?" her voice trembled. "No way. I won't do it."

"But you must," the Smart Man insisted. "If the court believes the allegation that you and the Secretary of State conspired to change the election, you might both be prosecuted and go to prison. Your life will be ruined."

"I feel like it's already ruined."

He nodded. "It would be very difficult, indeed, for Melissa Cooper to move on with her life in the swamps. But we'll help you leave all that behind. A new identity. A wonderful new home wherever you want. Lots of money. The freedom to travel. Doesn't sound so awful."

She looked at him. "Why so much? It sounds like a bribe. It's one thing to protect me from the people calling me a swamp monster. But what you're offering goes way beyond that."

He shook his head. "Bribe is such an ugly word. Let's call it a reward instead."

69

Henslowe Frappe was surprised when he arrived at the country club on Saturday and saw Judge Sly come out of the locker room with his right arm around the massive shoulders of a tall, stocky black man. They were both laughing.

The black man looked familiar, Henslowe thought, but he couldn't place him.

"Hey, Vesty," Henslowe said as he walked toward them.

"Good morning, Henslowe," Sly said good-naturedly. "I'd like you to meet a friend of mine. This is Roscoe Blackwell. Roscoe, this is Secretary of State Henslowe Frappe."

Roscoe Blackwell! He had been an All-American tight end at LSU about ten years ago - a finalist for the Heisman Trophy. He played for the Packers for three years before a nasty concussion ended his career.

Roscoe extended a huge hand and it swallowed Henslowe's. "Nice to meet you, Mr. Secretary."

Henslowe wondered if his hand might be gone when the handshake ended. "Please. Call me Henslowe."

"Yes, yes," Judge Sly intervened. "There's no need to be formal here. Roscoe is going to join us this morning."

Henslowe looked surprised. "Will the pro let us play as a fivesome?"

The judge shook his head. "No need. Billy Ray couldn't make it this morning. Which is just as well, because you and Roscoe have some important business to discuss."

Henslowe cocked his head in Roscoe's direction. "Business? What sort of business?"

"Lawyer stuff," Roscoe said.

"Roscoe here has agreed to represent you in that annoying little lawsuit you have going," Sly said. "And he's the very best at what he does."

"Nothing against you, Roscoe," Henslowe said, "but I'm being sued in my official capacity. The Attorney General will defend me."

Judge Sly put his hands up in a "stop" motion. "And I'm sure he'll do a fine job. But you need Roscoe here to defend your private flank. You don't want something coming out that could expose you personally. Now, give him a dollar Henslowe."

Stunned, Henslowe pulled a dollar out of his pocket and handed it to Roscoe.

"Okay, Henslowe," he judge drawled. "Now that he's on retainer, I suggest you ride in the same cart together and talk lawyer stuff. I'll be riding with Jackson."

That would be Jackson Stallings, chief of staff to the Attorney General.

"Johnny couldn't make it this morning, either?" Henslowe asked.

The judge stuck a cigar in his mouth. "You've got your business to discuss. And I've got mine."

At the first tee, Judge Sly was about to tee off when he looked at Roscoe and said, "You know, Roscoe, if you give me five strokes a side, we could put a bet down."

"Sure thing, Judge," Roscoe said.

"Shall we say five-five-ten?"

"Deal."

As they were driving down the first fairway, Henslowe looked at Roscoe and said, "Vesty said you're the best at what you do. What did he mean by that?"

Roscoe shrugged as he got out and reached for a nine iron. "I'm the best at throwing a golf bet without making it look too obvious."

Henslowe chuckled. "So you're gonna let old Vesty take twenty bucks off you today?"

Now it was Roscoe's turn to chuckle. "Not twenty bucks. Twenty grand."

"Twenty grand! What for?"

Roscoe shrugged again. "It's the least we can do to help elect a president. Plus, it's not my money. It's McHenry's money. And it's about to become the judge's money."

Then he hit a beautiful nine iron straight into the front right bunker.

70

Attorney General William Henry Carleton was seated at the right hand table, resplendent in a subtle, double pinstriped Armani suit. Secretary of State Henslowe Frappe sat to his right, also wearing his best suit, although he couldn't afford Armani. Men's Warehouse would have to do. Roscoe Blackwell was an enormous presence at the end of the table. His suit looked like someone had reduced him to molten metal and poured him into it.

At the other table sat Morton Benetton, a legendary trial lawyer who had extracted many millions of dollars out of businesses that dared to cross his path. He had three associates with him, all nervously digging through briefcases and shuffling piles of paper.

On the table in front of the Attorney General was a single piece of paper.

As the bailiff commanded all to rise and Judge Sylvester Sly breezed into the room, Henslowe caught him making eye contact with Roscoe. He thought he saw Vesty wink. Henslowe was the first to sit down, lest his knees buckle beneath him.

Henslowe wondered: would the true story ever be told? Would the history books tell the truth of how one side had bribed a federal judge to help elect a President? He hoped not.

Sly cleared his throat. "Good morning, gentlemen. We are here to establish an expedited schedule for Darling

v. Frappe, as time is of the essence. The people deserve to know who their President is going to be.

"Mr. Benetton, are you prepared to proceed?"

Benetton rose. "Yes, Your Honor. We are prepared to begin immediately, if necessary."

"Very good." Sly turned to the other table. "And you, Mr. Attorney General? Is the State prepared to begin immediately?"

Carleton rose. "Yes, Your Honor. In fact, the State begins by making a motion to dismiss."

"Objection!" Benetton jumped up so fast he actually left the floor for a brief moment. "On what possible grounds?"

Carleton walked to Benetton's table and showed him the piece of paper he was holding. "Your Honor, I have here a sworn affidavit from Melissa Cooper, swearing under oath that Secretary of State Henslowe Frappe had no prior knowledge of her decision to switch her vote to Governor McHenry, and that he never coerced her in any way."

"Let me see it," Sly commanded.

As Judge Sly was reading it, Benetton interjected. "Your Honor, this is outrageous! Surely the Attorney General knows better than to think a simple piece of paper will lead you to dismiss a lawsuit of such enormous magnitude! At the very least, I deserve the chance to cross examine this woman."

Sly set the paper aside and looked up. "I'm afraid he has a point, Mr. Attorney General. Is Mrs. Cooper available for cross examination?"

Carleton couldn't be happier. He had expected Mrs. Cooper to be put on the stand, but in this way, it was happening on his terms. He didn't know how Benetton had planned to start the proceedings, but it surely wasn't like this.

"Yes, Your Honor," Carleton said. "Might I suggest that Mrs. Cooper take the stand, read her affidavit into the record, and then make her available for cross?"

"Sounds reasonable," Sly said, turning to Benetton. "I'm sure you agree, Mr. Benetton?"

Benetton didn't agree, but what could he do? "Yes, Your Honor. We'll need some time to prepare."

Sly shook his head. "Were under the gun here. General Carleton, how soon can you produce Mrs. Cooper?"

"Within the hour."

"Wonderful. We will recess until 10:30 and then we'll hear from Mrs. Cooper."

The Smart Man was seated next to Melissa Cooper in the back of a black Suburban. As they pulled to a stop in front of the federal courthouse, Melissa was dismayed at the scene.

There was a mob. They were waving signs that read "Swamp Monster go home!" and "Traitor!" and even one that said "Die, bitch!"

"I'm afraid, Mr. Friend."

"I know. But you see the security, right? They won't let these people get to you. Plus, Darling's people probably hired them. To scare you."

"It's working."

He opened the door. "Let's go."

The jeers and boos and hisses blended together to produce a horrible sound. She caught a few words here and there, "Monster!" "Bitch!" And then she heard one guy with a very loud voice yell, "You're an asshole!"

The fear lifted, buoyed by anger, resolve, and determination.

"Let's do this, Mr. Friend," she said, her jaw set tight.

The Smart Man lit up his biggest smile. "Atta girl."

As they walked up the courthouse steps, the crowd fell into a chant: "Hey, hey! Ho, ho! The Swamp Monster has got to go!"

Inside, she could still hear the ruckus, but it was behind her. She entered the courtroom with confidence. She fought back a wave of emotion as she thought of her husband. "This is for you, Babe."

With everyone back in their places and Judge Sly situated, Sly banged his gavel and announced, "In the matter of Darling v. Frappe, the Court calls Melissa Cooper to take the stand."

She lost a little of her confidence as she strode to the stand, was sworn in, and sat down. Everyone was looking at her. The courtroom was full. There were no hisses, of course, but she could feel the cold steel in some of the stares.

Carleton approached and handed her the affidavit. "Mrs. Cooper, is this the affidavit you attested to yesterday?"

"Yes."

"Would you please read it into the record?"

She cleared her throat. "I, Melissa Joy Cooper, do solemnly swear that my decision to cast my Electoral College vote for James McHenry instead of Maurice Darling was my own. I was not coerced in any way by Secretary of State Henslowe Frappe, whom I had never met prior to the meeting of the presidential electors. He had no prior knowledge of my decision."

"And you are representing to this Court that the contents of this affidavit represent the truth and nothing but the truth?" Carleton asked her.

"Yes."

"She's all yours, Mr. Benetton."

Benetton rose. "So how does it feel to be labeled a Swamp Monster?"

Carleton shot to his feet. "Objection! Mrs. Cooper is here to be cross examined on her affidavit, not to be harassed!"

"Sustained," Sly said forcefully. "Mr. Benetton, I will not tolerate any nonsense here. You will confine your cross to the issues raised by the affidavit."

"Yes, Your Honor. So, Mrs. Cooper, you claim in your affidavit that Secretary Frappe did not coerce you to switch your vote. But he did assist you, did he not?"

"I don't know what you mean."

"Secretary Frappe deliberately had you sign the paperwork and allowed you to leave before the others knew you had betrayed them, correct?"

"Objection!" Carleton shouted. "There's no allegation of betrayal here."

"Oh, really?" Benetton countered. "What would you call it?"

Sly banged his gavel. "Overruled. Answer the question, Mrs. Cooper."

"Yes, he did," Melissa said softly, looking at Frappe. "Out of kindness, I suspect."

"Out of kindness?" Benetton sneered. "Wasn't the real reason to get you out of the room so you wouldn't come to your senses and vote for President Darling, as you promised you would?"

This time it was Roscoe on his feet, his voice booming. "Objection! There is no way for Mrs. Cooper to know what my client was thinking."

"Sustained. Keep to the affidavit, Mr. Benetton."

Benetton closed in on Melissa, resting an arm on the witness stand. "Do you expect this Court to believe that you simply woke up one day and decided to violate your oath and become a faithless elector? Someone had to convince you!"

"Someone did," Melissa said, looking him in the eye.

"Aha!" Benetton said, a finger in the air. "So someone did coerce you! Who was it?"

"I don't know about the word 'coerce.' It's an ugly word. I prefer 'convince.'" She looked at Mr. Friend and saw he was flashing his big smile.

Benetton chuckled. "Very well, Mrs. Cooper. Let's use your word. Who *convinced* you to turn your back on your President and cast your vote for Governor McHenry?"

Melissa paused, cleared her throat, and said firmly, "It was President Darling himself! He *convinced* me he's an asshole!"

It took a while for Judge Sly to restore order to his courtroom. It took less time for one of the reporters to fire off the first tweet: "#SwampMonster Melissa Cooper calls POTUS an asshole in open court! #RaginCajun."

After everyone calmed down, Judge Sly turned to Melissa. "Mrs. Cooper, I cannot tolerate such language in my Court. Please restrain yourself."

"Sorry, Judge."

"Mr. Benetton, you may continue."

"Thank you, Your Honor. Mrs. Cooper, I think you have some explaining to do here."

Melissa said nothing.

Carleton rose. "Your Honor, I didn't hear a question."

"Neither did I, General," Sly drawled. "Mr. Benetton? Do you have a question?"

Benetton did have questions, such as: What did the President do to earn your scorn? But how could that possibly help his case? The answer might very well be damaging.

"Mr. Benetton?"

"Uh, sorry, Your Honor. Yes. Mrs. Cooper, has anyone promised you anything for your testimony here today?"

"Promised me anything? Of course not. I wouldn't sit here and take this abuse for the *promise* of anything." Promise, no, she thought to herself. *Guarantee* is a better word.

Benetton was at a loss. He looked at Judge Sly in despair and said, "Nothing further."

Carleton stood. "Your Honor, it is clear there is no factual basis to the claim that Secretary Frappe coerced Mrs. Cooper to change her vote. Therefore, the lawsuit is without merit. The State renews its motion to dismiss."

"Granted," Sly said with a bang of his gavel. "All costs will be apportioned to the plaintiff. Secretary Frappe, you are hereby ordered to mail the Certificates of Vote immediately, to the end that they be counted before Congress on January 6th.

"We are adjourned."

71

"We'll have the appeal filed by close of business tomorrow," Kennedy said, pacing around the Oval Office. "All the way to the Supreme Court, if we have to."

"No, Kennedy," Darling said, seated at his desk. "It's time to stand down."

"Stand down? No way!"

"We can't win, Kennedy. Think about it. We can only count on four justices, and Tolliver tells me the Supreme Court has no appetite for getting in the middle of another election. They won't even take the case."

Kennedy stopped pacing and plopped into a chair. "Jesus. It's actually over."

"Yes. It's over."

Kennedy looked at his friend, a friend he had taken all the way from the mayor of Denver to the governor of Colorado to the White House. "What will you do?"

"Well, the first thing I'm going to do is concede the election to that bastard and try to sound like a statesman. Then I'm going to wish the nation Happy Holidays, fly off to Camp David, and get shitfaced."

"Got room on the helicopter for me?"

"Wouldn't dream of doing it without you, my friend." There was a lump forming in Darling's throat. "Now get McHenry on the phone before we start crying like we're on TV with Dr. Phil or some damn thing."

"My fellow Americans," Darling intoned, addressing the nation from the Oval Office. "Tonight, I phoned Governor McHenry and conceded the presidential election.

"I don't see the need or the value in putting Americans through any more of this drama, especially over the holidays. I congratulated the Governor and wished him well.

"This was the closest election in our history, and a lot of bad things happened and a lot of horrible things were said. And I know some of you may have strong feelings about it. But if America is to mean anything, it is to mean that we are able to rise above our differences at a time like this and unite for the common good.

"Governor McHenry faces a very difficult task in assembling his core team and cabinet in a very short amount of time. He needs and deserves our support.

"The close and sometimes crazy election divided us. Let the importance of this moment unite us.

"Thank you. Happy Holidays, and may God bless America."

"Holy shit, Lawson! We did it! The presidency!"

The celebration in the Governor's Mansion in Jefferson City was going strong. More and more friends were streaming in as the news of the President's concession speech spread.

Lawson adjusted his glasses after McHenry had nearly knocked them off. "Congratulations, Mr. President-elect."

"Lucas!" McHenry saw his chief of staff and they hugged fiercely. "We did it, old buddy! We did it!"

"Pretty exciting stuff, Jim," Lucas acknowledged. "But we have an awful lot of work to do."

McHenry pulled away. "Right you are, Lucas. I'm going to speak to the press shortly. I'm announcing that you will be my White House Chief of Staff, and that you and Lawson will head up the transition team, along with Gun. Obviously, I've been thinking about this and we have some excellent candidates for cabinet secretaries already."

He looked over their shoulders and saw Lydia Wade walk in wearing her shortest, tightest black dress.

"That reminds me. I promised Lydia a spot as a White House advisor. In the West Wing. Make it happen."

As McHenry walked off to meet with the press, Lucas and Lawson stared as Lydia removed her coat. Lawson adjusted his glasses and said, "Wow, Lucas. Guess what you get to look at every day?"

Lucas huffed and said, "She looks like trouble to me."

"Congratulations, Smart Man."

The director lifted his snifter of cognac and tipped it in Smart Man's direction. "We have our man, and we have our mole. Truly a night for celebration."

"Absolutely."

The director sipped, savored, and swirled his glass slowly. "Tell me. Has our brave heroine from the swamps of Louisiana decided who she is going to be and where she wants to live?"

"Her name will be Jenny Dean. We are already working on her documents and passport. As to where she will live, she hasn't decided. She wants to spend three months in the Caribbean. On us, of course."

The director chuckled. "Of course she does. What the hell. It's Uncle Sam's money, not ours. Where in the vast Caribbean has she set her eye?"

"Barbados. A friend of hers went there once for breast implants. Best in the world, she said."

They both laughed at this. The director said, "And I suppose we're paying for the new tits, too?"

"Of course. And some work around the face. She needs to become a new person."

"Indeed." The director drained his cognac. "See to it."

"Of course."

72

There was a light snow falling on Camp David. It was late. The First Lady had long ago wondered off to bed, along with the few other insiders who had been invited for one last trip to the Presidential retreat. The President's kids and grandkids would arrive in a few days for what would undoubtedly be a subdued Christmas. Kennedy and Darling were alone.

"Ah, Jesus!" Kennedy blurted. "I just remembered something!"

"Something important?"

"Well, yeah. Whatever happened to that guy you thought was the Mastermind? What was his name? Leo something."

Darling looked startled. "Holy shit! I forgot all about him. What the hell was his name?"

"We had the Secret Service lock him up, remember? As a danger to you?"

"Right, right. It was your idea. Because we couldn't admit that we messed up."

"So is he still locked up?"

"I guess so, Kennedy. I don't remember letting him go. I can't even remember his name!"

Kennedy was laughing. "Some innocent dipshit just spent the last month-and-a-half behind bars!"

"Jesus, Kennedy, it's not really funny. Call Secret Service. They'll know his name. Let the sonofabitch out!"

Kennedy reached for his phone. "At least he'll be home in time for Christmas." Then he stopped.

"What is it, Kennedy?"

"I can't give that order, Mr. President. Sarah has to do that."

"Well, call her."

"It's two o'clock in the morning. She'll be asleep."

"Then I'll do it. Get someone in here. He'll be out in time for breakfast."

"No," Kennedy said.

"What do you mean, no? The poor slob is innocent!"

"Exactly," Kennedy said as he started to pace. "You have illegally imprisoned an innocent man for six weeks. I'm complicit in it. So is Sarah. All to avoid admitting a mistake and losing the election. We could all go to prison, for God's sake!"

"What are you saying, Kennedy? That this poor guy has to stay incarcerated so we can cover our collective asses?"

"Do you have any better ideas?" Kennedy countered.

"Get him to agree to keep his mouth shut. Or pay him off. Or both. I don't care. Jesus, Kennedy! Keeping a guy locked up just to avoid the shame of arresting the wrong guy?"

A silence hung between them.

Darling had his head in his hands. "Do we tell McHenry?"

Kennedy was aghast. "Good God, no! He'll hang our asses from a tree!"

"Think about it, Kennedy. McHenry thinks we have the Mastermind - Barboni - in custody. What happens when he's the President and finds out what we did?"

Kennedy's face drained of color. "Oh, crap. We'll be busted for sure."

Another silence hung in the air.

"Wait a minute," Kennedy said. "I remember his name. It's Leo Snyder."

"So?"

"So the reason I couldn't remember it is that we almost never used it. The Secret Service was never told his real name. They think they're holding Barboni because that's what they were told!"

"Jesus. The circle of shame on this just got bigger."

Kennedy was smiling. "Like I said, I can handle the shame. Think of it. We're already holding the Soldiers of Allah in solitary confinement so they can't communicate. You need to order Snyder - but you'll refer to him only by number - held in solitary, too. Same facility as the others. No one is allowed to speak to him, not even the guards. After all, he's one of the terrorists."

"Good God, Kennedy! So we double down on this?"

"Exactly." Now Kennedy was grinning from ear to ear. "And we all know what McHenry promised to do to the terrorists! Problem solved."

"Jesus, Kennedy. We're going to execute an innocent man?"

"No, not us. McHenry."

73

January 18

Zulu was cautious as she climbed the stairs to the front entrance of the Westchester Garden Club. It had snowed. There were slick spots. And her stiletto heels made things even more hazardous.

She was the last to enter the private library. They turned as one to look at her. The only one who looked as high as her eyes was Omega. Alpha smiled wide.

"Good evening, boys," she said with a grin.

"You are lovely as usual, Zulu," Omega said as he hugged her. "And it has been too long since I've seen you."

Beta was his usual ball of frazzled nerves. He simply smiled and tipped his glass in her direction. Alpha was busy pouring her a glass of wine.

"I took the liberty of ordering your favorite brand of Chardonnay, my dear Zulu," Alpha said. "De Loach. From his private collection." He smiled wickedly as he handed it to her.

Zulu had never told him her favorite wine. But, she supposed, that was his point.

"How lovely of you, Alpha. Thank you."

"My lady," Alpha said, "and gentlemen, we are here tonight to celebrate. Our beautiful Zulu has been hired as a close advisor to President McHenry. She'll be three doors away."

"And, at times," he winked, "even closer."

Alpha raised his glass, and they followed suit. "To the Azalea Team! More powerful than at any time in history!"

After they had finished suitably congratulating Zulu and themselves, Beta spoke up.

"What are we going to do about finding a new guy from the newspaper world?" he asked. "Who will control the editorial writers?"

"Nonsense, Beta," Alpha scolded. "The newspapers are dying. We don't need them. You and Omega are the future. Find me anyone under the age of 30 who reads a newspaper anymore. Plus, with my connections to the intelligence world, and Zulu's hands quite literally on the throttle, we should be unstoppable!"

"Unstoppable at what?"

Alpha flashed his biggest smile. "I'm sure we'll come up with something!"

74

January 19

President-elect McHenry was having lunch with Lydia at the Hay Adams in Washington.

"I'm sorry, Lydia, my dear, that you have to miss the Inauguration Day festivities tomorrow."

"I wouldn't miss it for anything, Jim. What are you talking about?"

"Remember when we first met? I asked what you do and you said..."

"I get things done. Yeah, I remember." She gave him a wicked grin. "It was a magical night."

McHenry smiled back. "Yes, it was. It's still magical. And not having you there tomorrow will be a little sad. But I need you to get something done, and it needs to be done tomorrow."

"Why tomorrow?"

"To keep a promise. Actually, to keep two promises."

"I hope you enjoy Barbados, my dear Jenny Dean."

She looked at Smart Man with some sadness in her eyes. "I think this is the part where you tell me your real name and we hug and kiss and I beg you to go with me. I've grown quite fond of you, Mr. Friend."

He grinned. "You are a wonderful woman. But my job is to make sure you get on the plane, not get on the plane with you, as wonderful as that sounds."

"Maybe when I get back I'll look you up and see if you recognize me. If you do, I will have failed in my mission."

"That's a deal."

"And one other thing, Mr. Friend. See to it that McHenry follows through on his promise to investigate my husband's disappearance. I'm sure he's dead, but I want justice."

"I'll see to it."

75

Inauguration Day

"So help me God."

President James Madison McHenry lowered his right hand and accepted the congratulations of the Chief Justice. The crowd cheered.

Then, he approached the lectern, reaching inside his coat to retrieve a pen. He signed a document and handed to a Marine on the podium. After a quick salute, the Marine hurried off.

McHenry turned to the confused crowd.

"My fellow Americans, I have just kept my first campaign promise. That was an executive order declaring the Soldiers of Allah enemy combatants. I have ordered summary executions for all of them, by firing squad, which will take place as soon as possible today. Let the message be crystal clear: acts of terror against the United States will not be tolerated! Period!"

Lydia watched as eight men wearing prison orange and black hoods were led, shackled, into the exercise yard.

They had been told they were being transferred to a holding facility where they would be given new clothes and better food in preparation for trial. They were ordered to be quiet. All obeyed except for one who was annoyingly proclaiming his innocence. He kept it up even after one of the guards smacked his ribs with a baton.

"Wait here," the lead guard said. "I'll be right back." Then he scurried away, as did the others.

Lydia held her cell phone up, centered the frame and turned the video recorder on. The last in line was still bellowing for a lawyer. At one point he yelled, "Dammit to hell! Call Donnie!"

"Ready!"

The hooded men immediately turned to face the sound of the voice.

"Aim!"

Suddenly, all of them were shouting.

"Fire!"

Sixteen guns rang out. The wall behind the men lit up with blood. All were on the ground, still, except for the one claiming innocence, who was still on his knees.

"I'm not...Donnie..."

"Fire!"

All sixteen guns fired at the same man. After the echo died, everything was still.

Lydia uploaded the grainy video to YouTube - anonymously. President McHenry's order had specifically prohibited any video of the execution. But he had also ordered Lydia to violate the order.

"Clean up the mess," she said to the guards, "and incinerate the bodies immediately. Save the ashes in a vault, for the sake of history."

Outside, she got into the back of the black limo and was not at all surprised to see a man - a prisoner - sitting next to her. But he was shocked to see her.

"You!" was all Rafi could think to say.

"Hello, Rafi."

The driver was pulling away from the secret prison. Lydia raised the divider to give them privacy.

"Are you going to kill me?" Rafi was still wide-eyed, squirming against the door.

Lydia smiled. "Why would I kill you, Rafi? You're the second promise."

"What do you mean?"

"President McHenry promised he would let you go. It explains a lot, but I want to hear it from you. Why did you deviate from the plan?"

Rafi looked away, ashamed. "I couldn't do it. I couldn't shoot that little girl. The Butterfly Girl. Lucas - her father - is a friend of mine. Was, anyway. So I called McHenry. We used to be drinking buddies, you know. We set the whole thing up, even the timing, so it would mess up Darling's speech."

Lydia nodded. "So McHenry was never in any danger when he entered the house."

"Not at all. We had a couple of drinks, planned it out some more. Then we hit each other - to make it look good - and out we came."

"And he promised to let you go."

"Yes."

"What about the others?" Lydia asked. "Why didn't they fight?"

"I told them McHenry agreed to let us all go, after he got elected. But it was a lie."

"I assume you heard the firing squad, Rafi."

Rafi looked at his feet. "Yes."

"I videotaped it. Sent it to YouTube. Wanna see?"

"No! I betrayed them. I betrayed you, too. That's why I thought you were going to kill me."

Lydia tossed him a smile. "Relax, Rafi. It all worked out, even better than we planned. No hard feelings."

"But you told me the whole point of all this was to get Darling reelected!" Rafi protested.

"That's what I told you, Rafi, because that's what my superiors told me. But it became obvious the plan was flawed. Darling was flawed. So we switched horses. So, no reason to kill you, Rafi, but the world thinks you're dead."

Rafi looked sideways at her. "You videotaped it? And uploaded it to YouTube?"

"Yes. Wanna see?"

"No! But the world will see only seven being shot. There were eight of us!"

"Eight people got shot, rather splendidly. Wanna see?"

"No! Who was the eighth?"

"That boob you hired to drive the limo. The guy you fingered as the Mastermind. That was brilliant, by the way."

"You executed Ricky Barboni?" Rafi said, the relief washing over him. "That's awesome."

"I thought so."

"So how come you are doing McHenry's dirty work now? We were cut off from the outside world - no news."

"I'm one of his closest advisors, Rafi. Three doors down from the Oval."

Rafi was agape. "Jesus Christ! McHenry just executed everybody, but he's got the real Mastermind down the hall from him!"

"And in his bed."

Now Rafi was laughing. "No wonder you don't need to kill me! I actually helped you!"

The limo stopped in front of a bank.

"The world thinks you're dead, Rafi. You need to stay that way." She handed him a key. "Inside the bank is a safe deposit box with a new set of credentials, credit cards, a passport, and some cash. Disappear. Preferably in some other country. If you ever surface as Rafi Sayahd, you'll be dead for real."

"Will I hear from you again?"

"Only if I need a dead man. Someone half past evil." She smiled. "Which I might."

President McHenry sat behind the desk in the Oval Office. The feeling of satisfaction was intoxicating. He opened a drawer where, true to tradition, Darling had left him a handwritten note.

It was short. It read: "Things are seldom as they seem."

Huh. What the hell did he mean by that?

76

Millions of eyes around the world watched the firing squad executions of the Soldiers of Allah. Two of those eyes belonged to Rip Snyder, and he had a sick, unbelieving feeling in his gut.

He played it again. And again. He turned the volume way up and played it again.

"It can't be!" he said to himself.

"What, honey?" It was Carrie. She had heard the commotion after he cranked up the volume.

He looked at her sheepishly. "I don't know. It's probably stupid."

"What?"

Rip pointed to the screen. "This video of the firing squad. It..."

"I don't want to see it, honey."

Rip nodded. "I understand, Carrie. But I've been over it and over it and the one guy yelling for a lawyer sounds like my Uncle Leo."

Carrie's eyes went wide. "Your Uncle Leo was in the Soldiers of Allah!?!"

"No. Couldn't be. But it sounds like him. And then he says, 'Dammit to hell. Call Donnie.'"

"Who's Donnie?"

Rip looked at her with sad eyes. "My dad."

Again, Carrie was astonished. "You told me he was dead!"

"He is, Carrie. But he was always Leo's protector. You see, Leo was always kind of slow. He was always hollering for his older brother, Donnie, to help him out when they were kids."

Carrie shook her head. "So you're thinking that's your Uncle Leo in there, hollering for your Dad, and he gets executed? Sounds pretty far-fetched."

"I know," Rip replied, rubbing his chin.

"How long has it been since you saw your Uncle Leo? Or talked to him?"

Rip hung his head. "A lot of years. Too many."

"So call him," Carrie said. "You got his number?"

"I did that already," Rip said quietly. "No answer."

A long silence hung between them. Finally, Rip spoke. "I've got to track this down, Carrie. I need to prove it's not Leo."

Carrie nodded. "How?"

Rip looked at her. "I need to fly to Omaha."

The flight from Ft. Meyers to Omaha was uneventful. He took a cab to Leo's modest bungalow. He told the cabbie to stick around.

It was cold. The sidewalk in front of Leo's home had not been shoveled in some time, though it was matted down with foot traffic. Rip stomped through the snow to the front door and knocked.

"Leo!" He banged on the door. "Uncle Leo! It's Rip! Donnie's boy!"

Rip put his ear to the door and listened. Nothing.

"Leo!" More banging. "Leo!"

Rip walked around toward the back. He banged on the back door.

"I called the cops."

Rip spun in the direction of the voice. He saw an elderly man dressed in a flannel coat and a black stocking cap.

"You what?" Rip said, walking toward him.

"I said I called the cops," the old man replied, standing his ground. "I told 'em some crazy bastard was banging on the door of a vacant house."

"It's not vacant," Rip insisted. "My Uncle Leo lives there."

"Not anymore he don't."

"What are you saying?" Rip felt a chill climb his back.

"He got himself arrested here awhile back. November I think it was. I heard they caught him peeping in some windows across town. He ain't been back. Who are you again?"

Rip extended his hand. "I'm Rip Snyder. Leo is my uncle."

They shook.

The old man spoke. "I don't mean to offend you, Mr. Snyder, but you should know Leo had gotten pretty funny in the head here lately. Made everybody nervous. Kept calling himself the 'mastermind.'"

"The mastermind?" Rip felt the chill even stronger. "The mastermind of what?"

The old man shook his head. "Can't say. We pretty much ignored him. And then he gets arrested for peeping in windows, and we're all thinking it's Alzheimer's or something. Haven't seen him since."

There was a short bleep of a siren out front.

"That would be the cops," the old man said. "I'm sorry I called 'em now."

Rip said, "That's okay. I think I need to talk to them next, anyway."

Rip had paid the cabbie and ridden to the police station with the two officers who showed up. The elderly neighbor helped explain that Rip thought his Uncle Leo was still living there. He apologized for being so quick on the trigger. That's okay, they said, better safe than sorry.

At the station, Officer Stanton looked through the records and announced, "We have no record of arresting any Leo Snyder."

"Are you sure?" Rip prompted. "The old neighbor said it was back in November. Said he was peeping in windows and acting crazy. Called himself the mastermind."

Officer Stanton and his partner looked at each other. Stanton spoke. "The mastermind? Is that what he said?"

"Yeah."

Stanton rubbed the back of his neck. "We arrested a guy back in November who called himself the mastermind. The real mastermind. Identified himself as Ricky "The Mastermind" Barboni. You remember him?"

"Oh, yeah," Rip replied. "My wife and I, we have a history with him. A real badass."

Stanton nodded. "Right. So we arrested him and when he said his name was Barboni, we called the feds.

They came and got him right away. Sent two guys from the Omaha FBI office. Took less than ten minutes."

The cold shiver went up Rip's back again. He pulled out an old picture and showed it to Stanton.

"Is this the guy you arrested?"

"Yeah," Stanton said, then looked oddly at Rip. "Why are you carrying around a picture of this badass Barboni guy?"

Rip felt like the floor might swallow him up. "That's not Barboni. That's Uncle Leo."

77

Rip took another cab to the FBI field office, located in a boring looking white building. The Omaha police were nice enough to call ahead, so he wasn't completely unexpected.

After his identity was thoroughly checked, Rip was led to a small conference room and told to wait. After several minutes, two guys who could have been brothers walked in, both wearing navy suits.

"I'm SSA Settle," one of them said. He nodded at the other guy. "And this is Agent January. We're the ones who picked up Barboni from the locals."

Rip stood. "I'm Rip Snyder. Thanks for agreeing to see me." They all shook hands.

Settle took the lead. "Officer Stanton said you were poking around about the arrest of Barboni. What's your interest?"

"I think you made a mistake," Rip said bluntly. "I think you arrested the wrong guy."

Settle and January looked at each other. Here we go, the look said, another whack job.

"We didn't arrest anybody, Mr. Snyder," Settle reminded him. "The locals picked him up. When they realized it was Barboni, they called us. They did the right thing."

"And what did you do after you took custody?" Rip asked. "Did you verify his identity?"

Settle shook his head. "Our job was to get him on a plane to a federal corrections facility in Virginia. We did that. He was in the air within thirty minutes."

"You didn't question him?" Rip was incredulous.

"No," Agent January broke in. "Our orders were very specific: get him on the plane to Virginia. But he said plenty, even without asking. He kept yelling about being the mastermind and how all us assholes were gonna die. Shit like that."

"You didn't fingerprint him?"

"No," Settle replied. "All of that would be handled in Virginia. Tell me, Mr. Snyder, why do you think the man the locals arrested was not Ricky Barboni?"

Rip reached into his shirt pocket and showed them the picture. "Is this the man you picked up from the Omaha police?"

Settle grabbed the photo. "It's a bit old, this picture, but I believe so." He looked at Agent January. "Wouldn't you say, Don?"

January looked at the picture carefully and swallowed hard. "I'm sure of it. And you're saying that's not Ricky Barboni?"

Rip shook his head sadly. "Not even close. I know Ricky Barboni. He tried to kill my wife years ago. Well, she wasn't my wife then, but she is now."

January tapped his finger on the picture. "So who is this?"

Rip looked from one to the other with sad eyes. "That is my Uncle Leo. And I think he's dead."

Agent January went to get coffee. When he got back, Rip took them through it, from the firing squad video to his unanswered calls to Leo's house, to his banging on the door and the neighbor calling the cops. He even talked about Leo as a kid, almost retarded the way Rip's father used to tell it, always calling out for his big brother for help.

At one point, SSA Settle took out his smartphone and found the execution video. They watched it. When one of the hooded figures yelled, "Dammit to hell! Call Donnie," Rip said, "Right there. He's calling for his brother, Donnie. My father, deceased."

"How long has your father been dead?" Settle asked.

"Almost ten years now."

"So why would he yell about calling Donnie?"

Rip shrugged. "Maybe the stress of being incarcerated with a hood over his head? Plus, like I said, he was borderline retarded."

SSA Settle stood. "I'll go make a phone call."

When Settle returned, Rip thought he had lost some of the color in his face.

"Mr. Snyder, I'm afraid there is nothing more we can tell you. You need to go."

Rip was dumbstruck. "What? What did you find out?"

"I'm sorry, Mr. Snyder. We have our orders. No more talking to you. Agent January will see you out."

"It's true, isn't it? You found out it's true!" Rip was losing control. "And now the cover-up! Jesus Christ! You fuckers killed an innocent man!"

"That's enough. Agent January, escort Mr. Snyder out of the building. Better yet, drive him to the airport. He's done here."

Agent January had Rip by the arm, but it wasn't really necessary. Rip was smart enough not to resist.

"I'm not giving up on this," Rip promised as he was led out of the conference room. "Not by a long shot."

78

Agent January resisted all attempts by Rip to get him talking. Finally, January simply said, "Look, Mr. Snyder, I was in the room with you. I have no idea what SSA Settle found out on that phone call, if anything. I have nothing to add."

Rip brooded for awhile. "But you're curious, right?"

"Of course."

"And you know something isn't right."

January scowled. "Maybe you ain't right."

"Oh, I get it," Rip nodded. "The feds are closing ranks, covering their asses. But I'm not gonna let go."

January stopped the car at the passenger drop-off area. "Good-bye, Mr. Snyder."

Rip handed him a card. "Call me if you get an attack of conscience."

"Ain't likely."

Rip was not without friends in high places. All those years of stirring the pot for the Republican Party in Florida had its advantages. Waiting for his flight to board, Rip called the personal cell phone of Congressman Alberto Gonzalez. He was the first Puerto Rican Speaker of the House in the Florida Legislature, and rode that wave to Washington.

"Rip, old boy," Gonzalez said as he answered. "It has been entirely too long. I guess Carrie is keeping you busy!"

They shared a chuckle and made some small talk. Then Rip got straight to it.

"Al, I stumbled into something, something pretty serious, and I think I need your help."

"You got it, Rip. You know that."

Rip nodded into the phone. "Thanks. Are you in DC or Florida?"

"Miami. You know Congress, Rip. We hardly do anything anymore."

"Yeah, so I've heard. I need to come see you. Is tomorrow okay?"

"Sure. We can do lunch. Is that alright?"

"Perfect, Al. I'll swing by your office."

Back at the Omaha field office, Agent January was sitting across from SSA Settle's desk.

"Our asses are on the line here, Don," Settle said, his voice dead serious. "We are not to breathe a word of this to anyone, not even our wives."

"Girlfriends?"

That got a small grin out of Settle. "Especially not girlfriends."

"Okay," Agent January said. "So what are we not supposed to tell?"

Settle leaned forward. "Snyder is right. The local yokels arrested the wrong man, and we dutifully handed him over. When he got to Virginia, they printed him, and the prints didn't match Barboni.

"It was Leo Snyder, Don. Leo fucking Snyder."

"Jesus, Mary and Joseph."

Settle nodded. "The record shows inmate 65-xx3459fd was making specific and credible threats to the life of President Maury Darling. He was transferred to Secret Service custody and the FBI officially washed its hands of inmate 65-xx3459fd."

There was silence while they contemplated this. January said, "Pull up that execution video again. On your regular computer this time."

Settle did so and hit play, enlarging it to full screen. "There!" January said. "On the back of the prison jumpsuit! See the number?"

It was plain as day: 65-xx3459fd.

"Ah, fuck," Settle said.

79

On the way across Alligator Alley the next day, Rip thought ahead to his meeting with Congressman Gonzalez.

Gonzalez was not some back-bencher. He was on the Intelligence Committee, with more access than most to the levers of secrecy within the federal government. He had helped deliver Florida for President McHenry - or could claim to - which might come in handy.

To Rip's surprise, Gonzalez had arranged for them to have lunch at a large table in his Miami office, rather than finding one of the many nearby restaurants.

"You said it was serious, Rip," Gonzalez explained, "so I figured we could use the privacy."

Rip nodded. "Thanks, Al. This works great."

Over salads, Rip wasted no time. "Al, the story I'm going to tell you borders on the ridiculous. But bear with me."

Gonzalez spread his hands. "The floor is all yours, Rip. Let's hear it."

To his credit, Gonzalez didn't interrupt Rip once during the story. Then, he said, "You're right, Rip. It borders on the ridiculous."

Rip sighed. "I know, Al. But it's clear the Omaha cops arrested Uncle Leo, and the FBI agents put him on a plane to Virginia. After that, it's foggy, but I swear to God that's Leo yelling for Donnie on that execution video."

Gonzalez shook his head. "It makes no sense, Rip. Look, I was briefed by the White House about the summary executions of the Soldiers of Allah. The executive order lists only the eight Soldiers of Allah. Barboni wasn't listed, so there's no way Barboni would be in that line-up. So even if the mix-up you describe is true, it would only mean that Leo is still in custody."

Rip sat back. He had to admit, it was a serious hole in the narrative. "But why would one of the Soldiers of Allah be yelling for Donnie?"

"Lots of Donnies in the world, Rip. Look, let's assume your Uncle Leo is trapped in the system somewhere. We need to get him out. I'll make some calls, throw my weight around."

"Thanks, Al."

Ricky Barboni had long ago left the trailer on the outskirts of Miami, Oklahoma. It was too cold. He had migrated to a farmhouse south of Raymondville, Texas, where the owner had made the mistake of answering the door when Ricky knocked.

He still had the Harley. It was perfect for someone like him who traveled light and didn't want to waste money on gas.

The homeowner was in the basement, dead of a gunshot wound to the head. He would start to stink soon, but Ricky didn't plan to stay long. A life on the run had taught him that.

He showered, dressed in some of the dead man's clothes, and thoroughly searched the home for money and anything else of value. To his surprise, the old boy had a shoebox in the basement chock full of ten-ounce silver bars.

"Well, hot damn!" Ricky exclaimed to the dead man. "Won't that come in handy!"

Life on the run was looking up. He found a six pack of Shiner Bock beer in the fridge, and polished it off. He loaded the silver bars - fifty of 'em! - into one of the saddlebags on the Harley.

Time to raise a little hell in Raymondville, Texas.

Ricky fired up the Harley and headed north into town. It happened so fast, and with six beers sloshing around inside of him, Ricky couldn't react fast enough.

A pickup truck full of teenagers ran a stop sign. Ricky hit the truck straight on and went head-over-heels through the air. The saddlebags burst open and the silver bars went flying.

When the officers got there, they found Ricky unconscious, looking like a large bag of broken sticks on the road. They counted an amazing twenty silver bars lying about.

The ambulance hauled Barboni off, and the officers began their accident investigation.

It would rock the world.

80

The motorcycle came back registered to Brent Cooper of Happy Jack, Louisiana. The driver had no identification on him whatsoever, so the officers decided to fingerprint him to make sure it actually was Mr. Cooper.

It wasn't. The prints came back as Ricky Barboni, the one at the top of the FBI Ten Most Wanted list, with the notation that he was currently incarcerated in a federal facility.

"Well," the officer in charge grunted. "Ain't that somethin'."

So he called a friend of his at the FBI, who called his superior, who called the director, who called the Attorney General, who called Lucas Washington, the chief of staff to President McHenry.

"We got us a heap of shit," the Attorney General said. It was William Henry Carleton, from Louisiana, and he had been on the job all of a week.

"Well, hello to you, too, General," Lucas replied. "Which heap of shit are you referring to?"

"Well, there's a heap of shit lying in a Texas hospital bed with a broken pelvis, a broken arm, three smashed ribs and a busted jaw. His name is - I hope you're sitting down - Ricky Barboni."

Lucas stood up. "What the hell? How is that possible? Darling said they arrested him!"

"Yeah, right before the election," Carleton reminded him. "It's why he carried Louisiana. Well, until that Cooper woman switched sides."

Lucas sat back down. "Right. Melissa Cooper. She was pissed at Darling for not following up on her claims that Barboni killed her husband. But I'm confused. Did Darling openly lie about arresting Barboni to throw the election? Is that what we're looking at here?"

"Beats me," Carleton said. "Here's what I know. Barboni was riding a Harley registered to Brent Cooper of Louisiana. So it looks like Melissa was right about the sonofabitch killing her husband. Anyway, he wrecks the damn thing down in Texas and they fingerprint him. Bingo.

"As for what happened with the original report of Barboni's arrest, I get the distinct feeling that a bunch of feds are covering their asses on something. I gotta tell ya, Lucas, if I need to roll some heads on this thing I'm gonna roll some fucking heads."

Lucas was getting a headache. "Is it public yet? About Barboni?"

"I suspect it will be by morning," Carleton grunted. "That's when the shit hits the big fan."

"Mr. President? I have some rather disturbing news."

President McHenry simply arched his eyebrows at his chief of staff and waited.

"Ricky Barboni has surfaced in Texas."

It was like someone had swung a fencepost at McHenry's head.

"What?" McHenry stammered. "Lucas, that's impossible."

316

"I thought so, too. But it has been confirmed through fingerprints. One hundred percent match. He wrecked a motorcycle and is busted up pretty bad."

McHenry swiveled his chair so his back was to Lucas and gazed out at the Rose Garden. "Lucas, that can't be."

"But it is, sir. And it'll become public tomorrow. It'll become obvious to everyone that Darling lied when he told the country Barboni was in custody. We need a plan."

McHenry swiveled to look at his chief of staff. Lucas had never seen such panic in his boss's eyes.

"We'd better get Lydia in here," McHenry said, bile rising in his throat.

"I haven't seen her tonight," Lucas said. "I think she's already gone."

"Well, find her! She's a presidential advisor. She ought to be around to give me some fucking advice, or something."

"Or something," Lucas muttered under his breath as he went off to find the precious Lydia.

81

Lydia heard her phone buzzing inside her purse.

She was lying in bed with Richie and decided to let it go. A minute later, the buzzing started up again.

"I'd better find out what's going on," she said.

"Maybe gramps popped a Viagra, and he's looking for you," Richie said, moping.

"Stop moping." She looked at the phone screen. "Ah, shit. It's Lucas. Plus there's a text with 9-1-1 at the end."

Lydia hit the call back icon and Lucas picked up immediately. "Where are you?" he barked.

"Home, like most people this time of night. Why?"

"The President needs you here, right now," Lucas ordered. "We have a situation, and McHenry thinks you need to be in the middle of it."

"What's the situation?"

"Ricky Barboni. The Mastermind. He's in a hospital in Texas and by tomorrow the whole world will know he wasn't really arrested, like Darling claimed."

Lydia started pacing around her bedroom, naked. "Fuck that, Lucas. Barboni is dead. I watched him die. It's on the fucking video!"

Lucas was confused. "What? What do you mean, dead?"

Lydia suddenly realized McHenry had not shared his plan with his chief of staff. "How certain are we that the guy in the Texas hospital is Ricky Barboni?

"One hundred percent fingerprint match. Lydia, get in here, now."

Lydia's mind was racing. If the guy killed in the execution wasn't Barboni, who was he? She knew it wasn't Rafi. Her mind quickly sped to the most logical conclusion of what was going to happen. There was going to be a scandal, and every scandal needs a fall guy. And that fall guy would be her.

"Lydia? Are you there? For God's sake, get in here!"

"On my way, Lucas."

Lydia disconnected and threw her phone into her purse. She started dressing, quickly.

"What's this shit about Barboni being dead, but not dead?" Richie asked. "What the fuck is going on?"

"Forget everything you just heard, Richie. Everything. And I'm gonna disappear for a while. Do not come looking for me. Understand?"

"What do you mean, disappear? You just said you're headed for the White House."

"Well, I'm not. Good-bye, Richie. Lock up when you leave."

With that, she grabbed her emergency go bag and was gone.

"She's on her way," Lucas said. "But there's something you're not telling me."

"What do you mean?" McHenry was stalling.

"Lydia said she watched Barboni die, and it's on the videotape," Lucas said, as he watched his boss's eyes falter. "I can only assume she means the anonymous execution video. So, what gives?"

McHenry's shoulders sagged. "Have a seat, Lucas. You're not going to like what I'm about to tell you."

Before McHenry could launch into his story, his secretary interrupted. "Mr. President, it's Attorney General Carleton on the phone. Says it's extremely urgent."

Grateful for the interruption, McHenry put the call on speaker. "General, it's me and Lucas. What's up?"

"Mr. President, I've been knocking heads over this Barboni deal. Then out of the blue I get a phone call from Congressman Gonzalez. You know him?"

"What's that gasbag want?"

"So you do know him. Mr. President, between what I've pieced together and what Gonzalez was able to provide, it turns out the man arrested by the feds right before the election was actually some Omaha retard named Leo Snyder. He claimed he was Barboni, bragged about killing people and what-not. By the time the feds figured out who he was, it was Election Day, and Darling didn't want to admit the mistake."

McHenry wanted to puke. "So they just kept him locked up?"

"Apparently. Now Gonzalez is trying to get this Snyder fella out of prison. Could be a win-win-win for us, Mr. President. We get Barboni, Darling looks like a monster, and we help Gonzalez put together a family reunion."

McHenry was staring off into space. "General, you'd better come to the Oval. We got some serious shit to figure out."

82

"Where the hell is Lydia?" McHenry snapped.

McHenry was doing everything he could to put off telling Lucas about the execution swap.

"It has been over a fucking hour since she called you back," McHenry groused. "Fuck it, I'll call her myself."

He picked up his mobile phone and hit speed dial.

Lydia had been expecting it. She had checked into a hotel and gone through her transformation. Her hair was cut short. She wore a too-small sports bra that flattened her breasts, for the most part. Over that was a starched white shirt, Brooks Brothers suit, a silk tie and polished wingtips.

She was a man, though an awfully attractive one. Her passport identified her as Lyle Spokes.

Lydia answered the phone. "Hello, Jim."

"Where the fuck are you, Lydia? We're in a shit storm here."

"I'll bet you are. Is Lucas with you? If he is, you should send him on an errand."

"Like hell I will! Dammit, Lydia, it's becoming increasingly obvious to me that you disobeyed my direct orders regarding the execution of the Soldiers of Allah. You need to get in here and explain yourself!"

Lydia smiled. "You didn't tell him, did you? And now you're going to tell him a lie by letting him listen to your half of the conversation. Okay, fine. Here's how it is.

"I recorded that conversation at the Hay Adams, Jim," Lydia lied. "I record lots of conversations. So I have you on record telling me to swap Barboni for Rafi and let Rafi go. I followed your orders to the letter, except now we know it wasn't Barboni for some reason."

McHenry could hardly breathe. "You bitch."

Lydia laughed. "Yes, Jim, and here is how the bitch is going to play it. I'm going to be the fall guy on this; I get that. So you can denounce me and call for my arrest, but you'd better not find me. If you do, the truth will come out, and the truth will not exactly set you free."

"We're going to hunt you down, Lydia, and throw your ass in the slammer," McHenry said.

Lydia cooed. "Very good, Jim. Sell it to Lucas. Bye-bye now."

It was highly unusual for the Smart Man to go to the director's house, but it was late, and this was an emergency.

"We've been tapping Lydia Wade's cell phone," the director said.

"Of course."

"We now know she let Rafi Sayahd go on the orders of McHenry. We know the eighth man on the execution video was supposed to be Barboni. We know from Congressman Gonzalez - we tap his phone because he's on the intelligence committee - that the stand-in was actually an innocent man wrongly arrested in Omaha, and Barboni was free to commit more crimes until he landed in a Texas hospital."

"Sounds like the White House is drowning in shit," the Smart Man observed.

"Absolutely," the director nodded. "And so is Darling, if the truth ever comes out. And this presents us with a unique opportunity. We protect everybody and they leave us alone."

"Of course."

"I'm headed to the White House shortly. We will solve this for everybody," the director said. "Barboni escaped from federal custody during the hoopla of the inauguration, probably with inside help. This fact was not disclosed to the public to avoid raising undue alarm and with the hope that Barboni would lead us to the parties responsible.

"Our investigation determined that Lydia Wade and Rafi Sayahd are longtime associates. She sprung him from prison in direct violation of her orders from McHenry. In Rafi's place, a known drug dealer and pedophile was executed instead.

"Our investigation also determined that Lydia was an operative in a secret organization called the Azalea Team that has been working for decades to overthrow the government and bring about a fascist regime. While Lydia is still on the loose, two other operatives - known as Beta and Omega - were killed in a fierce gun battle with our agents. We believe the Azalea Team has been destroyed."

The Smart Man nodded. "This fierce gun battle. It has already occurred?"

The director glanced at his watch. "I believe so."

"What do you want me to do?"

"Contact Maury Darling," the director ordered. "Make sure he plays along, and his people, too. After all, we're pulling his ass out of the fire."

"I'll see to it."

"And when this is all over," the director said, "you've earned some down time. I'm thinking a trip to Barbados is in order."

"Barbados?"

"Yeah," the director said with a smile. "Tell the nice lady that justice will, in fact, be served on behalf of her late husband. And when she gets all grateful with you, check out our investment."

"Our investment?"

"The new tits, man. Make sure we got our money's worth."

83

The next morning, the news broke with ferocity all over the world. The White House got out in front of it, and spun it as best they could.

There was a lot for the media to digest, including the disclosure of the existence of the fascist Azalea Team.

The McHenry Administration was fully on board with the story, as was Darling and Kennedy Jackson, because it kept them out of prison.

Rip Snyder was another story. He was livid at the notion that his Uncle Leo had been wrongly arrested, and mistakenly executed, and apparently no one would be held to account.

Alberto Gonzalez was there, in Rip and Carrie's home, helping them through it.

"Jesus, Al, I'm supposed to act like nothing happened?"

"What happened was a tragedy, Rip. But think about it. All evidence of Leo's arrest will be destroyed. His body was cremated. There is no evidence he was ever in federal custody. If you try to make a stink about this, Rip, you'll be labeled as a kook. Or worse."

Rip looked alarmed. "What are you saying?"

"One man, with no evidence other than a crappy video, against the current administration, the previous administration, the FBI, and the NSA, all covering their asses. And these people play for keeps, Rip. You don't stand a chance."

"And what are you getting out of this, Al? Why are you playing along with this horseshit?"

"Political capital, Rip. Piles of it. One of these days, I'll cash it in."

Rip started pacing. "Alright, I'll keep my mouth shut. But don't expect me to like it."

"Nobody likes it, Rip. Nobody. But you've made the right decision."

"What do I get for keeping quiet, Al? Everybody else is getting something."

Gonzalez smiled. "I thought you might get around to that, so I came prepared, courtesy of President McHenry."

Rip grimaced at the sound of it, but he finally said, "Spit it out."

"Have you ever been to Monaco?"

Lydia Wade, as Lyle Spokes, breezed through immigration and customs at the Cozumel airport.

The condo overlooking the Caribbean was just as she remembered it: paradise. It was the penthouse unit, with a private rooftop terrace, shaded with a large palapa. It was the perfect spot to sit with a cocktail, relax, reflect, and plot.

She was in no hurry.

The Smart Man was at the baggage carousel in Barbados. He had his bag, and was looking around for Melissa Cooper as Jenny Dean, but she was nowhere in sight.

Finally, a woman about thirty feet away smiled and held up a sign that said, "Mr. Friend."

He flashed her his biggest grin and said, "My God! I would not have known you! That is amazing!"

"Do you like it, Mr. Friend?"

"Of course! You are even more beautiful than before!"

She giggled. "I'm so excited you're here, Mr. Friend. And thrilled to hear about Barboni, that he will be prosecuted for the murder of Brent."

"Indeed."

The Smart Man couldn't keep his eyes off her. "I think you are the most beautiful woman I have ever known."

"Thank you, Mr. Friend."

"It's Jeff."

"Excuse me?"

"My real name," he said with a grin. "It's Jeff."

She leaned in and kissed him, hard, passionately. Later, back in the states, he would report to the director that the investment was indeed a good one.

The Final Chapter

Ricky Barboni was having the strangest dreams.

He blamed it on the painkillers. To most people, the dreams would more accurately be called nightmares. Whenever he drifted off to sleep, he saw clearly the faces of all the people he had killed over his lifetime, and there were many.

Ricky felt no remorse, but he was struck by the fact that for most of the victims, he had no clue about their names. They were just people who either had gotten in his way or needed killing for some reason.

And now this. A new doctor hovered over him. He looked Cuban, with an enormous grin. The man bent down close.

"Ricky Barboni," the man in the white coat said, "you have been sentenced to death for your crimes against America. Do you have anything to say for yourself?"

What? Crimes against America? Ricky struggled to speak, but he was so groggy.

"And," the man continued, still smiling, "I personally am here to administer justice on behalf of Brent Cooper."

The face of Brent Cooper found its way into Ricky's mind. The motorcycle guy.

The Cuban suddenly pulled up, looking around as if startled, a tinge of fear evident in his eyes. Then he frowned, and injected a syringe full of something into Ricky's IV.

"Pentobarbital," the Cuban said, smiling again, though still shaky. "It won't take long."

Ricky barely had time to react before his eyes drifted shut. Suddenly, the room was swirling with bats, gruesome bats, with human faces. They were the faces of the murdered.

They landed on him, tearing at him, biting him, drinking his blood. The squealing sound was horrible.

Then, even with his eyes closed, Ricky saw the biggest bat land on his chin. It cocked its head and leaned closer, and the screaming inside Ricky's head wouldn't stop.

The bat had the laughing, sneering face of Satan.

The Smart Man was outside the hospital, trying hard to breathe clean, fresh air into his lungs.

He found a bench and hit a speed dial number on his phone. The director answered immediately.

"Yes?"

"It is finished," the Smart Man said. "Barboni is dead."

"Excellent. Dead men tell no tales."

"Of course."

"Are you okay?" the director asked. "You sound winded."

"I'm fine. I had to hurry out of the hospital to avoid being seen."

"I see. Good work, then. See you back at the office."

The Smart Man returned the phone to his pocket. He was sweating, but not from hurrying.

He had sensed the very essence of evil in that hospital room, and thought for sure he had seen fleeting shadows and heard the horrible sound of a swarm of bats.

My mind is playing tricks, he thought; shake it off. But it took him a long time to get his breathing back to normal.

##

About the Author

Daryl Duwe is a grizzled veteran of the political battlefields in Missouri, Florida, and nationally. He has the scars to prove it. Prior to working in politics, he spent two decades working in radio. He currently runs a successful government relations firm in Jefferson City, Missouri.

When he's not dreaming up wild plots for political novels or pulling levers in the Capitol, he's usually outside annoying the golf gods.

Daryl and his wife, Yolanda, live in Missouri.